Rotten Bananas

and

the Emerald Dream

Muriel Ellis Pritchett

Black Rose Writing | Texas

ISBN: 978-1-68433-365-3
PUBLISHED BY BLACK ROSE WRITING
www.blackrosewriting.com

Library of Congress Control Number: 2019908899

Printed in the United States of America
Suggested Retail Price (SRP) $18.95

Rotten Bananas and the Emerald Dream is printed in Chaparral Pro

To Celestia Elizabeth Purcell Killingsworth Arrington, my nonagenarian friend, who found the perfect place to enjoy her golden years

Acknowledgments

I am deeply grateful to Celeste Arrington, Ronald Musselwhite, Freda Stearns, Jerry Mitchell and many other residents of retirement communities in Georgia, Florida, California and Virginia who graciously toured me around their apartments and cottages, answered my many questions about their lives, introduced me to their friends, responded thoughtfully to my survey, shared humorous stories about their lives, invited me to dine with them, and allowed me to participate in some of their many daily activities. I could not have written this book without their time, support, and contributions.

As always, I am indebted to my long-time editor, Judy Purdy, who spent long hours working on my manuscript to turn it into a good read. This included one long evening on the phone making final corrections, while she was terribly sick. Thank you, my friend!

And many thanks to the women in my writers' group – Gail Karwoski, Susan Vizurraga, Emma Stephens, and Debra Harden, who enthusiastically critiqued my manuscript, chapter by chapter, over many, many months of weekly meetings. Your thoughts, suggestions, and comments helped bring my story to fruition.

I also want to thank rock and gem gurus, Gail and Chester Karwoski, for walking me through the world of emerald crystals, emerald mining, and emerald smuggling; and much love and thanks to my amazing, computer guru husband, Hal Pritchett, for patiently keeping my computer up and running.

Rotten Bananas

and

the Emerald Dream

Chapter One
The Villas at Kensington Grove

Carolina Cunningham sat on her perfect bed in her perfect bedroom and squished the perfect plush carpet between her toes. After a morning shower in her perfect bathroom, she rummaged through her walk-in closet for a pair of loose, comfy pants and her favorite pullover shirt with the University of Georgia Bulldog on the front.

Unable to avoid looking in the mirror as she brushed and tried to calm her frizzy, silvery hair, Carolina studied the image of the non-perfect 62-year-old woman staring back at her. When she was fifty-something, Carolina thought the image in the mirror looked like her mother. But lately, it was her grandmother gazing back at her with gray eyes offset by dark circles—a side effect of her glaucoma drops. Better to have dark circles than to be blind, she decided.

Carolina fussed at the wrinkled face in her mirror and sighed deeply. "For gosh sakes, Carolina Cunningham! Of course, you don't look like you did when you were forty. Suck it up. Move on." After all, it wasn't like she was a twenty-something trying to find the right man online. Her beloved Arthur had been dead over two years now, and the thought of having romantic feelings for any old man was terribly disturbing.

Giving up on her hair, Carolina headed to her perfect kitchen and made herself a bowl of oatmeal in the microwave, because her doctor insisted oatmeal for breakfast was a weapon against a thickening waistline. By the time she stirred in the butter, brown sugar, cinnamon, half 'n half, and sliced bananas, she doubted her doctor would still consider it healthy. If the Villas at Kensington Grove was truly what the residents said it was—God's waiting room—what the dickens did it matter what she ate? But then, if Carolina had any say in the matter, she wanted to reside in God's waiting room for at least two more decades. She had long-range plans that included seeing her young grandchildren graduate from college, get good jobs, and possibly marry and give her great-grandchildren.

One touch of an app on her iPad screen brought up a digital copy of the Savannah morning newspaper. Soon Carolina was reading a news story about a Wilmington Island couple who retired at age 70, sold everything they owned, bought a 32-foot sailboat, and set sail for the Caribbean and the West Indies. "Omigosh!" Carolina spluttered. "What were those people thinking?" Retiring for a risky life at sea was ridiculous, she thought. If the sea really was calling them, then a cruise ship would have been a better option for two old geezers.

After finishing breakfast and reading more news than she really wanted to know, Carolina headed into her perfect living room, opened the curtains on her perfect floor-to-ceiling windows, and greeted the sun as it rose over the Marshes of Glynn. This was her favorite time of day. From the fifth floor of her high-rise independent-living apartment, she could see Saint Simons Island on her left, Jekyll Island on her right and, straight ahead, a blue sliver of the Atlantic Ocean. She sighed softly and sat down in her recliner with a second cup of coffee and the daily program of activities at the Villas at Kensington Grove—the absolutely perfect place to live out her active golden years.

Carolina's monotonously perfect morning was interrupted by a FaceTime call from her son Charter Cunningham. She touched the "accept" button, and her son magically appeared on the screen. Even though he was over 80 miles away in Savannah, she could almost believe she was sitting in his editorial office at Varendoe Communications. "Good morning, Charter."

"Top of the morning to you, Mom. How are you feeling today?" He looked away and accepted a file from a young woman, who stepped into his office and quickly left.

"Gracious me, Charter, you know I'm having another perfect day here at the Villas."

Charter smiled and shook his head. "So you keep telling me. What does your schedule look like today?"

"Same as last Wednesday. Nothing changes around here." She switched the view on her iPad so Charter could see the daily schedule on her lap. "See? It's Walking with Becky at 9; Bridge Club at 10; lunch with my friends at 12:30; gentle yoga at 2; field trip to Harris Teeter at

3:30; dinner at 6; concert by the Rose Dhu College Orchestra at 7:30; and reading until bedtime."

Charter raised an eyebrow. "What happened to Poker Night?"

"That's Thursday night after bingo."

He chuckled and leaned back in his chair. "Mom, that sounds relaxing and stress-free. Something I could get used to."

"You know what they say, Charter—too much of a good thing can quickly become a bad, boring thing." She sipped her coffee.

Charter's smile widened and his dimples popped out. His daddy's dimples. His daddy's dark brown eyes. His daddy's dark curly hair. "Say, you aren't getting any ideas from that spy series you're reading, are you? What's the character's name?"

"Mrs. Craycraft." Carolina wished she had never shared her love of the book series with her son. He once told her the idea of an elderly widow leaving the safety of her comfortable apartment to become a spy for excitement was utterly amusing, yet totally ridiculous. Like many young professionals, Carolina understood that he had an entirely different definition of "elderly" than she did.

Charter laughed. "Ah, yes. Now I remember. How many books have you read in the series now?"

"I'm on book fifteen, *Mrs. Craycraft Cruises Away*." Going on a round-the-world cruise had been at the top of Arthur's bucket list—at least before her husband dropped dead on the golf course. The EMT said he was probably dead before his body hit the 10th hole green. Too bad he didn't live long enough to go on a cruise with her.

"Enjoy the books, Mom, but please don't get any ideas about going on a cruise yourself. Too many bad things can happen to older women on a cruise. Passengers fall overboard and get lost at sea. Ships can catch on fire or run aground and sink. You see it on the news all the time. You could even get some exotic disease. And let's not forget about pirates and terrorists who love to hijack ships. Remember, you moved into the Villas for a secure and perfect life in your retirement."

Carolina felt herself bristling. A slight disturbance rippled through the bottom of her stomach. How much boring perfection, happiness, and security would she be able to take? But, she had to admit, moving to the Villas had been all her idea. It wasn't like her children sold her home out from under her, and shoved her kicking and screaming into the retirement community. No, she went willingly, and for many of the same reasons as her friends who chose to do this before her. They were tired of taking care of homes or they were lonely after losing a spouse or they wanted security and the social life a retirement community offered.

Carolina felt much joy and relief after selling her house and downsizing into the Villas. She didn't want her son Charter and her daughter Caitlyn saddled with selling the family home and getting rid of everything she and Arthur had accumulated over the years. When she asked them if they wanted anything from the house, they adamantly said no. But she did insist that they take all of the boxes they had stored in the basement when they left home. Neither Charter nor Caitlyn was happy at the loss of this free storage space.

"Mom," a frustrated Caitlyn had whined, "what am I supposed to do with all of this?" She lived in a small condo on Tybee Island, not far from the Coast Guard Station, where she served as a petty officer first class. Her work covered everything from rescuing fishermen from sinking boats and passengers off of grounded casino boats to arresting drug smugglers and illegal aliens. It sounded like dangerous work to Carolina, but Caitlyn loved it. Carolina liked to think her daughter inherited her free spirit and love of adventure from her. Arthur had always leaned toward the cautious side of life.

Charter complained about the boxes, too. "Mom, Boopie and I don't have room to store this stuff." Charter, Boopie, and their twin daughters Carey and Cinnamon lived in a small two-bedroom/one bath bungalow in an affluent historic neighborhood in Savannah. The storage space in Charter's home was almost as bad as in her two-bedroom unit at the Villas, where some residents stored Christmas decorations and other belongings in bathtubs, dishwashers, and kitchen pantries.

"Children, let me be blunt. These boxes belong to you. They are not moving with me to the Villas. Throw it away. Give it away. Rent a storage unit. I am returning your stuff to you." Carolina bit her lower lip to prevent herself from laughing out loud as she remembered. Arthur would have enjoyed the moment, too.

What had started Carolina's search for the perfect retirement community was a *eureka* moment in the middle of the night.

Somewhere down the road, she realized, she might not be able to live alone. She had already seen it happen to some of her friends. They broke a hip or didn't bounce back from heart surgery or they were diagnosed with Alzheimer's. This could happen to her, too.

What would be her options if something happened to her? She couldn't move in with her daughter. Caitlyn never knew when she would receive orders to a new duty station. That was probably why she'd never married. As for Charter, his house barely had enough room for the four of them.

The right answer—the responsible thing to do—was clear to Carolina. She would retire from teaching art at Rose Dhu College, sell her house, and live happily ever after in the perfect retirement community.

Carolina's search took several months of visiting retirement communities in Georgia and Florida, but she couldn't connect with any of them. The Villages in Ocala and Sun City in Tampa were too big, too busy, and way too far from her church, friends, and doctors. Some retirement communities she visited in Georgia were depressing with terrible odors, and sad men and women sitting in wheelchairs in lobbies, and cramped, small rooms. She didn't want to feel like she was living in a college residence hall or a small hotel suite. She needed space to breathe. And active, vibrant friends.

She saved the Villas at Kensington Grove for last, because it was close to Savannah, where Carolina had lived her entire life. Once her beloved Arthur died—leaving her a widow at age 60—any dreams of an adventurous life together in retirement went out the window of possibility.

Four months after she buried Arthur in the spring, the air-conditioner died. Not a good thing to happen during a Savannah summer when the humidity can drown you. Before the end of the year, the 'fridge, the clothes washer, and the dish washer all croaked. But it was after a bathroom pipe ruptured, and one entire wall and the floor had to be replaced, that Carolina realized her life needed to change. After 36 years teaching ceramics in the college's art department, Carolina's financial advisor gave her the green light to retire. Carolina immediately began her search for the perfect retirement community.

At 10 o'clock that morning, as Yasuko Crane dealt cards for the first bridge hand of the day, Carolina was still remembering how she ended up living at the Villas. But her thoughts were interrupted when she fanned out the cards in her hand. Carolina's eyes widened as she counted 25 points. "Heavens to Mergatroyd," she whispered under her breath. She had never had a hand with that many points in all her years of playing bridge. Could this be an omen of things to come?

Carolina glanced across the table at her partner Eula Mae Davis, whose forehead was deeply furrowed and her lips tightly pursed, as she arranged her cards and groaned loudly. Eula Mae had moved into the Villas shortly before Carolina did. Before that, Eula Mae had lived several years with her daughter, Georgia Davis, who handled public relations at Rose Dhu College on Wilmington Island. But after Georgia married some rotten scoundrel, who also worked at the college, Eula Mae decided to let the happy couple live in married bliss without her. She didn't want to be the fifth wheel.

As the "new kids" in the Villas, Carolina and Eula Mae quickly became friends and bridge partners, along with other newcomers and fellow bridge players, Yasuko Crane and Lilly Sigman.

"Well, ladies, I guess I dealt this mess, so that means I should bid or pass." Yasuko folded her cards and thumped the table. "One heart."

"Good for you," mumbled Eula Mae. "As usual, I have nothing. Pass."

Yasuko brushed her shoulder-length, straight black hair back out of her face. She was 72 and not one strand of gray hair could be seen. Carolina knew Yasuko dyed it, because she saw it being done in the Villas Salon. The dyed hair, the flawless makeup, her stylish outfits, and lots of high-end jewelry made Yasuko stand out among most of the other women living at the Villas. She reminded Carolina of the boyfriend's mother in the movie *Crazy Rich Asians*.

Yasuko's story for ending up at the Villas was straight off the front page of the Savannah newspaper. Her husband, the infamous Hirohito "Harry" Crane, was arrested and convicted by the Feds for swindling and defrauding his investment firm clients out of their life savings. All property and money owned by the Cranes was seized. Even though Yasuko was cleared of any wrong-doing, she was left penniless and homeless. Her only child and grown son, Takahito Crane, helped his mother get a divorce and paid all expenses for her to move into the Villas. Each month, he deposited a check in her account to cover her expenses.

"Maybe my partner has all the points you don't have," said Yasuko, looking hopeful in Lilly Sigman's direction. Everyone turned to look at Lilly, who was a little bit fluffy around the edges and always had a smile on her face. She was one of those people who never met a stranger. But today she had no smile. A big fan of the character Penelope Garcia on the TV series "Criminal Minds," Lilly had purple and pink shoulder-length hair with long bangs, and wore brightly colored outfits. With her usual flair for the dramatic, she leaned over and banged her head on the table. Thud. "I have nothing." Thud. "I pass." Thud.

Lilly might not have any points in her current bridge hand, but she did get points for having something most of the women living in the Villas did not have—a husband, Archie Sigman, who retired from the U.S. Coast Guard after 28 years of service. They had been living at the Villas for 18 months. Lilly, who was 56 and the youngest person living at the Villas, was a computer guru of the highest caliber. Carolina suspected Lilly could hack into anywhere and find out anything about anybody. Already today she had used her magic fingers to hack into Chef Jean-Paul's grocery shopping list and add five gallons of Death by Chocolate ice cream—Lilly's favorite flavor.

Carolina and Eula Mae, the newest members of the Tuesday Bridge Club, figured out after only one bridge session that Lilly was a beginning player, while Yasuko was a card counter and the most serious, shrewdest player in the group. It was also rumored that she played cut-throat mahjong on Fridays.

Carolina saw Yasuko's eyes narrow after Lilly's tirade. It was no secret now who had the rest of the points. Raising and lowering her shoulders a few times to release the tension in her neck, Carolina eyed the attractive Asian woman on her left and took a deep breath. "Courage, Grasshopper," she whispered to herself. "Well, okay. Guess I better say something or Yasuko will be forced to play one heart."

Eula Mae raised an eyebrow and sighed. "I knew you'd bid something, Carolina. You never know when to pass."

Yasuko leaned forward, brushing back her black hair, and smiled. "I don't mind playing one heart," she said sweetly.

"I'm sure you don't, Yasuko. However, if you want to play those hearts, you'll have to bid higher because—" Carolina paused and tucked both feet under her chair, in case Eula Mae tried to kick her in the shins. "I bid four spades."

"What!?" shrieked Eula Mae, jumping to her feet. "Weren't you listening?" She gripped the edge of the card table and leaned over as far as she could. "I have nothing, Carolina! I don't have a pot to pee in! Not one single point! I have a void in spades! We are so going down."

Lilly looked at her partner hopefully. "You mean we have a chance to win?"

"Of course, we have a chance, Lilly." Yasuko glared at Eula Mae and rolled her eyes. "Eula Mae Davis, will you quit your whining? I pass. You're the dummy, so sit down and act like one."

It was at that moment—when Eula Mae dropped to her seat and laid out her pointless hand—that Carolina accepted that her perfect life in retirement wasn't all that perfect. She sighed loudly. Her perfect life was lacking something. Like a banana split without the whipped cream and a cherry. Like a chocolate éclair without the Bavarian cream. Carolina wanted something more. There had to be more. If Mrs. Craycraft could find excitement and adventure on a cruise, then so could she. She just needed to find the perfect cruise and convince her perfect partners in crime to go with her.

Chapter Two
The Emerald Dream

Taking advantage of Lilly's computer skills for two nights running, Carolina poured over cruise websites for Oceania, Royal Caribbean, Norwegian, Princess, Regency, and more. Lilly and Carolina played around with the computer app "iCruise," using filters to search for the ideal price and itinerary. Finally, Carolina found a cruise that was nearly perfect in every way.

The *Emerald Dream*, a small ship with less than 700 passengers, offered an eight-day cruise in the Caribbean for less than $1,000 per person. The price included a suite with twin beds and a queen sofa bed, a free beverage package, all gratuities, $200 onboard ship credit, and free shore excursions. Ship activities for young and old included everything from cooking lessons, art and crafts, and a wet T-shirt contest—Carolina paused to picture herself braless in a wet Tinker Bell T-shirt and shuddered—to a variety of games, like bingo, mahjong, and bridge with cash prizes. Plus, the ship cruised out of the Port of Jacksonville, which was only a 75-minute drive from the Villas.

Carolina planned to wait until after dinner to spring her cruise plans on Eula Mae and Yasuko. She knew she could lure them back to her room with the promise of chocolate peanut-butter cup gelato and café latte.

Carolina, Eula Mae, Yasuko, and Lilly always sat at the same table for six. She remembered the awkwardness of her first dinner at the Villas. Entering the dining room, she stood just inside the large cavernous room full of tables with either four or six-place settings. She had been impressed with the Villas dining room during her first visit. Each table was covered with a white linen cloth, fine china plates, good silverware, folded cloth napkins, and faux-crystal glasses. There was no buffet line. Everyone received a menu with lots of choices. A box by the door allowed residents the opportunity to submit suggestions for entrees, side dishes, salads, or desserts.

But that first evening meal at the Villas did not go well for Carolina. After looking around the room at full tables, she spotted a table for six that was empty, except for one woman. Smiling pleasantly, Carolina slowly approached the sole occupant of the table. "May I join you?" she asked.

The woman replied by slamming her cane on the table top. "Nope. Can't you see this is a full table?"

The scrawny woman had unruly copper-red hair—Arthur would have called it bed-head hair—and a scowl on her face that would have scared off any mugger. Carolina eyed the woman for a few seconds, thinking of a response. "I only see you and five empty seats." Carolina continued to smile.

The woman lifted the cane and pointed it at her. "I'm the gatekeeper for this table. I say there aren't any empty seats."

Carolina's eyes widened and her jaw dropped. How rude! So much for the perfect dining room at the perfect Villas at Kensington Grove, she thought. Then she felt a gentle hand on her shoulder and turned around to see the friendly face of Eula Mae Davis, whom Carolina had met earlier at the new residents' reception.

"Heavens to Betsy, Temperance Spencer, what is going on here?" Eula Mae asked the redhead.

Temperance took her cane off the table. "This interloper here was trying to take one of our seats. I told her we had a full table."

Eula Mae nodded. "That was true. We did have a full table at one time, Temperance, but with Mary Frances in rehab and Ozella gone on to meet her Maker, I think it would be polite to let our newest Villas resident join us for dinner. Right?"

Temperance grunted in agreement, Carolina thought, but she wasn't going to sit down until she knew which seats were not taken. Eula Mae pulled out a chair at the end of the table and sat down, followed by Yasuko Crane and Lilly Sigman, both of whom she also met at the reception. They sat in chairs on either side of Eula Mae.

"I think it would most likely be in your best interest if you sat in Ozella's seat," said Eula Mae, pointing to the seat next to Lilly. "We know for sure she won't be back."

That evening, Carolina bonded with her new friends, Eula Mae, Yasuko, and Lilly. She learned that dinner was the time to talk and catch up. No subject was taboo. The discussion topics included politics, religion, health issues, the weather, and lots of gossip. Dinner was an opportunity to learn from others and to contribute any knowledge recently accrued. The juicer the better.

That first dinner at the Villas, Carolina learned that EMTs made several trips a day to the Villas (mostly to pick up residents who'd fallen and couldn't get up); that Julia St. Claire was the best of the housekeepers, because she vacuumed up dust bunnies and didn't eat any chocolate candy lying around; that Livie Vinson would get right into your personal business and post it on the Internet; and that a few of the single male residents chased after new female residents for evil reasons. Temperance did not participate in the dinner conversation. In fact, she ignored everyone at the table and, as soon as she took the last bite of chocolate pudding, she left the table without a word. She was odd, and a good gatekeeper, but not a person who would consider going on a cruise, even if she were invited.

As soon as Temperance left the table and dinner was officially over, Eula Mae, Yasuko, and Lilly followed Carolina back to her apartment. While everyone dug into bowls of gelato, Carolina spread pictures of the *Emerald Dream* cruising in the Caribbean on her dining room table.

"My friends," Carolina began her spiel, "it has come to my attention that as perfect a place as the Villas is, something is missing."

Yasuko swallowed a spoonful of gelato. "Yeah, we could use a few more good men around here."

Lilly licked her spoon thoughtfully. "Strong men. Healthy men."

"We have quite a number of men here," said Eula Mae.

"Oh yeah?" Yasuko asked. "Name some."

"Dicky Wilson and Alan Pinholster," said Eula Mae.

"They don't count," said Yasuko. "They're married."

"How about Fred Umbry or Henry Jones?" suggested Eula Mae.

Lilly rolled her eyes upward. "Fred is deaf and half blind."

"And Henry only has 50 feet of tubing on his oxygen tank," said

Yasuko. "His portable oxygen tank weighs a ton. He needs a wheelchair for field trips to carry it with him. Not to mention he keeps telling the same stupid jokes over and over."

"What about Harlan Wilson?" asked Lilly.

Eula Mae spluttered. "Are you talking about the guy on the sixth floor with the harem?"

Carolina cringed. She met Harlan once. He reminded her of Jack Nicholson in his slimiest role with narrow eyes, devilish grin, and a toothpick dangling from his mouth. According to gossip at the Villas, Harlan had season tickets to all stage productions and concerts in Savannah and Brunswick. By playing the field of single women living in the Villas, he had collected more than a dozen women—jokingly referred to as his harem—who were more than eager to accompany him to a performance.

"That man is the worst of the worst," Yasuko said.

"Maybe you're just jealous because he hasn't invited you to join his harem?" asked Eula Mae.

Carolina, realizing she had lost control of the meeting, stood up and shouted, "Stop it!"

Everyone stopped talking and stared at Carolina. "Geez, Louise, you asked us what was missing around here," pointed out Eula Mae.

"Yes, I know I did. The lack of a few good men is something I will add to the list." And she did. "But something else is missing. Can't you see that?"

The women looked at each other and shook their heads. "What?" asked Eula Mae.

"We have the best food prepared for us by Darryl, an award-winning chef we stole from a four-star restaurant."

"Our accommodations were voted the best in the state," Lilly said. "The best salt-water pool. The best clubhouse. The best grounds. The best lobby. The best activities and recreation."

"We have more activities than we have time to participate in," pointed out Yasuko. "The Villas at Kensington Grove is the perfect place to live. I don't understand what else we could possibly want, need or ask for?"

Carolina plopped down cruise photos taken of the *Emerald Dream*. Photos of older passengers lying around the ship's pool, silver-haired couples dancing the night away, gourmet food platters, an outdoor climbing wall, slot machines in the casino, Broadway entertainers on stage, and a room full of happy bridge players. "This, Ladies, is what we are missing—excitement, adventure, and thrills. The ports of call represent different countries, cultures, music, and people." They stared at her. "Pay attention people—cruises offer a doorway into other worlds," she enthused. "Don't you get it?" She handed them a list of ship activities. "Check this out."

Eula Mae glanced down the list, looking underwhelmed. "Sounds like what we have here—Scrabble, mahjong, art classes, photography—" She stopped mid-sentence. "Well butter my butt and call me a biscuit!" she exclaimed. "Contract <u>and</u> duplicate bridge, <u>and</u> classes with one of the world's most renowned bridge masters?"

"What?" Yasuko snatched the brochure out of Eula Mae's hands. "Not the winner of the Bermuda Bowl? Not the winner of the triple crown of bridge?"

"Yes!" squealed Eula Mae. "Steve Goodwill! One of the Open World Grand Masters!" She leaned back in her seat. "Help! I think I'm going to swoon!"

Carolina laughed. Yes, she congratulated herself. Thank you, Steve Goodwill and the *Emerald Dream* for helping sell your cruise to my friends. "All right, ladies, is anyone interested in going on this Caribbean cruise with me and Steve?

Six weeks later, Carolina, Eula Mae, and Yasuko loaded their luggage into the back of Carolina's 4Runner, and headed south down I-95 towards the Port of Jacksonville. Lilly ended up cancelling, when Archie decided to have his knee replaced on their departure day. But she promised to be their eyes and ears at the Villas while they were gone. Basically, the high-techie computer guru at the Villas, Lilly had downloaded the "WhatsAp" on her friends' cell phones. This app, she explained, would enable them to swap texts, photos, and international phone calls, plus do face-to-face chats for free. That way Carolina, Eula Mae, and Yasuko would know what was going on at the Villas, and Lilly could experience their cruise adventures vicariously. Not to mention passing on their adventures to other interested parties in the Villas.

The weekend before their departure, Eula Mae's daughter and son-in-law, Georgia and Carl Overstreet, stopped by the Villas to wish them a good and safe trip.

Georgia gave Eula Mae a departing hug. "Mother, I know I can't talk you out of this, so I'll just say, 'Have fun, but try to stay out of trouble.'"

Eula Mae raised her eyebrows and threw up her hands. "Shucks, Georgia, how much trouble can three old ladies get into playing bridge all day?"

Carl gave Eula Mae a hug. "Actually, I cringe at the thought. So many possibilities come to mind."

Carolina grabbed Yasuko's shoulders and nudged her over to Georgia and Carl. "This is Yasuko Crane, the group chaperone, who will keep us from doing anything stupid—like getting drunk and falling overboard."

Yasuko rolled her eyes. "That's true. I have more common sense than both of them put together."

"If we do get into trouble, Yasuko has a black belt in karate," explained Carolina, not knowing if that were true, but hoping Yasuko might have grown up taking a martial arts class or two—like some girls take dance or piano lessons. Carolina had hoped that Yasuko's son might drop by, so she could meet him, but that didn't happen. Takahito said he was too busy. However, he did send a courier with a cash envelope and a note, notifying her that he had taken out a health and travel insurance policy on her. In case anything happened to her during the cruise, her medical bills would be covered, and her body would be shipped back to Georgia.

Carolina, of course, had not mentioned to either her son Charter or her daughter Caitlyn about the impending cruise. She knew if she did, they would both try to talk her out of going. Her children apparently saw her as this aging, fragile old woman, who needed protecting. But this cruise adventure was Carolina's idea, and it was up to her to keep everyone safe and return them to the Villas in one piece. The three of them would play bridge every day, and she planned to read about the adventures of Agent Craycraft. Eight days of cruising the Caribbean and enjoying the moment. Like Eula Mae said—what could possibly go wrong?

Chapter Three
Spy Next Door

After a late lunch in the *Emerald Dream*'s Jade Café, Carolina, Eula Mae, and Yasuko headed to their cabin suite on Deck 8. Carolina pulled out her multi-purpose ship's card, which served as a "door key." It could also be used to make purchases in the ship's shops, to buy drinks in the bars and restaurants, and to buy tokens for casino gambling. Most importantly, the card's bar code—when scanned by security—brought up the passenger's name and face on the ship's computer, allowing each passenger to disembark or embark at each port.

"Wow!" said Carolina, as the three women walked into their two-room suite for the first time. A large flat-screen TV attached to the wall was already turned on. On screen, a ship's officer welcomed everyone aboard the *Emerald Green* and reminded passengers about the lifeboat drill at 5:15 p.m.

"Look," pointed out Yasuko, "our luggage is here, waiting to be unpacked."

Eula Mae ambled through the living area and into the bedroom, pounced on one of two twin beds covered with white comforters and pillows, and stretched out. "I claim this one. I'm as happy as a dead pig in the sunshine! Happier than ol' Blue layin' on the porch chewin' on a big ol' catfish head!"

Yasuko shook her head. "I am so happy that you're happy, Eula Mae." She sat down in the middle of the sofa and ran her hands over the cushions. "Nice. I bet this makes into a queen bed in the evening. This will work for me. You two enjoy your twin beds."

Carolina eyed the remaining twin bed and dropped her carryon on the comforter. "Then I guess this one must be mine. Process of elimination."

Eula Mae squealed and headed for a gift basket on a table by glass-sliding doors that led to a veranda. "Well, hot damn and shiver my timbers." She pulled a bottle of red wine and three glasses out of the basket. "Hey, the card says 'Welcome aboard the *Emerald Dream*.' Bless the Captain's pea-pickin' heart. He sure knows about Southern hospitality."

Carolina slid open the veranda doors and the three women stepped outside with their wine and a dish of chocolate-covered strawberries. Three chaise lounge chairs were lined up side by side. Leaning over the ship's railing, the women had a bird's eye view of the Port of Jacksonville terminal building and a steady stream of passengers pulling luggage along the gangway, through security, and onto the *Emerald Dream*.

"Lordy, Lordy!" exclaimed Eula Mae. She pointed below. "Look at that odd-looking woman creeping up the gangway."

Carolina set down her wine glass on a small glass-top table and followed Eula Mae's finger to a woman who did, indeed, look out of place. Everyone coming onboard the *Emerald Dream* looked like normal people going on a Caribbean cruise. But this woman was wearing a trench coat, a wide-brimmed straw hat, and large sunglasses. Who did she think she was? Some character in a spy thriller? Oh no, no self-respecting secret agent in the world would wear a trench coat in the Port of Jacksonville in June. Talk about attracting attention, Carolina thought.

Eula Mae took another sip of wine. "Sure as my mama was raised on a pig farm, I'm telling you that woman is up to no good." She licked melted chocolate off her fingers and chomped on a strawberry.

"Maybe she's cold-natured or maybe she's wearing her coat so she won't have to carry it," said Yasuko. Then she yawned and stretched out on her chaise lounge.

Eula Mae shrugged and followed Yasuko's example. "Might be. Maybe she only has one oar in the water. Who knows?"

Carolina stayed by the rail and watched the suspicious woman follow four passengers up the gangway. Then suddenly the suspiciously dressed passenger turned abruptly around and headed back to the terminal, disappearing into a crowd of embarking passengers and crew members.

"How weird is that?" Carolina muttered out loud. Eula Mae was right. The woman was obviously up to no good.

"What's weird?" Yasuko asked, not bothering to look up from her new book, *Playing Cut-Throat Bridge*.

"Oh, nothing." Carolina reached for her glass, sipped some of her wine, and grabbed one of the chocolate-covered strawberries. She took a big bite of the strawberry, savoring the creamy richness of the melting dark chocolate. Letting out a contented sigh, she leaned over the rail, again, searching for the mysterious woman.

Just as Carolina bit into a second strawberry, she saw the same woman returning to the gangway. "Look, here comes that woman in the trench coat."

"What about her?" asked Yasuko, not looking up from her book.

Carolina couldn't take her eyes off of her. "Doesn't she look suspicious? Maybe she's working undercover for Interpol. Or she's on the trail of an international spy ring."

Yasuko looked up, rolled her eyes, and turned back to her book. "Seriously, Carolina? You've been reading too many of those Craycraft spy books."

Eula Mae, napping in her chair, let out a jarring snort of a snore.

Carolina turned her attention back to the mysterious woman— a.k.a. Interpol agent—who walked up the gangway next to an older, plumpish woman struggling with a large red carry-on. No other passengers were in sight. Four feet from security check, the spy intentionally stuck out her foot and tripped the woman. Carolina gasped as the passenger landed shrieking, butt-first on top of her suitcase. The carry-on collapsed and ripped, spilling toiletries and clothes all over the gangway.

"Poor woman," said Yasuko, joining Carolina, who was focused on the drama below.

It was obvious to Carolina that the Interpol agent was trying to distract the security guard. Sure enough, as soon as the security guard left his post to help the distressed older woman, the spy disappeared— undetected—into the ship. Carolina shook her head. "Did you see that, Yasuko? She just snuck onboard."

"What are you talking about?"

"The woman in the trench coat. She didn't go through security. She's a stowaway."

"That's not possible," said Yasuko.

"That woman is a stowaway," Carolina explained. "Don't you get it? She didn't scan in an ID card. She's not in the ship's computer."

"So? That's not our problem." Yasuko returned to her seat and opened her book.

"But no one knows she's on board." But I know, Carolina thought, and she turned to watch the crew pull in the gangway and cast off the mooring lines. Slowly the *Emerald Dream* eased away from the pier, pulled from her berth by powerful side thrusters. Their great adventure had begun.

As Jacksonville slowly receded into the horizon, Eula Mae and Yasuko left the veranda and went inside. Carolina rose from her seat, but paused at the sound of sliding doors opening on the other side of the privacy wall that separated their part of the veranda from that of their neighbors. She slipped to the rail and saw a tall man leaning over the railing to her left. His thick, graying hair was tousled by the wind. He had the rugged good looks of an older James Bond spy, Carolina thought, admiring his bulging shoulder muscles that strained against a tight yellow polo shirt. She saw no evidence of a concealed weapon, but she supposed his Glock could be lying on the bed. When he glanced her way, she stopped breathing. As their eyes met, she noticed his were a stunning shade of blue. She felt the tiniest ripple in her abdomen. Then just as quickly as he had appeared, he disappeared. She heard his sliding door close, and the spy next door was gone.

"How about dinner?" Eula Mae's voice sounded behind her.

Carolina turned away from the rail. "I guess I can do that." She followed Eula Mae into the suite. She would worry about the spy and the stowaway after dinner.

Chapter Four
The Purser

The Poseidon Room, the main dining area on the *Emerald Dream*, stretched from one side of the ship to the other. Circular and rectangular tables topped with white linen cloths, fancy china, fine silver, and crystal glasses filled the room. Much fancier and more impressive than the dining room at the Villas, Carolina thought. Floor to ceiling windows showed an endless stretch of ocean. Carolina couldn't remember ever seeing anything like this. Not even the fancy wedding dinner she attended with Arthur at the Savannah Yacht Club—their last big social event before his untimely death. For once, even Eula Mae and Yasuko were at a loss for words as they waited to be seated for dinner.

"This is an awfully swank place," Eula Mae finally muttered. "I feel like I'm in high cotton. Will I have to eat snails or raw fish? What if I pick up the wrong fork or knock over a crystal goblet?"

Carolina grabbed Eula Mae's arm. "It's okay, Eula Mae. Relax. They serve regular food here."

Yasuko turned and glared at Eula Mae. "Please restrain yourself. This is not Billy Bob's BBQ House. Get a grip."

Carolina rolled her eyes. Please, God, just get us through this meal without incident. She took a deep breath as the hostess approached them. Her name tag said she was Yin from Myanmar.

The young woman asked for their cabin number, checked a seating chart on her computer screen, and smiled. "I believe I have the perfect table for you," she said, picking up three menus. "Do you mind sharing a table?"

"No problem," Carolina said.

"Does it have a view of the ocean?" asked Eula Mae.

"Definitely," the hostess answered with a smile. "Every table has a view of the ocean." She handed three menus to a young man in uniform. "Table 24."

The three women followed the young man through a sea of laughing, talking, happy passengers. Many of the women wore elegant dresses and expensive jewelry. Most of the men wore suits and ties or at least a dinner jacket. On the way to their table, Carolina spotted their neighbor, the gray-headed, blue-eyed man—a.k.a. Mr. Hunky Spy—sitting alone at a table for two. She couldn't help but notice that he wore typical spy clothes: black trousers, black shirt, and black jacket. Definitely a man who was up to something, she thought—him and that weirdo lady in the trench coat. Something was afoot, but what?

The young man stopped so suddenly, Carolina almost rear-ended him. "Madams, your table for the evening."

An older man wearing a ship's officer's uniform rose from his seat at the table for four. He had snow-white hair, thick jet-black eyebrows, and dark-brown eyes. Carolina guessed he was in his early sixties. He smiled, bowed, and clicked his heels. "Lieutenant Peter Lieberson at your service."

Carolina stared at Yasuko, who was gushing and swishing her black-dyed hair. *My gosh,* Carolina wondered, *does she think she's a femme fatale?*

Lieberson shook Yasuko's hand and held it a little bit too long as far as Carolina was concerned. Sure, he looked all charming and handsome in that white, crisp uniform, but he was obviously the stuffy British type. No James Bond here, just a boring ship's officer. Carolina glanced back at the spy. Ah, yes! Now that man was the perfect picture of danger and adventure. The thought sent a tremble down below, which shocked Carolina. It was a feeling she had not felt in a long, long time.

"I'm the ship's second engineer officer, and, with your permission, I'd like to join you for dinner tonight." Lieberson finally released Yasuko's hand.

"A pleasure to meet you, Lieutenant Lieberson. I'm Carolina Cunningham, and these are my traveling companions, Eula Mae Davis and Yasuko Crane."

Mr. Boring Officer extended his right hand in Carolina's direction. Not wanting to be accused of having bad manners, she shook his hand, but pulled back before he could get a tighter grip.

Eula Mae reached out and grabbed Lieberson's hand tightly. "Pleased to meet you. That's a mighty fine-looking uniform you have on. Looks pretty stiff and scratchy though. How much starch do you put in it?"

The lieutenant pulled his hand from Eula Mae's grip and laughed. "I guess that would be a question for the crew in laundry services."

"Madam?" The young man—Andries from Ukraine, according to his name tag—pulled out a chair on the left side of Lieberson. Carolina plopped clumsily into it. When she tried to pull herself up to the table, Carolina only succeeded in setting the chair leg down on the head waiter's foot. She smiled apologetically. He grimaced, spread a napkin in her lap, and handed her a huge leather-bound menu card.

Mr. Boring Officer pulled out Yasuko's chair on his right side. "Is this your first cruise?"

Carolina noted that Yasuko sat down gracefully and seemed to float on the chair as Mr. Boring Officer slipped it closer to the table.

"Yes," replied Yasuko. "My very first cruise. Does it show?"

In the meantime, Eula Mae—not waiting for Andries' assistance—seated herself and spread her napkin across her own lap.

Oh bother, Carolina thought, watching Yasuko gush and goo. Utterly unbelievable that a man in a white uniform could bring out such behavior in a woman. Especially an older woman.

"Yes, it shows all over your lovely face," Mr. Boring Officer said.

Carolina's eyes widened. Her jaw dropped. Was Yasuko actually blushing? This was too painful to watch. Carolina turned her attention to the menu. And what a menu it was! No wonder people gained weight on cruises.

"I researched cruise ships before the trip," Yasuko confessed.

"What do you think so far? Is this cruise everything you expected?"

Carolina dropped her menu in her lap and interrupted the flirting. "Frankly, I'm not taking another cruise, if things don't improve."

"What's the problem?" Mr. Boring Officer asked, turning his attention to Carolina. "Your cruise should be perfect, so you'll sail with us again. We've barely left port. Whatever has displeased you?"

Yasuko's eyes narrowed, but Carolina didn't seem to notice. "First of all, the security on this ship needs to be tightened."

"Excuse me?" he asked, frowning.

"Pay no attention to her," Yasuko said. "She reads too many spy novels, like the Craycraft series. She sees spies and government agents in every dark corner."

Mr. Boring Officer laughed and relaxed. "You have nothing to worry about, my dear lady. We thoroughly check every passport. I'm sure no more than one or two spies slipped on board today."

"Please, Lieutenant Lieberson, she needs no encouragement," Yasuko said.

"Call me Peter and don't worry, I have an 80-year-old aunt who loves that Craycraft series about the old woman who wants to work for the CIA because her life is boring. Nothing your friend says will surprise me."

Eula Mae peered over the top of her menu. "Yasuko is not the only person to research cruise ships. I cannot believe the shenanigans that happen on cruise ships nowadays. Why some ships are nothing but floating dens of iniquity—regular Sodoms and Gomorrahs."

Lieberson, who had just taken a sip of water, snorted, choked, and coughed. He wiped his mouth with his napkin. "Mrs. Davis, let me assure you that the *Emerald Dream* has a top-notch reputation and impeccable security."

"Horse pucky!" Eula Mae spat out the words. "How about that gang of jewelry thieves arrested on your Panama Canal cruise? Or the young female officer who disappeared and might have fallen overboard?"

Carolina gasped out loud. Her eyes widened. She was absolutely shocked. Eula Mae did not seem like the kind of person who would do research on anything. Maybe bridge strategy or recipes for making buttermilk pound cake or cheese grits, but crime onboard cruise ships? Seriously? She jumped as a male voice sounded directly behind her.

"Good evening, my ladies; good evening, Lieutenant Lieberson."

Carolina jerked her head around and looked up at a short, thin man with a dark complexion, black wavy hair, and a pencil-thin mustache that curled up on each end. Funny, but he reminded her of a Loony Toons cartoon character.

"Good evening," Peter said. "Ladies, your table steward, Dominic."

Dominic's toothy smile stretched from ear to ear. "Ladies, it will be my pleasure to serve you throughout the cruise. What would you like to eat tonight? Do you have any questions?"

Carolina peered at Dominic over the top of her menu. "You remind me of a Mexican spy I saw in a cartoon once."

Dominic smiled and curled the ends of his mustache with his fingers. "Ahh, my lady, how do you guess? I will now demonstrate my version of the Mexican hat dance." Everyone laughed as he danced around the table, but the appearance of the head steward brought the entertainment to a halt. "Thank you, thank you, thank you. I will now give you demonstration of table steward getting you something to drink." He turned around and walked sedately through the galley door.

Carolina realized then that meal times in the Poseidon wouldn't be boring.

"That Dominic is a mess, but don't believe anything he says," Peter said. "He isn't even Mexican; he's from Goa, India."

While Peter concentrated on his menu, Carolina watched Yasuko studying him. Carolina shook her head negatively and mouthed the words, "Too old." Yasuko frowned.

Dominic returned from the galley with three glasses of iced tea, stopping next to Carolina. "You, my lady, look the hungriest."

"I doubt that," butted in Eula Mae. "But I'm hungry. I could eat the north end of a south-bound polecat."

Peter laughed. "That's a good one. I love to hear Southerners talk. It's like you have your own language."

"I believe that also applies to the British," Eula Mae responded.

Dominick cleared his throat. "Back to you, Mrs. Cunningham. What would you like to eat?"

Carolina touched her finger at the top of the menu. "I'll start off with banana soup." She had never eaten banana-anything that tasted bad. She ran her finger down the menu. "I'll have the prime rib, medium rare, and a baked potato with lots of butter, sour cream, and cheese. And for dessert, Decadent Triple Chocolate Pie."

Peter shook his head. "That's a lot of food."

Eula Mae sighed and nodded. "You haven't seen anything yet."

After Dominic cleared away the last of the dishes, he placed a bowl of large red strawberries with sour cream and brown sugar in front of

Carolina, who picked up a plump berry, dipped it into the sour cream, then into brown sugar, and plopped it into her mouth. "Mmmmmmm," and other contented sounds emerged from her. Carolina closed her eyes to maximize the enjoyment of the mingled flavors exploding her taste buds. She swallowed and sighed happily.

Peter grinned at Carolina and sipped his coffee. "I didn't realize eating strawberries could be such a—uh—delicious experience." Then he turned his attention to Yasuko. "Tell me, why did you choose this particular cruise?"

When Yasuko hesitated, Eula Mae jumped in. "It seemed like the perfect cruise for three women living in an old folks home."

"Eula Mae!" Yasuko spluttered.

Peter looked surprised. "You ladies don't look old enough for a retirement home."

"How old do I look?" asked Eula Mae.

"Sixty, maybe."

"Such a sweetheart! I'm 78; Carolina is 62; and Yasuko here is—"

"Eula Mae, stop right there. I'm sure Lieutenant Lieberson could care less how old we are."

"But—"

Yasuko glared at Eula Mae. "Put a lid on it. Change the subject."

Eula Mae sniffed. "Fine. We could talk more about crime onboard cruise ships."

"I don't think that—" began Peter, just as the ship lurched and pitched.

Yasuko turned pale. "Oh my."

"Yasuko, you don't look so hot," Eula Mae said. "What's wrong?"

"I don't feel well," Yasuko said, holding a napkin to her mouth.

"Probably a touch of *mal de mer*," said Peter, leaning toward her.

"Is that something serious?" Carolina asked. She had never seen Yasuko look so pale. Pale with a hint of gray. Normally, with all of her makeup, her face color was ivory pale. Had Yasuko been poisoned with plutonium or nerve gas by a Russian spy, while she ate her dinner?

"Seasickness," Peter translated. "Dramamine might help. Also, try to keep something solid in your stomach."

"Seasickness?" Yasuko groaned. "Will it be like this the entire cruise?"

"No, it's because we're entering the ocean shipping lanes. The sea's a little rough here. Once we reach calmer waters in the Caribbean, you'll feel much better."

Yasuko, with the help of Dominic, pushed her chair back from the table. "Sorry, but I need to lie down."

"Probably not a bad idea," Peter agreed, taking her arm.

"This is embarrassing. I've never been seasick before."

"You've never been on a ship before," Eula Mae pointed out.

"Yes, lots of passengers get seasick their first time on a cruise ship," Peter said. "Look, I'm on my way to my cabin, myself, since I have to be on duty at 4 a.m. Please allow me to escort you to your suite."

Carolina quickly maneuvered herself between Yasuko and Mr. Boring Officer. "Thanks, but I can take care of her." Carolina put her arm around Yasuko's tiny waist and steered her toward the exit.

"Good night," Carolina said.

"Good night," Peter replied. "Trust me, you'll feel better in the morning." He quickly left the dining room.

"Wait up." Dominic ran toward Carolina with a bowl of strawberries. "For Madam. Should you get hungry later."

Carolina accepted the bowl from Dominic, just as the ship lurched, again, catching her and Yasuko off guard, and sending Carolina stumbling into Mr. Hunky Spy, who was also heading for the exit.

"Sorry, I'm not used to the floor moving," Carolina apologized.

Mr. Hunky Spy raised his right brow. "I can see that," he said. "Will you be able to manage or do you need help?"

Carolina straightened herself up and reached for Yasuko, who was starting to look a pale, grayish green. "Thanks, but we'll be okay."

Mr. Hunky Spy nodded, flashed her a wide smile of perfect teeth, and walked away, leaving her with a weird feeling in her abdomen. Was she getting seasick, she wondered, or could it be something she had not felt in years?

Eula Mae, who had remained seated, walked over to Carolina and Yasuko. "Who was that?"

"An international spy, of course." Carolina handed the strawberries to Eula Mae. "Now, please help me get Yasuko to our suite before she throws up."

After Carolina and Eula Mae rolled Yasuko moaning and groaning into her bed, they stepped outside onto their veranda. Eula Mae sat on a chaise lounge, while Carolina leaned over the railing and looked below at the ship's bow cutting through the ocean swells. With the roar of rushing water in her ears, Carolina closed her eyes and inhaled the smell of the sea and felt her hair being tossed and blown by the wind.

Carolina stepped away from the rail. "Eula Mae, where are my strawberries?"

Eula Mae bolted to a sitting position. "Oops."

"What do you mean, 'oops'?"

"I'm afraid I left them in the passageway, so I could help you get Yasuko into our suite."

"That's okay. I doubt if our steward would pick them up." Carolina walked briskly to the cabin door and opened it in time to catch a glimpse of the stowaway in the trench coat scurrying away—a bowl of strawberries in her hand. "Hey," Carolina yelled after her, but the a.k.a. Interpol agent didn't even look back.

"Those are my strawberries!" Carolina chased after her. Not only to retrieve the strawberries, but to question the stowaway and get some answers. She pursued her straight down the corridor, halfway through the length of the ship. At a major intersection, the stowaway looked left, uttered a high-pitched yelp, and kept running straight. Seconds later, Carolina passed through the same intersection and collided with a big-bellied, gray-headed man in a white uniform.

As Carolina fell on top of the ship's officer, she caught a glimpse of the disappearing stowaway. Had she taken his strawberries, too, Carolina wondered? What a desperate woman.

"I'm sorry, sir." After making sure nothing was broken—like a hip or a leg—Carolina rose from the floor, as slowly and as gracefully as possible for an older woman. "I was chasing my strawberries."

Grunting and puffing from his efforts, the opulent ship's officer stood up. A dark blush crept up his neck and across his sweaty face. "Bloody hell, you let her get away!" He rubbed his nose gingerly. "You hurt my bloody nose."

Carolina cringed at his burst of temper and stared in fascination as a trickle of blood oozed down his upper lip. Wow, she marveled, she'd never bloodied anyone's nose before. "Who were you chasing?" Carolina asked in a soft, calm voice—something she'd discovered worked better than screaming back. "Sorry about your nose. Are you okay?" Carolina tried to sound sympathetic.

The man, who looked even older than Lieutenant Lieberson, took a deep breath and let it out slowly. He wiped his nose with a white handkerchief from his pants pocket. Slowly the color of his face returned to normal. "I'm sorry, Madam. And you are?"

"Carolina Cunningham."

"Yes, Mrs. Cunningham. Please excuse my rudeness. I shouldn't have been running, and I shouldn't have raised my voice."

"Apology accepted, mister—?"

"Alvin Greene, the ship's purser."

Carolina smiled and held out her hand. "Does that mean you're in charge of the Purser's Desk?"

Greene shook her hand limply by the fingertips. Totally icky, Carolina thought.

"Yes, that's correct. We're open 24/7, serving as a bank, post office, information booth, and customs and immigration authority."

"I'm sure my suite mates and I will see a lot of you."

"Yes, I'm sure." He glanced in the direction the stowaway had taken.

"Nice to meet you, Mr. Greene." She almost purred her response. It was advantageous to be polite and well-mannered in such a situation. It always caught any suspects off-guard.

"Please excuse me. I have matters to attend to. Good evening."

Carolina watched him hurry away. "Talk about a man with an agenda," she mumbled out loud. Did the stowaway have an agenda, too? Or would she be glad she escaped the purser's clutches and foiled his plans?

Chapter Five
Day at Sea

Dominic curled his mustache and smiled, as Carolina, Eula Mae, and Yasuko slid breathlessly into their seats for breakfast. "Dominic happy to see his ladies this morning. Did everyone have a good evening?"

"Yes, thank you," Carolina replied, accepting the breakfast menu. She felt no need to share her evening yet. Eula Mae and Yasuko had been asleep when she returned to the suite. Crawling into bed seemed better than waking her friends. She had considered calling Lilly on the WhatsApp, but decided to wait until after breakfast.

"The ship rocked me to sleep. I don't think a cyclone would have awakened me," said Eula Mae.

The ship suddenly lurched, and a small groan escaped from Yasuko. She waved away the menu. "Just a Coke for me, please."

"Better to have solid food, Mrs. Crane," Dominic said. "Squall coming through this morning."

Yasuko rubbed her forehead. "Uh-uh—no way—I need a Coke."

"Yes, ma'am. One Coke. And for you, Mrs. Cunningham?"

"The fruit plate, please, and super-size it." Carolina pointed to the list of fruits on the menu. "No raspberries, please, but bananas and strawberries." Carolina looked over the other offerings. Eggs Benedict? Cherry Blintzes? Smoked Salmon? Where was the regular breakfast food? Her eyes finally spotted something. "Blueberry pancakes with bacon." She gave the menu a final once over. "Oh, and a glass of orange juice, and a cup of jasmine green tea."

"Ahhh, now that's a good breakfast." Dominic wiggled his thick black eyebrows and turned to Eula Mae. "What would Mrs. Davis like for breakfast?"

"I'm starving. Must be the ocean air. I'll have a cup of coffee. Black. None of that fru-fru stuff." Eula Mae shook her head. "Too much fancy food on this menu, Dominic. Is it possible to get two plain fried eggs with grits, bacon, and biscuits?"

"Certainly. Anything else for you?"

"Strawberry jam? Orange juice?"

Dominick curled his mustache. "It will be my pleasure to serve that for you." He smiled his toothy smile, gathered the menus, and headed for the galley.

"Sorry I bailed out on you guys last night. Did I miss anything?" Carolina asked.

Another waiter arrived and served them one Coke, two glasses of orange juice, a cup of black coffee, and a white porcelain teapot with one jasmine green tea bag and a lemon slice on the side.

"I tried to stay awake, but you never came back with your strawberries," Eula Mae said, between sips of juice and swallowing several pills.

"The stowaway stole my strawberries."

Eula Mae strangled on her juice. "What?"

"Carolina," Yasuko said, "Stop it right there."

Carolina paused dunking her tea bag in the hot water. "I'm serious! I'm not making this up. When I opened the door to get the strawberries, they were gone."

"I bet the cabin steward picked them up," suggested Yasuko. "What's his name? Mr. Gallenkemp? He told us it was his job to tidy up after us."

Carolina pictured the tall, thin, balding older man who introduced himself to them when they checked into their suite. He said he would be making up their room and dropping off clean towels every day. The perfect picture of a British butler—like the old actor David Niven. But, somehow, she could not picture him as a strawberry thief. "No, the stowaway took them." Carolina took a deep breath. "I chased after her. I would have caught her, too, except I collided with the ship's purser. Gave him a bloody nose."

Eula Mae gasped. "Please tell me you're joking!"

"I swear I didn't see him. He was chasing the stowaway, too."

"Why?" asked Yasuko.

"I'm not sure. I only know he was furious. His face turned nearly purple, and you could see this big fat vein throbbing in his neck."

Carolina pointed to the side of her neck. "Right here."

"I refuse to believe this," Yasuko said.

"Believe it. He yelled at me."

"Well, dang it all, Carolina," Eula Mae said, "you did knock him down and bloody his nose."

"But it was an accident, and I'm a guest on this ship. He's supposed to be polite."

"Hmph! This isn't Disney World," pointed out Yasuko.

Dominic returned with a large platter of fruit for Carolina, who quickly forked a slice of banana, chewed it thoughtfully, and frowned. "Dominic, this banana is green!"

"Yes, Mrs. Cunningham. The bananas are always brought aboard the ship green, but slowly during the cruise they will ripen."

"You know how bananas are, Carolina. Tomorrow they will be a little bit riper. By the end of the cruise, they will be rotten." Yasuko closed her eyes and sipped her Coke as the ship gently rocked.

"Yasuko's right, Dominic." Carolina said. "I understand. Bananas are a fruit that ripen fast, so they need to be green when they reach the ship."

"Thank you for understanding. Did you enjoy the strawberries last night, Mrs. Cunningham?" Dominic twisted his mustache and smiled.

Carolina forked a strawberry and sighed. "Afraid not, Dominic. The stowaway ran off with them."

Dominic's eyes widened. His mustache quivered. "Stowaway? What stowaway? We have no stowaway." He looked over his shoulder at the head steward.

Carolina tilted her head and stared at him. "Really?"

Dominic pinched at his mustache nervously. "Eye-yi-yi. I know nothing."

Carolina's eyes widened. "Did you hear that, Eula Mae? Yasuko? There's a stowaway onboard the *Emerald Dream*."

"Huh? I didn't say that." Dominic's eyes bulged. "Please don't get me into trouble."

"I saw her last night, and the purser did, too. Tell us what you know, and we'll do the same." Carolina crossed her fingers, hoping that Dominic would give them the whole scoop.

"Ladies, Dominic cannot do that." He looked over his shoulder at the head steward, again. "I get into 'mucho' big trouble."

Carolina motioned to him with her finger. He leaned towards her, and she whispered in his ear, "We won't tell a soul."

"Carolina, Dominic is only teasing," Yasuko said. "It's not possible for a stowaway to be onboard."

Dominic grimaced. "Ahh, but it is easy thing to do," he whispered. "Last cruise, a steward's girlfriend sneaked onboard."

"Definitely no problem getting food," Carolina said.

"But the hostess asked for our cabin number at the Poseidon door this morning," Yasuko pointed out.

"But not in the Jade Café yesterday," Eula Mae said. "Or afternoon tea in the library. Or the buffets around the swimming pool. A stowaway could eat, and no one would be the wiser." When it comes to food, Carolina thought, Eula Mae always knows it all.

"But where would a stowaway sleep?" asked Yasuko.

"Everywhere," said Dominic. "Outside. Inside. In lounges throughout the ship. On chaise lounge chairs around the pool. We can't accuse sleeping passengers of being stowaways, no?"

Only if they're wearing trench coats, Carolina thought, wiping her mouth with her linen napkin. "I can't wait to get home and tell my friends how easy it is to stowaway on a cruise ship. What an inexpensive Caribbean vacation."

Dominic's jaw dropped. His eyes bulged. "No, Mrs. Cunningham, please don't do that. I would get fired for sure."

"Relax, I'm only joking."

Dominic sighed and straightened up. "You had me worried. I could see me back in Goa working in my uncle's coconut grove."

Yasuko set down her Coke. "It's possible we saw the stowaway slip onboard yesterday. What have you heard?"

Carolina looked at Yasuko in surprise. Had she heard correctly? Had Yasuko admitted to seeing a stowaway?

"Ah, yes, the woman in the trench coat you saw sneaking on board," agreed Eula Mae.

Dominic glanced around cautiously. "The captain says a woman stole onboard during an incident on the gangway," he said in a hushed voice. "All crew members must report anyone suspicious."

Carolina mentally filed away this information.

The ship lurched, again. Yasuko sipped her Coke and turned pale. "I'm starting to feel really awful, again."

Carolina pushed back from the table. "Yasuko, Eula Mae. Back to the suite."

"No. Please finish your breakfast. I can get there by myself. But would you mind stopping by the ship's store and getting me something for seasickness? I can't spend the whole cruise in our suite."

"Will do." Carolina watched Yasuko disappear out of the dining room. Then she poured warm maple syrup on her blueberry pancakes, while worrying about the safety of herself and her traveling companions. With the number of possible spies, secret agents, and stowaways onboard the *Emerald Dream*, Carolina needed Yasuko and Eula Mae to be prepared for any trouble that might lie ahead.

After sending Eula Mae back to their suite to check on Yasuko, Carolina headed to Deck 5, where the ship's map showed the location of four boutiques. One sold jewelry and watches, and gold and silver chains by the foot. A second one sold tropical clothing: bikinis, shorts, tops, sun hats, wind-breakers, sun dresses, and casual outfits. Another shop sold souvenir items, ranging from coffee mugs to towels with the ship's logo. The fourth shop carried everything else—from paperback books to large bags of M&M's and toiletries.

A box of Dramamine prominently displayed by the cash register caught her eye. Obviously a bestseller during rocky sea days, she figured, as she grabbed a box. Waiting to check out, Carolina added a brown leather journal with the image of a sailboat on the cover. Light beige, lined pages inside the book were bordered with palm trees. The perfect spy journal, she thought—very much like the one Mrs. Craycraft had. A place to write down notes, clues, discoveries about the stowaway, and any other pertinent, sinister happenings onboard the ship.

Returning to their suite, Carolina found Yasuko lying on her bed, a damp cloth rolled up across her forehead. She handed her the Dramamine and a glass of water, and joined Eula Mae on the veranda.

For a few moments, the two of them watched as a light rain began, and the Atlantic waters turned dark gray and choppy.

"No wonder Yasuko's stomach feels queasy," Eula Mae said. "Just looking at all them swells rising and falling makes me feel a might woozy." She and Carolina went back inside.

"I hope the Dramamine works," said Yasuko, placing her empty glass on the nightstand. "The Captain's cocktail party is tonight. I can't miss it."

"Me either," agreed Eula Mae. "There's bound to be good wine and tasty appetizers."

"*Hors d'oeuvres*." Carolina said.

"Huh?"

"*Hors d'oeuvres*, Eula Mae. That's the fancy word for appetizers."

Eula Mae grunted. "More like the fancy word for inedible."

Carolina grinned, sat down at the small desk, and pulled out her new spy journal.

"What's that?" Eula Mae asked, looking over Carolina's shoulder.

"It's my journal for the cruise," she answered, opening the book and picking up a pen. Across the top of the first page she carefully printed:

Agent Carolina Cunningham's Journal

Eula Mae grunted.

Carolina turned the page and wrote, **Day One**. She smoothed the paper with her fingers and started to write:

Mysterious woman in trench coat, wide-brimmed hat, and large sunglasses knocks down older passenger on gangplank and sneaks onboard ship undetected.

Stowaway - a.k.a Interpol agent - steals strawberries. While in pursuit, I knock down rude Purser, Alvin Greene, who is also chasing stowaway.

Possible male secret agent onboard staying in cabin next to ours.

Questions: Why is stowaway onboard? Why was purser chasing her?

Yasuko lifted her head. "What are you doing? Writing your own spy novel?"

"No, this is my travel journal." Carolina held up the cover so Yasuko could see the image of the cruise ship. "I thought it might be cool to write about our adventures."

"That's nice, Carolina." Yasuko lay back down. "In ten years—if we're still alive—you can read it out loud at our trip anniversary party to remind us of how much fun we had. Especially the part where I was seasick the entire week."

Carolina closed her journal with a snap. "You are correct, Yasuko, that's exactly what I had in mind." She reached for her cell phone. "But right now, we need to call Lilly and let her know we're still alive."

With Eula Mae looking over her shoulder, Carolina brought up the WhatsApp on her cell phone and clicked the camera image for a face-to-face call. In seconds, Lilly's smiling face appeared on the screen.

"Hello!" Lilly greeted them. "I see Eula Mae, but where's Yasuko?"

"I'm lying down," Yasuko mumbled from her bed.

Carolina reversed the camera, enabling Lilly to see a miserable-looking Yasuko in bed. "She's feeling a little bit seasick at the moment," Carolina said, reversing the camera back. "How is Archie? Did his surgery go okay?"

"Yes, no problems. No rehab for Archie, either. We've only been home about an hour. He's napping, and I'm trying to get his pills organized. He has about a dozen pills to take each day."

"That's a lot of drugs," Eula Mae said. "Any Oxy in the bunch?"

"Yes, but he's not supposed to use it unless his pain level is 8 or above. He's only taking some ultra-painkiller called tramadol today," Lilly explained. "Physical therapy starts in the morning."

"Besides Archie's knee replacement, anything exciting going on at the Villas?" Eula asked.

"Harlan and his harem went to the photo exhibit at the Brunswick Mall," Lilly said.

Carolina rolled her eyes. Harlan Wilson was probably the most popular bachelor at the Villas. What made him so special? Besides being funny and charming, and having a little more hair on his head than most of the other single men at the Villas, he only had a small belly. Not to mention he played the guitar and sang with a sexy, smoky voice.

The women in Harlan's harem ranged in age from 81 to 90 and loved him passionately. They "doted" on him, as Eula Mae was prone to say. They fussed over him. In return, Harlan took them to concerts, stage performances, the movies, and even to restaurants for dinner or Sunday brunch.

"I can't believe he took his entire harem to Brunswick Mall. How did they get there?" asked Eula Mae.

Lilly laughed. "You'll love this. He paid his grandson to chauffeur them there and back in the family mini-van. But that's enough of news from the Villas. What's going on with you? Do you like the ship and your suite? Have you met any good-looking men yet?"

Eula Mae took the phone from Carolina's hand. "Lordy, Lordy, have we met good-looking men!" she said. "Yasuko is already in love with a ship's officer."

"I heard that," Yasuko called out from her bed.

"And we saw a stowaway sneak onboard the ship," Eula Mae continued. "Carolina chased after her for stealing her strawberries. In the process, she knocked down the purser and bloodied his nose."

Carolina snatched back the phone. "It was nothing," she insisted.

"Wow!" was all Lilly could say. "Omigosh! This sounds like a chapter in an Agent Craycraft book." Lilly looked at her husband, who had pushed his walker up behind her. "Got to run give Archie his drugs. Call, again, tomorrow."

Just as Carolina closed the WhatsApp, Yasuko let out an indignant squeal. "Oh crapola!"

"What's wrong?" asked a concerned Eula Mae.

Yasuko waved the day's program of events angrily in the air. "Steve Goodwill has cancelled all bridge classes."

"What?" Eula Mae snatched the program out of Yasuko's hands and read the boxed note: *Due to a series of unfortunate events, Steve Goodwill will be unable to make the cruise. We apologize for the cancellation of all bridge sessions and any inconvenience this may cause.*

"Unbelievable!" fussed Yasuko. "The opportunity to learn from Steve Goodwill is the only reason I signed up for this cruise. If I'd known he wouldn't be onboard, I'd have stayed at home."

Eula Mae continued to look over the program of events. "It's too late now. We'll just have to make the best of it. We have a very nice suite, and we'll be visiting Caribbean islands we've never been to."

Yasuko made an odd sound in the back of her throat. "My

apartment is much bigger, and I don't share it with anyone."

"The food's delicious," pointed out Eula Mae. "Also, there are lots of activities beyond bridge. We could go to lectures on each port, and learn about the island's history and how to shop."

"I wouldn't know about the food, since I've been too seasick to eat anything," said Yasuko, still looking over the program of activities. "Wait a minute. Hey, this looks interesting. Mahjong sessions and lessons every morning at 9 a.m. Maybe the instructor could give me some pointers to up my game."

"If that doesn't sound like something highfalutin' and fancy," said Eula Mae. "What the dickens is mahjong?"

"Do you know how to play rummy?" asked Yasuko.

"I've played it a time or two."

"Well mahjong is similar, but instead of cards, you play with bamboo and ivory tiles. You build a wall with the tiles and draw tiles instead of cards. Got it?"

Carolina rubbed her temples as her two roomies argued back and forth. Then she grabbed her key card and walked over to the door. "I need to get out of this cabin and walk around."

"But it's raining," Eula Mae pointed out.

"I don't plan to walk outside," explained Carolina.

"I'm not going anywhere until my stomach settles," Yasuko said, closing her eyes. "Please don't get into any trouble without us."

"I'll stay here with Yasuko," Eula Mae said.

"Not to worry, you two. I'll just walk around and look for the stowaway."

Yasuko's eyes popped open. "That's tantamount to risky behavior, Carolina. Read one of your spy novels. Live vicariously."

Carolina frowned. "Where's the thrill and excitement in that?"

"Save your breath, Yasuko," Eula Mae said.

Yasuko covered her eyes with the wet cloth. "Fine. Go chase your spies, secret agents, and stowaways. Get your throat slit or yourself thrown overboard. See if I care."

Carolina smiled and opened the door. "Who knows what evil lurks in the hearts of men? I'm off to find out. Ta ta!"

Half an hour later, after wandering around several lower decks, Carolina stopped in front of a large map of the ship and searched for the Green Springs Pool. The pool brunch area seemed a good place to search for a hungry stowaway. She had to eat, Carolina reasoned. That small bowl of strawberries wouldn't last long.

Carolina turned away from the map and couldn't believe her luck. The trench-coat clad stowaway, running full speed, rounded the corner right in front of her and dashed into the women's toilet. Before Carolina could follow her, one very flustered, red-faced purser—huffing and puffing from exertion—rounded the same corner. *Deja vu* all over again.

The out-of-breath purser halted in front of Carolina. After a few gasps for breath, he managed to speak. "Ah, yes, Mrs. Cunningham, I believe."

"Yes, that's right, Mr. Greene. Good morning." Carolina decided to be cordial, too.

He rubbed his hands together. "Did you perhaps see a woman in a raincoat come this way?"

"Yes." Carolina knew if she said otherwise, he'd know she was lying.

"Jolly good! Did you see which direction she went?"

"That way." Carolina pointed beyond the restroom. "And left toward the elevators."

Without a word of thanks, he rushed past her. When he was out of sight, she pushed open the restroom door. "Hello? He's gone. You can come out now."

Seconds went by before she heard the sound of a stall door unlocking. When the stowaway peered out cautiously, Carolina gasped aloud in surprise. She wasn't a woman. "You're a girl!"

"Well, duh! If I were a boy, I'd be in the other toilet."

The girl's face appeared pale in the subdued bathroom lights. Unkempt brown hair hung down the middle of her back in one plaited braid; dark circles underlined her hazel eyes.

"No, no, no. I mean I thought you were a woman, not a teenage girl."

"Well, I am a woman. I've had my period. My mom says that officially makes me a woman. How about you? You gone through menopause yet?

"That's none of your business," Carolina said indignantly. She didn't even know the girl's name and already this teenager was asking personal questions. "<u>Who</u> are you?"

Ignoring Carolina's questions, the young stowaway brushed by her, cracked the restroom door, and looked up and down the hallway. "Like you said, that's none of your business." She opened the door wide.

"Stop! You hold it right there. I just saved your butt from the purser, so talk to me."

"No time for talk. Later." She looked Carolina in the eye, stepped into the corridor and put her finger to her lips. "But thanks for your help." She hurried back around the corner.

Carolina ran after her, but by the time she rounded the corner, the stowaway was gone. What a rude teenager, Carolina thought. Maybe next time she saw her, she'd just let the purser catch her.

Frustrated, Carolina walked out onto the deserted pool deck at the stern of the ship. Even though it had stopped raining, the sky remained overcast and the air chilly. She walked over to the side rail and looked down at the water as the *Emerald Dream* cut through the choppy waves. The wind bit through her clothes and blew her hair up and away. Shivering as a cool mist off the ocean covered her face, she licked the salty spray off her lips and knew why no one else was on deck.

Carolina dragged an abandoned deck chair over to a sheltered spot out of the wind—between a ventilation shaft and a storage room door. After wiping off the chair with a dry pool towel, she sat down and opened her new spy thriller, *Mrs. Craycraft's Arabian Adventure*. The sun peeked out between the clouds and chased away the chill. Soon the roar of the ocean, the gentle rocking of the ship, and the persistent vibration of the ship's engines lulled her to sleep.

Sometime later, she was awakened by voices of two men carrying on an intense conversation nearby. Even over the noise of the ship, she clearly heard the deep voice of one man.

"She's in our way."

A second man responded with no emotion. "Then dispose of her."

Feeling her heart beginning to race, Carolina peered cautiously around the ventilator shaft. One of the men was the purser; she could only see the back of the other man. Suddenly, her book slipped off her lap and hit the deck with a thud. *Uh-oh.*

The purser frowned and looked straight at Carolina. "Hey, you there."

With the purser in pursuit, Carolina jumped out of her seat and ran down the deserted deck as fast as an out-of-shape sexagenarian could. She had been a track star in college, but apparently her older body had lost the memo. Gulping down the chilly, salty air, Carolina felt her chest tighten. and the pain in her arthritic knee went from a 5 to an 8. Just as she glanced behind to see how close the purser was, a man stepped out of the shadows and grabbed her by the shoulders, catching her off balance.

Closing her eyes, Carolina screamed and struggled to free herself from his grasp before he could garrote her or do her in. "Let go!" Like any well-trained agent, she brought up her knee to hit him where it would hurt, but only managed to slam her knee into his thigh. She wished then that she had signed up for those senior martial arts classes at the Y.

The man shook Carolina hard. "Mrs. Cunningham, are you all right?"

Wait, Carolina thought, she knew that voice. She opened her eyes. "Peter?" She grabbed him ferociously, promising herself never to call him Mr. Boring Officer, again.

He pushed her away at arm's length. "What's wrong? You're shaking all over."

Over Peter's shoulder, Carolina saw the purser approaching, his breaths coming in gasps. She was thankful he was in worse physical shape than she was. He came to an abrupt stop next to Peter.

Still breathing hard, Carolina pointed her finger at the purser. "That man—" She paused to catch her breath. "—is plotting to kill someone."

When the purser took a threatening step toward her, Carolina rushed behind Peter for protection.

Peter looked from Carolina to the purser. "Crikey, Mr. Greene, what's going on here?"

The purser furrowed his brow and glared at Carolina before looking at Peter. "No idea, sir. I was talking with a friend by the pool, when this woman took one look at me and ran off like a frightened rabbit. I followed her to make sure she was okay." He stretched out his arm.

"And to return the book she dropped."

Peter took the book from the purser. "Mrs. Cunningham, is this your book?"

Carolina stepped from behind Peter and grabbed her book. "Yes, but he really was talking about murdering someone." She pointed a shaky finger at the purser. "That man chased me to shut me up."

The purser threw his head back and laughed. "What a preposterous story. My friend and I were discussing an American detective series on the telly, that's all. I think this woman has had too much salt air, not to mention having an overactive imagination."

"Excuse me?" Carolina said as indignantly as possible. Just because she had frizzy gray hair and a few wrinkles didn't mean she was a dotty old lady and wacky in the head.

The purser shook his head and smiled. "I must be getting back to work, lieutenant. Mrs. Cunningham, have a good afternoon and evening."

Peter flashed Carolina a sympathetic smile. "Come along, Mrs. Cunningham. How would you fancy a nice cup of tea with some biscuits. Tea, coffee, orange juice, and pastries are served in the Horizons lounge until 10 o'clock. Pick up the pace, we don't want to arrive too late."

Fifteen minutes later, Peter and Carolina were sipping English tea and munching on scones with clotted cream and jam. Carolina thought she could really get used to this. Nothing like a mid-morning snack. Glancing across the tea room, she locked eyes with Mr. Hunky Spy. Before she could give him her full attention, she was distracted by a passing tray of gooey sticky buns with caramel and nuts. Carolina took two of them from the tray and looked back at Mr. Hunky Spy, who stared back at her. But when she smiled at him, he glanced down at his cup of tea.

Peter nudged Carolina. "Are you feeling better now? The shakes all gone?"

"I'm fine, lieutenant. Thanks for suggesting tea." She looked at him over the top of her cup. He definitely looked distinguished in that uniform, she thought. No wonder Yasuko flirted with him.

He chuckled. "Please. Call me Peter."

"If you call me Carolina."

"Agreed. Now, Carolina, tell me what really happened between you and Mr. Greene?"

Carolina sucked the sweet, sticky caramel off her finger. "I told you already. I know what I heard, and I know what I saw. That man has been chasing this teenage girl all over the ship. Maybe he's a pervert or a pedophile."

Peter spluttered tea down the front of his white uniform shirt. "Girl?" He blotted the tea spots with his napkin.

"Uh-huh. She's about 15 or 16."

Peter rubbed his chin, leaned closer to Carolina and lowered his voice. "Carolina, this isn't public knowledge, but the Captain has put out a stowaway alert. Might this teenager be the stowaway?"

"The stowaway no one knows anything about?" Carolina popped the last of the sticky bun into her mouth.

"Yes. Shhhh. Not so loud. You think you saw her?"

Carolina took in a long breath and let it out slowly, trying to decide if she should go with the truth. "Not only did I see her, but I saved her from Mr. Greene—twice." She waited for his reaction.

Peter set his cup down noisily in the saucer. His eyes narrowed. "I say there. Preventing the purser from carrying out his official duties is not good, Carolina. You could get into serious trouble."

Seeing that he wasn't too happy with the truth, Carolina decided to follow up with innocent ignorance. "I didn't know she was a stowaway. Last night I saw a fat, red-faced, older man chasing a scared girl. For all I knew, he was a pervert planning to have his way with her."

Peter raised an eyebrow. "Have his way with her?"

"He certainly wasn't chasing her to award her a free cruise."

A steward presented a tray full of croissants, but Peter waved him away. "I see." He cleared his throat. "Tell me, did you really bloody his nose?"

Carolina squirmed in her seat. Ouch, how did he find out about that? "Well, yeah, but it was an accident."

"And did you lie to him today?"

She bit her lower lip and sighed. "Sort of. Actually, I was merely misleading. I simply failed to mention she was hiding in the restroom."

"You admit you misled him."

"Possibly, let's face it, Mr. Greene isn't a likeable individual. He needs to take classes at the Disney school. Or some kind of charm school." She wondered if it was obvious to Peter that she disliked the purser?

Peter chuckled. "Yes, one could say he has a few personality flaws."

Carolina dropped her elbows on the table and leaned forward. "I don't care if the man has personality flaws. We're talking about a frightened teenage girl." She didn't mention the teenage girl was rude and disrespectful to her elders. Why complicate the situation?

"First of all, Mrs. Cunningham—"

"Carolina," she reminded him, thinking how annoyed Yasuko would be if she knew she were sitting here drinking tea with Peter. But Peter did not appeal to her. In fact, she thought, no man other than Arthur had ever interested her romantically. Her Arthur had been gone over two years now. No man could compare to him.

Peter sipped his tea and started over. "Carolina, trust me when I tell you this—that young woman isn't as helpless as she looks. Secondly, it's part of the purser's job to keep the ship free of stowaways. This teenage girl needs to be found, turned over to the authorities, and returned to her parents."

"I understand that, Peter, but I'm not going to apologize to him."

"Did I say you had to apologize to him?"

"No. And I'm not. At my age, reserving one's dignity is important." Carolina took a sip of her tea. "I think something more is going on here than a mere stowaway." For one second, Carolina thought she saw Peter stiffen. Could something sinister be afoot after all?

"Like what?" Peter asked.

"I'm not sure. But when I find out, I'll let you know."

Peter sighed. "Carolina, please let the ship's officers handle the situation. All right?"

How odd, thought Carolina. Was it her imagination that he seemed agitated and anxious? That his face appeared a little bit flush and his right eye twitchy? Carolina sighed. "Sure, if you insist." She didn't like giving in so easily, but maybe he had a promotion on the line and he needed to catch the stowaway himself.

"Yes, I insist. Stowing away on a ship is a criminal offense. Aiding a stowaway is, also."

"All right. I'll leave all the stowaway catching for you and Mr. Greene." At least she didn't promise to tell him, if she saw the stowaway, again. The good agents always keep their options open.

Chapter Six
Suspicions Arise

As Peter correctly predicted, the ocean calmed down enough for Yasuko to join Carolina and Eula Mae for lunch. While Yasuko sipped on vegetable soup and nibbled on a freshly baked croissant, Carolina had the chicken salad plate and a scoop of chocolate brownie ice cream; Eula Mae ate her way through a plate of French fries, a quarter-pounder cheeseburger, and a hot fudge sundae, topped with whipped cream and cherry.

"How was the soup?" Carolina asked Yasuko.

"It was perfect. I was getting tired of drinking Cokes,"

"Hmph! I bet you were getting tired of feeling sick, too." said Eula Mae.

"Dominic is glad his ladies look and feel well." He winked, twisted his mustache and carried away the dirty dishes.

After Dominic disappeared into the kitchen, Carolina updated Eula Mae and Yasuko on the stowaway, the latest run-in with the purser, and warnings from Peter. "What do you think we should do?"

"Listen to Peter," Yasuko said.

"I agree with Yasuko on this," Eula Mae said.

"But I think we should help this girl. This whole thing doesn't feel right."

"Maybe it's part of an episode for reality TV," suggested Eula Mae.

Carolina sighed and looked through the floor-to-ceiling windows at the gray-blue ocean. "You're wrong, Eula Mae. This is <u>much better</u> than reality TV. This is a spy thriller in the making. Mark my words. Something sinister is happening on this ship."

"Carolina, what you read in your spy novels is fiction," said Eula Mae.

"Yes," Yasuko agreed. "This is real life. Don't you know the difference?"

"Of course, I do," Carolina said. "But can you explain why the purser seems to be the only ship's officer intent on catching the stowaway? And I also know what I heard. Those men were talking about murder."

"When was the last time you had your highfaluting hearing aids checked?" asked Eula Mae.

"My hearing aids are working just fine, thank you!"

"But what if they really were talking about a TV show?" asked Yasuko.

"But they weren't." Carolina's voice rose in pitch and loudness. She could feel her frustration increasing.

"Calm down," said Eula Mae. "For the sake of argument, let's say you're right."

"No," shouted Yasuko. "She's not right. We should listen to Peter. He's a smart man."

Of course, he seemed smart and good-looking to Yasuko, Carolina thought, because she had the hots for him. "But what if I'm right? Then what?"

"Then to play it safe, I guess we shouldn't walk in any dark places," answered Eula Mae. "And we better stay close to the other passengers."

Yasuko tapped her cheek with her finger. "Since the bridge classes are cancelled, we could play mahjong in the game room."

"How about bingo in the Horizons lounge?" suggested Eula Mae. "They start selling cards in 15 minutes."

Carolina stared at them in disbelief. "Mahjong? Bingo? We may as well have stayed at the Villas. Did we not come on this cruise for a little excitement?"

"Excitement, yes," said Eula Mae, "but we didn't sign up for stowaways and secret agents. We signed up to play bridge with Steve Goodwill."

Carolina sighed. These two old women could be so obstinate and stubborn, she thought. But she needed to take their thoughts and feelings into consideration. After all, there might be a slight chance they were right. She threw her arms in the air. "Fine. To be safe, we'll hang out with lots of people doing whatever boring activity they do."

Yasuko and Eula Mae relaxed.

Carolina's brow furrowed in thought. "Maybe the stowaway is

having the same thought. Who would try to harm her in front of witnesses? Let's do it. Mahjong or bingo?"

Yasuko waved the daily program excitedly. "Wait! Change of plans! It's time for the Mr. Emerald Dream contest on the pool deck. We can't turn down a chance to ogle a few young hotties."

That evening at the Welcome Aboard cocktail party, Carolina, Eula Mae, and Yasuko had their photo made with Captain Oliver Burbage. At Yasuko's insistence, they wore identical floor-length black silk palazzo pants with black long-sleeve, V-neck tops—purchased at Chico's especially for the occasion.

"We look like triplets," said Eula Mae earlier, looking at herself in the suite's full-length mirror.

Yasuko shook her head. "Maybe more like the Andrew sisters. I'm the youngest, of course," she said, circling her flawless makeup one more time with her face-powder brush.

"Seriously?" Carolina asked. "We look like three old women in matching outfits out for one more good time before croaking."

The Captain was no spring rooster either, Carolina noticed. He reminded her of that old dead movie star her parents liked so much—Cary Grant, with thick white hair, immaculately styled and groomed. Burbage had enough hair to share with two bald men and still have plenty leftover, she thought. His smile was pleasant, and he seemed happy to shake hands and pose for photos. But that was probably why he was paid big bucks. Carolina figured they had the Captain's full attention for at least thirty seconds. Not bad, considering what they paid for thirty seconds of his time.

Lieberson stood straight and tall at the end of the receiving line. "Ahh, ladies," he said, and led them off to the side. "You three look quite glamorous tonight."

"Yes, sir, they certainly do," came a man's voice from behind Carolina.

Recognizing the voice of Mr. Hunky Spy, Carolina turned and saw him making his way to her through a sea of passengers. For some unexplained reason, that old movie "10" popped into her head.

Specifically, the part where Bo Derek runs down the beach in slow motion, her hair braids tossed by the breeze, as Ravel's "Boléro" plays in the background. Carolina swallowed hard and cleared her head of the image.

"Good evening, ladies," Mr. Hunky Spy said. "Ronald Dunten, freelance writer from Atlanta, at your service."

Carolina could not help but notice that Mr. Hunky Spy had replaced his spy clothes with black pants, white dinner jacket, and black bow tie. Not bad, she thought. Not bad at all. James Bond would be proud. She felt a slight quiver down below. Omigosh, what was it about this man?

Carolina extended her hand. "Carolina Cunningham, Mr. Dunten."

Mr. Hunky Spy smiled and shook her hand. "It is a pleasure to meet you, Mrs. Cunningham."

Carolina pointed to her suite mates. "Eula Mae Davis and Yasuko Crane."

He shook Eula Mae's hand. "Pleasure to meet you Mrs. Davis." Then he reached for Yasuko's hand. "And Mrs. Crane. Are you feeling better today?"

Yasuko gave him the once over with her dark brown almond-shaped eyes. "Yes, thank you for asking. The ship seems to be rocking less tonight." She tilted her head. "What exactly do you write?"

"Spy novels, of course," suggested Carolina. Anything else would be a waste of Mr. Hunky Spy's time. She jumped when Eula Mae elbowed her in the ribs.

Mr. Hunky Spy laughed and raised his right eyebrow. "Maybe when I retire. At the moment, I'm doing a series of articles on cruising for a travel magazine."

Peter stepped forward. "Peter Lieberson, the ship's second engineer," he said, bowing slightly and clicking his heels together. The men shook hands. "Pleasure to meet you, Mr. Dunten."

"Good to meet you, too," Mr. Hunky Spy replied. "Please call me Ron."

"Peter keeps the ship sailing," Carolina said.

Peter laughed. "How kind of you to say so, Mrs. Cunningham. However, it takes many officers and crew members to do that."

While Mr. Hunky Spy and Mr. Boring Officer discussed the difficulties of ship maintenance, Carolina listened to the orchestra play

"Some Enchanted Evening" and watched stewards serve glasses of champagne, red and white wine, and fruit punch. Other stewards passed out canapes and *hor d'oeuvres*.

Carolina yawned. This was turning out to be a wearisome, boring evening. No stowaway or ugly purser in sight, and the spy had turned out to be a writer.

Eula Mae edged over to Carolina. "I can only take so much of this testosterone conversation," she whispered. "Why don't you sashay over and change the subject?"

"Allow me," said Yasuko. "We're old enough now that we can be blunt. Isn't it freeing not to have to be diplomatic and nice all the time?"

Eula Mae grabbed Carolina's forearm. "Should we try and stop this?"

"Why not see how far she'll go," replied Carolina, suspecting Yasuko could go quite far.

Yasuko walked up next to Ron and waited for the men to look her way. "Tell us, Ron, are you married?"

Ron's eyes widened in surprise. "Wow. Now that's not a question I get asked a lot." He smiled broadly.

His white-tooth smile dazzled Carolina. Her dentist had never been able to lighten her teeth that bright. Goodness knows she'd paid him an exorbitant amount of money twice to get a brilliant Hollywood smile. Her teeth did come out a few shades lighter, but nothing to write home about. Guess it was because her teeth were too old to brighten.

"Well? Are you married or not?"

"No, Mrs. Crane, I am not. How about you three?"

"Carolina and Eula Mae are widows. I'm divorced from a con artist who wanted to live the lifestyle of the rich and famous by stealing their money. He's now rotting away in a federal prison."

Carolina and Eula Mae gasped. Peter's jaw dropped. Ron chuckled. "Interesting. If I weren't writing this travel article, I would consider doing a feature article on you and your ex for the *National Inquirer*. I bet you have lots of juicy tidbits to share?"

"You don't know the half of it. I did enjoy feeling rich for a short period of time, but all good things must come to an end. Are you rich by any chance?"

"This is beginning to feel like a major interrogation," Ron said and winked.

Carolina grabbed Yasuko's arm. "All right, Yasuko! That's enough! What is it with all of these personal questions?" It was so out of character for Yasuko and couldn't be blamed on too much alcohol since the reception had just started.

Ron laughed, again. "Not a problem, I've been asked worse."

A subdued Yasuko hovered nearby, whispering with Eula Mae. Carolina took a deep breath. Maybe the evening was headed away from disaster. Maybe they could enjoy the night after all.

Peter thoughtfully eyeballed Ron for a few seconds. "I say, Ron, what specifically are you writing about? The gourmet cuisine? Onboard entertainment? Exciting ports of call?"

Ron focused on Peter. "I spent the entire morning on the bridge. Fascinating! All that radar equipment, buttons, gadgets, and alarms."

Carolina didn't think that sounded fascinating at all, She had hoped Ron might be interested in crimes committed on cruise ships. Eula Mae's research in that direction had roused her curiosity.

"Say, Peter, perhaps you could answer a question for me?" Ron reached into his jacket pocket and pulled out a small notepad and pen.

"I'll try," Peter said. "What would you like to know?"

Ron flipped back a page and checked his notes. "One of those alarm systems was for fire anywhere on the ship. The other one was for ship emergencies. What would constitute an emergency?"

Peter stroked his chin. "Have you noticed the alarms on all outside decks? Man overboard alarms, we call them."

"Yes, I know the ones."

Peter swallowed the last of his wine. "If you see anyone fall overboard, pull the alarm, throw over a life ring, and shoot off a flare. The alarm automatically relays to the bridge."

Carolina's eyes widened. Whoa. Now this was good stuff, she thought. You never knew when you were going to see someone fall—or get thrown—overboard. "Is it common for someone to fall overboard?" she asked. Out of the corner of her eye, she saw Eula Mae and Yasuko moving next to her.

"It happens occasionally. Last New Year's Eve we had a male passenger, who enjoyed one too many drinks, fall overboard."

"Did you save him?" Carolina asked, disappointed nothing that exciting had happened on their cruise—at least so far.

"We didn't know he was gone until we reached port. His wife was hysterical. We cruised back the way we'd come, and there he was, still bobbing around after six hours. Lucky for him it was daylight, and the sea was calm. We figure if he hadn't been so drunk, he'd have died from shock."

"Or been eaten by a shark or drowned," pointed out Eula Mae.

"From shock, huh?" asked Ron, jotting down a few notes.

"Most people who fall overboard go into shock because they think the ship has left them," Peter explained. "Ships this size don't stop on a dime. That's why it's important to throw out a life ring and flare so they'll know someone saw them."

"What about that female officer who fell overboard last month?" Ron asked.

Carolina sucked in her breath sharply. "Really? A ship's officer fell overboard?"

"What about her?" Peter replied. His smile disappeared.

"Was she drunk or high on drugs?" probed Ron, tapping his pen lightly on the pad.

"Some crew members believe she might have jumped." Peter glanced at his watch impatiently. "Oops, look at the time. Please excuse me, but I need to get back to greeting passengers. Ladies, maybe I'll see you later at dinner." Peter bowed and returned to the receiving line with the Captain.

"He certainly left in a hurry. Was it something we said?" asked Ron. "Guess I'll have to interview the three of you now." He yawned, patted his mouth, and winked.

"I doubt if we're important enough for that," said Carolina, but she certainly didn't mind the opportunity to spend more time with Mr. Hunky Spy, a.k.a. Ron Dunten the travel writer. "Not to mention, we know nothing about nothing."

"You should let me decide that." He smiled and winked, again. Carolina felt warmth on her cheeks.

"Yeah," said Eula Mae. "Just because you know nothing doesn't mean Yasuko and I have nothing to say."

"Are you interviewing anyone important tomorrow?" Yasuko asked.

"Only the Captain's goldfish. That's why I wanted to talk to the really important people on my list today. Goldfish are always a tough interview."

Everyone laughed loudly, but stopped abruptly when the purser seemed to appear from out of nowhere. A feeling of dread and apprehension formed in Carolina's stomach. She gripped Eula Mae's shoulder and leaned toward her ear. "We need to leave. Now!" she hissed.

"Carolina, don't be absurd," Eula Mae said. "The evening is just starting to get interesting."

Yasuko frowned. "What's going on? I'm not ready to leave."

Carolina grabbed their arms and began pulling her friends away from the oncoming purser.

"Hey!" yelled Ron. "Don't leave yet. You haven't answered my questions."

"Sorry!" Carolina said, pushing Eula Mae and Yasuko toward the other exit door. "We'll try again later."

Too late. The purser, who was making a beeline for the three women, pushed his way through a group of passengers and cut them off before they could reach the door.

"I say, do wait up, Mrs. Cunningham," he called out nicely. "How frightfully jolly good to see you, again. And these lovely ladies would be your suite mates?" He took Eula Mae's hand. "Alvin Greene, the ship's purser. And you are?"

"Eula Mae Davis. How did you know we share a suite?"

"Oh, my dear lady, I know all about my passengers, but I don't think I've met your friend here," he said, indicating Ron, who had followed the women across the room.

"Ron Dunten," Carolina said, her entire body in flight mode.

Ron and the purser shook hands.

"Sorry to disappoint you, Mr. Greene," Carolina said, "but he's not a stowaway. He's writing a magazine article about the activities on <u>this ship</u>," she said, emphasizing the last words.

Ron raised his right eyebrow.

The purser turned back to Carolina. "Such an imagination you have Mrs. Cunningham. Maybe you should be a fiction writer."

"No, I think an investigative reporter would be more like it for me." Carolina and the purser glared at each other.

Finally, Mr. Greene pasted on a phony smile and stepped back.

"Mrs. Cunningham, it has been a pleasure seeing you, again, and meeting your friends and fellow passengers." He nodded to Ron, Eula Mae, and Yasuko. "But before I leave, please allow me to introduce you to my good friend, Mr. Smith."

A blah, unremarkable-looking man stepped out of the shadows, where he had been standing unnoticed. "Mr. Smith handles my problems, leaving me free for more enjoyable things." No one said anything. The purser laughed and led Mr. Smith away. "Good evening," he called over his shoulder.

Carolina started to tremble. This could not be good, she thought. The purser was flaunting his personal thug in public. If she were Agent Craycraft, she would already have a plan.

"You're right, Carolina, he oozes pure nastiness," Eula Mae said.

"What a creep!" Yasuko said.

"I told you so. He's simply a horrid man. Now do you believe me?"

"Being nasty does not make one a murderer," pointed out Eula Mae.

"Anyone want to tell me what's going on here?" asked Ron, who had been standing quietly, listening to them talk. "I think I missed the beginning of this conversation."

Carolina looked at Eula Mae and Yasuko, and hesitated. "Should we tell him?" she asked them, as though Ron wasn't there listening.

"Tell him what?" asked Eula Mae. "That the purser gets a burr in his saddle every time he sees you? That Alvin Greene is lower than a snake's belly in a wagon rut? Or that he wants to do you in."

"It may be to our advantage to tell as many people as possible. Then the purser might not be so quick to harm us. Especially—" Carolina pointed to Ron. "—if we tell all the facts to a magazine writer, don't you think?"

"Carolina, stop it," Yasuko said. "No more silliness tonight. No one is planning to murder you or us."

Ron shook his head. "Hey, remember me? The invisible writer?"

Argh! Carolina could not believe that in the face of mounting evidence, her friends were in denial. She turned to Ron. "Okay, we'll tell you, but not here."

"Carolina!" Eula Mae almost squealed.

Carolina looked at Ron conspiratorially and whispered, "Our room or yours?"

Half an hour later, in the empty Star Dust lounge, Carolina could tell that Eula Mae was quietly simmering in her seat. Her eyes were all scrunched up, and her mouth was so tight, her lips had disappeared. Carolina glanced at Yasuko, whose arms were crossed tightly against her chest. Something she did at dinner at the Villas, if her food didn't arrive fast enough to suit her. "Why do we continue to pay an exorbitant amount of money, if we have to wait forever to be fed," she would complain loudly.

Ron sat in front of the three women, notebook and pencil in hand. "All right, you three, what's going on?"

"We saw this young woman in a trench coat, hat, and sunglasses board the ship without going through security," Carolina began.

His right eye brow went up. "How did she manage that?"

Eula Mae leaned forward. "She tripped this poor old woman on the gangway."

"As soon as the victim fell down," broke in Yasuko, "her suitcase popped open, and her personal items went everywhere."

"When the security guard went to help, the stowaway snuck onboard while everyone else was distracted." Carolina took a deep breath and the words rushed out. "After dinner last night, she stole my strawberries. When I ran after her, I collided with the purser who was chasing her, too. Only he got mad at me because I bloodied his nose and the stowaway got away."

Ron stopped writing and looked at Carolina. "What? You bloodied Mr. Greene's nose?" He shook his head and looked amused.

Carolina nodded. "But it was an accident. I got hurt, too."

"I believe you. But this explains his attitude toward you. Go on."

"This morning, I saw him chasing the stowaway, again. She hid in the restroom, but I didn't tell Mr. Greene."

"Of course not, stowaways have to be protected," Ron said. "Makes sense to me. So you went into the restroom and confronted the perp— uh—helpless stowaway?"

Carolina glared at him. He wasn't taking her seriously. She took another deep breath. "The stowaway is a teenage girl."

Ron's eyes widened. "How old, you think?"

"Maybe 15?"

"Are you sure?"

"I know an adolescent girl when I see one."

Ron wrote down something. "Did you talk to her?"

"No, she rushed out. I tried to follow, but I lost her. I went out on the Green Pool deck to read. That's where I overheard the purser talking to this other man about killing someone who was getting in their way. Then he saw me and chased me until I ran into Peter."

"Second engineer, Lieutenant Lieberson?"

Carolina nodded. She noticed that Eula Mae and Yasuko were listening intently. Some of what she was telling Ron, they had not heard.

"You tell him what you thought you heard?" Ron continued.

"Yes, but the purser told him I heard wrong."

"What was his story?"

"That he and his friend, Mr. Smith, were talking about a TV show."

"You didn't believe him?"

"No, but Peter did. Now he thinks I'm either imagining it or overreacting." Carolina sighed, her shoulders sagged. She thought of her son Charter. If he were here, he'd laugh and make a smart-ass remark about her beloved book series.

"Peter could be right," Eula Mae pointed out. "You were probably napping at the time and woke up confused over what you heard."

"True, they did wake me up, but I heard what I heard," Carolina said in her own defense and wondered why Eula Mae didn't seem to believe her story. "And you yourself agreed that the purser is a slimy, sinister person."

"You're missing the point," Yasuko said. "You can't arrest a man because he doesn't have a sunshiny personality. If this is a simple case of a stowaway onboard, then Mr. Greene is only doing his job, and we're wasting Mr. Dunten's time."

Ron raised his eyebrow and tapped his pen lightly on his pad. "Let's look at this logically."

"All right," Carolina agreed. "Let's do that."

Eula Mae and Yasuko nodded.

"First of all. Does everyone agree there is a teenage female stowaway onboard the *Emerald Dream*?"

"No doubt in my mind," Carolina said.

Yasuko nodded.

Eula Mae took a deep breath and released it slowly. "All right, it looks that way."

"Question: Why would the purser want her dead? What would be his motive? Why not just arrest her, contact her parents, and drop her off at the next port?"

Eula Mae pointed her finger at Carolina. "See, I told you there's nothing going on. The man has no motive."

"It doesn't matter. I tell you, he wants her dead," Carolina insisted.

"Why?" asked Ron.

Everyone stared at each other in silence. The seconds ticked by, but no one could think of a single reason.

Eula Mae glanced down at her watch. "I hate to break up this brainstorming session, but we're going to be late for dinner."

"Oh no!" yelped Yasuko. "We can't miss dinner. We'd starve to death before breakfast."

Carolina rolled her eyes, stood up, and headed for the exit. Although Yasuko was being sarcastic, she knew that her suite mate did not want to miss an opportunity to see Mr. Boring Officer.

Ron followed the three women out of the lounge.

"I'm sorry we bothered you, Mr. Dunten," Eula Mae said, looking at him over her shoulder."

"Ron, please."

"Yes, Ron. I was hoping you could anchor Carolina firmly to the floor of reality. Thanks for listening to her," Eula Mae said. "She means well."

Ron slid his note pad into his pocket. "You know what they say? Where there's smoke, you'll probably find fire."

Eula Mae nodded thoughtfully. "You're right. It's also possible that we could all be murdered in our sleep tonight."

Ron smiled and raised his right brow. "You probably stand a better chance of falling overboard and getting eaten by a school of piranha."

"You know I can hear you, right?" Carolina asked, stepping back next to Ron.

Ron grinned. "I was hoping that might be the case. I would like to continue my interview with you ladies. If you share your table at dinner,

I'd like to join you."

"We would love having you join us," Carolina said. She figured he would keep the assassins away.

"But what about Peter?" asked Yasuko. "Will there be room for five of us?"

"I know for a fact this ship has tables that will seat six," Ron said.

"Oh, then it's all right with me if you join us, Mr. Dunten," Yasuko said.

"You have my vote, too," Eula Mae chimed in.

Carolina stood by the door to the dining room tapping her foot impatiently. "Now that we've all agreed that Mr Dunten may share our table, shouldn't we go inside and get seated?"

Ron chuckled. "I really love a take-charge kind of woman." He held out his elbow to Carolina, and winked. "Shall we?"

Carolina hesitated. Was Mr. Hunky Spy really offering to escort her into the dining room? It means nothing, Carolina Cunningham, she told herself. He's just being a gentleman. Not to mention you're not ready for anything more than that.

Carolina watched Ron charm the hostess with his soft voice and humor. Then the hostess handed a paper slip to a waiter. "Table 45, Raka. They will be sharing with the lieutenant."

Raka—from Myanmar, according to his name tag—led the party of four to a round table set for five, where Peter was waiting. Yasuko preened as Peter pulled out a chair for her. Ron pulled out a chair for Carolina. Eula Mae frowned when Dominic pulled out her chair, but she allowed him to push her to the table, spread a napkin in her lap, and hand her a menu.

Carolina sighed with relief. She had spent 15 minutes explaining to Eula Mae how to handle this. "Pretend you are Queen Elizabeth. The waiter is helping you to the table out of respect—not because he thinks you're feeble and older than dirt."

As Dominic collected the menus, Yasuko leaned toward Carolina. "You missed Lilly's phone call."

Carolina selected a sesame seed roll from the basket and placed it on her bread plate with a seashell-shaped pat of butter. "Oh? What did she have to report? Everything all right at the Villas?"

"Laura Lee moved in with Colonel Sneed," offered Eula Mae.

"Seriously?" Carolina asked. She knew that they were an item at the Villas. They shared a table at lunch and dinner, and they were often seen in the main lounge holding hands and whispering to one another. Both of them were in their 90s and going strong.

"Yes," said Yasuko. "Seriously. Get this: Laura Lee says they were married by a Justice of the Peace, but that she is not taking his name."

"Nope," said Eula Mae. "She does not want to become Laura Lee Sneed. She wants to stick with her maiden name—Appleton."

"Maybe they didn't really get married," suggested Carolina. "Maybe they just said that so they can live together without all the gossip."

"Lordy, Lordy, that's what everyone said. Let me tell you that did not sit well with Laura Lee. Not at all," said Eula Mae. "To stop all the yapping, Laura Lee taped the marriage certificate to their door."

Ron suddenly burst out laughing. "That is one funny story. Sounds like living in a retirement community can be pretty lively on occasion."

"Oh," Yasuko said, "you haven't heard the best story."

"That's right," Eula Mae took over the conversation. "The maintenance supervisor found out why Dorothy Pearson has mice in her apartment."

"Because she lives on the ground floor on the end?" Carolina guessed. Dorothy's glass sliding patio doors opened only a few feet from the edge of the marsh grass, which was full of wild life. Dorothy's patio was often covered with hermit crabs.

"That's partially it," agreed Eula Mae, "but the real problem is that Dorothy feels sorry for the mice and leaves them treats—like a French fry or a piece of cheese or grapes."

"In other words, Dorothy is an enabler," added Dunten.

Yasuko nodded. "Exactly!"

By the time Dominic had served the main course to everyone, Ron was steering the dinner conversation to discuss the purser and the stowaway.

"The purser does act peculiar on occasion, but let me assure you that he is a man of integrity," Peter said and sniffed.

"Integrity? No, there's something sinister going on with him, I can feel it," Carolina insisted.

"As a writer," put in Ron, "I have to deal with facts, Carolina. You're talking about gut feelings."

Carolina mulled that thought over for a second. "So, if I looked at the facts in a logical way, then it's highly unlikely Mr. Greene would harm anyone?"

"That's right," Peter said.

"Does everyone think I let my imagination run wild?"

Yasuko and Eula Mae rolled their eyes. Ron smiled and said, "Of course not."

Peter rubbed fingers across his lips. "No, but you may be overreacting."

Ron scribbled something down in his ever-present notebook. "How about the old saying where there's smoke, there's fire?"

Peter forced a laugh. "Sure, but why would Mr. Greene want to murder anyone, much less a teenage girl—stowaway or not? A perfect stranger to him?" He looked around the table at each person in turn.

Everyone at the table fell silent for a moment. Carolina looked at Eula Mae who was chewing her bottom lip thoughtfully. Carolina sighed. Here we sit, she thought, back to that motive thing, again. Why would a respected ship's officer resort to murder? Who was this teenager anyway? What was she doing on this ship?

"Well ..." Eula Mae started to speak. Every eye turned to her. "Maybe she isn't a stranger to him. Maybe he knows her."

Carolina's eyes widened. "Yes! That's it!" she cried out excitedly, moving to the edge of her seat. Instantly everything became clear. "She knows something bad about him. Maybe she found out he's a double-agent. Maybe she's blackmailing him, and he has to kill her to shut her up?" Carolina smiled brilliantly.

Ron turned to Peter. "Is that motive or what?"

"A double-agent? How utterly ridiculous," Peter said.

Ron laughed. "Now, now, Peter. You asked for a motive. You didn't say it had to make sense."

Suddenly, Carolina looked around. The dining room was almost empty, the tables were being set for breakfast, and Dominic was nowhere in sight.

"Should we leave before they turn out the lights?" Yasuko asked, pushing back from the table.

"How about a stroll around the deck, ladies?" asked Peter.

"I'll second that," said Ron.

"That would be good," Carolina said. "We could keep an eye out for—"

Eula Mae grabbed Carolina's elbow. "You know, it might be chilly walking outside. I think we should stop by the suite for sweaters."

Carolina frowned. She didn't need a sweater, but she didn't want Eula Mae to go by herself. Mr. Greene and Mr. Smith might be lurking in a corner somewhere. "Sure, I'll come with you."

"Yasuko, do you want to get a wrap, too?" asked Eula Mae.

"Thank you, but I'll be all right."

Carolina turned to Peter and Ron. "Why don't we meet you in the Reception Hall in fifteen minutes?"

"Splendid," said Peter with a slight bow.

Ron nodded. "Don't keep us waiting too long."

Carolina felt a tingle on the back of her neck, when she saw the door to their suite was ajar. Was some intruder inside their darkened suite lying in wait for them?

"I know I locked the door when we left for the reception," Eula Mae said, pushing the door open a few inches with one finger.

"I'm almost certain you did, too." Goosebumps broke out on Carolina's arms. The hair on the back of her neck stood up.

Eula Mae hesitated in front of the door. "Maybe Mr. Gallenkemp forgot to lock up after he turned down the beds."

Carolina thought that sounded reasonable. "Maybe. Let me check it out. You stay here. If I scream, run for help."

"Very funny, Carolina."

"Who's being funny?" Carolina nudged the door open and walked into the pitch-black room. Immediately, the door slammed shut behind her, and she heard the safety lock click into place. A good secret agent wouldn't have let that happen.

Eula Mae began banging on the door. "Carolina! Open up! This isn't funny!"

Standing in the darkness, Carolina could hear someone breathing behind her. She was not alone.

Chapter Seven
Stowaway Revealed

"Who's there?" Carolina felt a chill run down her spine.

The cabin lights snapped on. Carolina turned around, expecting to find herself face to face with Mr. Smith and a Walther PPK "James Bond" spy special with silencer. Instead, between her and the door stood the stowaway with pale face and dark circles under her eyes. Carolina's jaw dropped.

The stowaway reached out her right hand. "Remember me? I'm Colleen Burgess—the infamous stowaway."

Carolina clasped Colleen's hand. Even though it trembled slightly in hers, she had a strong grip. But Colleen seemed less spunky than the girl she'd seen in the restroom. "How did you get in here?"

"The cabin steward left the door open when he went for clean towels." Colleen swayed slightly.

Carolina quickly placed her hand behind Colleen's back to steady her. "Are you okay? Why don't we sit down?" Carolina guided her to a bed, noticing that the teen was wearing dark knit pants and a royal blue polo shirt that looked suspiciously like her own. She read the embroidered logo: Rose Dhu College. Yes, definitely her shirt. Carolina sniffed Collen's damp brown hair. It had the same fruity smell as her own brand of shampoo. Colleen had obviously made herself at home.

Colleen sat down on Eula Mae's bed and waved Carolina off. "I'm fine. Just tired from running and hiding."

"Where do you hide besides restrooms?" Carolina sat down next to her.

Colleen's shoulders sagged and her whole body slumped forward. Carolina thought she looked exhausted.

"I like the library. The sofas are comfy." She pulled her hair behind her neck and fastened it with a scrunchie. "I guess you've noticed I'm wearing your clothes?"

"Yes, I did, young lady. I also see they're a little bit large on you."

Her face blushed. "I'm sorry, but after I showered, I wanted to put on clean clothes, and yours were the best fit."

"And you thought 'why not'?"

Colleen laughed awkwardly and looked down at her hands. "Something like that."

Suddenly someone pounded on the cabin door, and Peter's voice called out urgently. "Carolina, are you all right?"

"Yikes!" Carolina hissed. "Eula Mae called for backup."

Colleen jumped off the bed and grabbed Carolina's forearm with more strength than seemed possible. "Please, no one must know I'm here."

Carolina realized she needed a plan. How would a good agent handle this situation? "Quick, into the closet." As the closet door shut behind Colleen, Carolina opened the door. At the same time, Peter and Ron charged into the suite, nearly knocking her down. Ron lost his balance and fell against Peter, who slammed his knee into the corner of the desk.

Eula Mae and Yasuko followed the men into the suite. Eula Mae grabbed Carolina by the shoulders. "Are you okay?"

Carolina mustered up a pathetic voice and matching facial expression. The same ones she had used on Arthur when she didn't want to go to Lowe's or Best Buy. She moaned slightly to increase the effect. "Yes." She grimaced and held the back of her head. "I think so."

"Is this some sort of joke?" asked an annoyed Peter. "Mrs. Davis said you were in trouble."

Clutching her head, Carolina backed up, collapsed on the bed, and sighed pathetically. "Sorry you were dragged into this. The cabin door was open, so I came inside to check for assassins." She sighed, again, for good measure.

Ron raised his right eyebrow and shook his head. "You planned to disarm an assassin by yourself?" Carolina noticed his sarcasm was barely masked.

"Why didn't you open the door for me?" asked Eula Mae.

Carolina leaned over and groaned. "I tripped in the dark and fell. Knocked the breath out of me. I opened the door as soon as I could."

Carolina looked at the three of them through half-closed eyes. Were they going for it? Ron looked amused. Peter still looked annoyed. Eula Mae and Yasuko looked concerned. Now if she could only get all of them to leave, she thought. But how could she accomplish that?

"You scared me to death, Carolina," Eula Mae said, feeling the back of her head. "I don't feel a lump."

"Hey, stop that! You're hurting me." Carolina scrunched up her eyes like her daughter Caitlyn would do when she was a toddler. Right before the crocodile tears would flow, and she'd accuse her brother Charter of doing some wrong.

Eula Mae backed off. "Sorry."

"You had us worried," Peter grimaced and massaged his knee.

"Think you'll be okay?" Ron sat down next to Carolina.

"Maybe you should see the ship's doctor," Peter suggested. "You might have a concussion."

"<u>No</u> doctor." Carolina adjusted her face to look a little less pathetic. A little less in pain. "I'm just a little shaken, that's all."

Yasuko gave her a strange look. "Maybe we should call it an evening."

"You do look a little pale, and your hands are shaking," Ron observed.

"I'll talk to Mr. Gallenkemp about leaving your door unlocked," Peter said.

"Please, don't make a fuss," Carolina said. "Everything's fine. I just need to lie down for a few minutes." Why couldn't they take the hint and leave her alone?

Eula Mae gently touched Carolina's upper arm. "Sure you don't want to see the doctor?"

"No, Eula Mae, I'm fine. Really."

Ron nudged Peter out the door and nodded to Eula Mae and Yasuko. "Come along, you two. Here's your chance to spend time with two good-looking men and make the other female passengers jealous."

"Lordy me, Mr. Dunten!" Eula Mae exclaimed.

Yasuko put her arm through Peter's. "Count me in. I'm ready for a good time tonight."

Ron grinned and winked. "Good evening, Carolina!"

"Hope you're better tomorrow," Peter said.

Carolina left the bed and listened at the door. "Okay, it's safe to come out now."

Colleen slipped cautiously out of the closet. "Thanks." She plopped down on Carolina's bed. "I'm so tired of running and hiding. The purser is relentless." Her eyes filled with tears. "Can't believe this seemed like a good idea when I first thought of it."

Carolina patted her shoulder. "Tell me what's going on, child. How can I help?" She sat down next to Colleen. "Start at the beginning. Why are you stowing away on this ship? You can find really cheap cruises online."

Colleen wiped her nose and almost smiled. "This isn't a vacation. I'm here looking for answers."

"Answers to what?"

"My sister Garland disappeared off this ship on the last cruise."

Could she have been the ship's officer Ron had asked about? "What happened?"

"They say she fell overboard." Her voice cracked. "That she was lost at sea."

"Oh, my goodness, Miss Agnes. How did that happen?"

"No one knows. They say it was an accident. Or suicide." Her voice lowered to a whisper. "But I think she was murdered."

Carolina gasped. "Murdered?" She knew something sinister was afoot on this ship. "But why?"

"She knew about the smuggling ring."

"Smuggling ring?" Carolina felt her spirits soar. Stowaways, smugglers, and secret agents! Oh my! This cruise could be more exciting than her wildest dreams. "Are you serious?"

Colleen nodded. "Dead serious."

Carolina tried to contain her excitement. "What were they smuggling? Drugs?"

"She wasn't sure. Maybe she finally found out."

Carolina sat in silence for a moment, while her mind absorbed this. "How did she find out about a smuggling ring?"

"She overheard something she shouldn't have. But she didn't say what. Now she's gone."

"You talked to her before she disappeared?"

Colleen wiped her nose with the back of her hand and nodded. "She called home whenever the ship was in port. We were very close."

Carolina handed her a tissue from a box on the desk. "Why didn't she tell the Captain what was going on?"

Colleen blew her nose. "She thought some of the ship's officers were involved, but she wasn't sure who."

Thoughtfully, Carolina paced to the cabin door and back. "You're saying you slipped onboard and stowed away to snoop around?"

She nodded. "I couldn't come onboard as a passenger. Many of the officers and crew members would recognize me as Garland's little sister."

"You've cruised with your sister?"

She nodded. "My whole family has cruised on this ship several times."

"Where are your parents now?"

"At home. Numb and in shock. Grieving. I couldn't involve them. They think I'm staying with friends."

Carolina pulled her journal out of the bottom drawer. "Look at this." She said, sitting down next to Garland and opening the journal.

"What is it?" Colleen looked at the hand-written notes.

"Thoughts, clues, questions, and things on this ship that don't add up." Carolina glanced at her. "Sinister, suspicious stuff. Maybe if we put what you know with what I know, we can figure out what really happened to your sister."

"I know what happened. The purser's friend killed her, but I can't prove it."

Carolina's eyes widened. Could it be? "Mr. Smith?"

She nodded. "You know him?

"Unfortunately, I've met him." Carolina shivered, as she remembered the scary Mr. Smith.

"Garland told me he was having secret meetings with the purser on deck."

Swinging her head around, Carolina pointed to her journal, a.k.a. spy notebook. "And I bet I know where—Deck B by the Green Springs Pool?"

"Yes, but how did you know that?"

"I overheard them talking there myself." Carolina's head felt dizzy from sorting through so much information.

"Mr. Smith is bad news. I know he threw my sister overboard."

"They never found your sister?"

"No. The Captain told my parents the authorities looked for several days."

"Maybe you should talk to the Captain."

"But what if he's one of <u>them</u>?"

Scuffling sounds at the cabin door distracted Carolina. "Shh!" She jerked open the door and ran out into the hallway—smack into the restraining arms of Ron Dunten.

"You enjoy hurling yourself at people?" he asked with a big grin.

"Were you snooping at my door?"

Ron laughed. "*Moi*, snoop? Why, Carolina, I was worried about you. Just wanted to make sure you're okay."

"Why didn't you knock?"

"I was about to, when you rushed out. Did you think I was listening at your door?"

"Maybe. Can you prove you weren't?" she asked.

"Probably not."

The cabin door across and down from their suite opened, and an elderly man in green-striped pajamas stepped out. "Could you please have this conversation somewhere else? My wife and I are trying to sleep."

Ron walked over to the man. "We're sorry, Mister?"

"Klepner . . . Arnold Klepner."

"Ronald Dunten, freelance writer." He shook Mr. Klepner's hand. "I'm interviewing passengers about privacy onboard cruise ships. Do you keep up with the comings and goings of your neighbors?"

"What?" The man spluttered. "The very idea!" He backed into his cabin and slammed the door.

Ron grabbed Carolina by the elbow. "Okay, talk to me."

Carolina's eyes widened. She didn't like the serious tone in his voice. "Talk to you about what?"

He nudged her back into the suite and shut the door. Immediately, he opened the bathroom door and looked behind the shower curtains. He knelt down and looked under both beds. Then he opened the walk-in closet doors.

Carolina grabbed his arm. "What are you doing?"

"Making sure no assassins are hiding in here." He shoved the hanging clothes aside. "Hmmm. Anyone in here?"

Slowly, Carolina released the breath she didn't know she'd been holding. Tension in her neck muscles eased. Obviously, Colleen was not in the closet. "Well, Mr. Dunten, are you having fun? Why are you really searching our suite? If you're missing something, we didn't take it."

"Not 'something,' my dear Mrs. Cunningham, 'someone.' And you are just as surprised as I am that no one is in the closet." Ron smiled wickedly, walked over to the suite door and locked it. "Now, my dear Mrs. Cunningham, it's just the two of us. The door is locked. Let's get to the truth."

Chapter Eight
Friend or Foe?

Carolina backed away from Ron, alarmed. "Why did you do that?" She didn't like the serious turn this one-on-one was taking.

Ron, no longer smiling, pointed to the bed. "Sit, please."

Feeling very uncomfortable about this situation, Carolina sat down. She knew she was out-manned, outgunned, and without a game plan. What else could she do short of screaming bloody murder and gouging his eyes out?

Ron straddled the desk chair backwards and faced Carolina. "I'm tired of playing games. I know the stowaway was hiding in this suite."

Carolina's eyes widened. How did he know that? She opened her mouth to speak.

"Don't say a word. I can see by your face it's true. You hid her in the closet, but she ran as soon as she had an opportunity to slip out unseen."

Carolina looked down at her fingers and her very short nails. She didn't know what had happened to Colleen, but she realized even if she told him that, he wouldn't believe her. She considered all of her options. She really liked the idea of gouging out his eyeballs, but she doubted if she had the strength or courage to do it. Not to mention she was beginning to like him. What was she going to do? What would Agent Craycraft do?

Ron left the chair and grabbed her shoulders. "Carolina, this is serious business. This is not fiction. This is all about real people and situations."

Carolina stared into his riveting blue eyes and gulped. Ron obviously wasn't your ordinary spy. Ron was a super agent. But a super agent for whom?

"You and I both know she'll be back," Ron said, releasing his grip on her shoulders. "When she returns, I want to talk to her. Do you understand? Her life may depend on it."

Ron stopped talking at the swish of a keycard in the lock, but the deadbolt was in place. Someone pounded on the door, and Eula Mae began shouting, "Carolina Cunningham, if you don't unlock this door, I'm going to knock you into the middle of next week looking both ways for Sunday."

Carolina had never been so glad to hear Eula Mae's voice. "Help!" she yelled.

Ron muttered something under his breath and unlocked the door.

Eula Mae gaped at Ron. "What's going on here, Mr. Dunten?"

Yasuko, who was barely 5 feet tall, peered around Eula Mae. "What's happening? They naked? Having sex?"

"Hold your horses, Yasuko, and I'll get to the bottom of this." Eula Mae turned back to Ron. "Why was this door locked? I thought you were going to your cabin to write?"

"I remembered something I had to ask your suite mate. I didn't realize the door was locked. Sorry."

Eula Mae looked from Ron to Carolina. "Lordy, Lordy! Carolina, is that true?"

Ron raised his eyebrow and shot Carolina a warning glance.

Carolina bit her lower lip. If she told the truth—that Ron was trying to scare her into spilling the beans about the stowaway—would Ron pull out his Walther PPK and shoot them all? Or drag them out on deck and throw them overboard? To save herself and her friends, Carolina decided to play along. "That's right, Eula Mae, and he was just leaving. Weren't you, Mr. Dunten?"

Ron smiled coldly. "Yes, I'm leaving, but you remember what I said."

Carolina smiled back. The tables had turned. "I'll certainly consider it." In the meantime, she would definitely come up with a better plan.

Carolina was on her knees looking under the bed when Eula Mae came out of the bathroom in her Moana nightie and Maui slippers. She stared first at Carolina and then at Yasuko, who was seated at the desk rubbing a special wrinkle-preventing cream all over her unlined face. Then she looked back at Carolina, who was searching through the bed covers on all the beds. "Lordy, Lordy, Carolina. What are you doing?"

Carolina froze. "What? Is there a problem?"

"For gracious sakes, what are you looking for?"

"Isn't it obvious, Eula Mae? She's a crazy woman looking for invisible spies." Yasuko cackled.

Carolina opened and shut the closet door, sighed, and bent over to look under the bed, again. She could not figure out where Colleen had gone. How could she disappear like that?

"Stop it right this minute, Carolina," Eula Mae said. "This has gone far enough. There are no spies in our suite."

Carolina fell back onto her bed and sighed. "But the stowaway was in here, and now she's gone."

"What?" Eula Mae and Yasuko yelled.

Carolina sighed, again. Even though she knew she'd regret doing it later, Carolina propped herself up on her elbows. "I have a confession to make. The stowaway was in our suite earlier. She shut the door behind me and locked out Eula Mae."

"You didn't trip and fall?" asked Yasuko.

"No. Sorry I lied, but I couldn't let Peter and Ron find her."

Eula Mae sat down next to Carolina and eyeballed her. "What did she tell you?"

"Colleen—that's her name." Carolina sat up on the edge of the bed. "Her sister Garland was the crew member who was lost overboard last month."

"The one Ron asked Peter about?" asked Eula Mae.

Carolina nodded and kicked the bed with her heel. "Colleen thinks Mr. Smith threw her sister overboard because she knew about the smuggling ring."

"Smuggling ring?" Eula Mae grabbed her forehead and fell backward onto the bed. "Hells, bells! I don't believe this."

Yasuko covered her ears with her hands. "I don't want to hear about any more evil."

"You better listen up because it only gets worse. Colleen says she's here to find the truth about what happened to Garland. And Ron knows Colleen was in our suite."

Eula Mae sat up so fast, she almost banged heads with Carolina.

"Did Ron threaten you?"

Carolina stood up. "No. He suspected Colleen was in our suite and returned to see for himself."

Eula Mae stood up. "How did he know Colleen was in the suite?"

"Spy intuition?" Carolina surmised.

"No such thing," said Yasuko.

Eula Mae rolled her eyes. "Did he talk to her?"

Carolina smirked remembering. "He wanted to. He searched the entire suite, but he couldn't find her."

"She wasn't in the closet?"

"Nope."

"You checked under the beds and the covers, and in the bathroom and everywhere?"

"Absolutely everywhere."

"Then where is she?"

Carolina didn't like Eula Mae's tone. She made it sound like she'd lost the stowaway intentionally. "I don't know, unless—"

"Unless what?" asked Eula Mae. "Come on, Carolina, spit it out."

Suddenly Carolina knew how Colleen had escaped unseen. "When Ron and I were yelling at each other in the hallway, this older man across the way asked us to move. Colleen must have slipped out while Ron was talking to him."

"Why does Ron want to talk to her?" asked Yasuko.

Carolina paused. She couldn't tell them she suspected they were dealing with a super agent spy. She decided it was best for everyone if she went along with Ron's own cover story. "He's a writer, remember? He wants an exclusive interview with a gutsy stowaway."

"Ah, yes. I get it," Eula Mae said. "He's hoping for a Pulitzer and a better job with *Newsweek* or *TIME Magazine*. Travel writing couldn't be that satisfying for a man like him."

A man like him? Did Eula Mae know more than Carolina thought she did? "What do you mean?"

"He's not a wuss. I can't imagine him covering the Keukenhof tulip exhibition or the Pillsbury Bake-Off. World Cup, maybe. Or the Presidential Election. Or—"

Carolina tuned Eula Mae out and glanced down at her watch. She knew from experience that when Eula Mae started ranting, it could go on forever. Besides that, Carolina realized she was hungry. "How about a snack?"

"Snack?" asked Yasuko, who was already in bed with her face greased.

"We can get food and drinks in Horizons," Carolina pointed out. She already knew this forward lounge would become her favorite spot to relax. With its floor-to-ceiling windows and a 180-degree bird's-eye view, you could hang out with friends, play bingo, take a nap, enjoy high tea at 4 o'clock, or view each port from on high.

"How can you eat at a time like this?" asked Eula Mae.

"I don't know. I just can. Besides, I think better on a full stomach. I want you to go with me. If I go alone and something happens to me, you'll regret it the rest of your life."

Yasuko's muffled voice sounded from beneath her bed covers. "If anything happens to Carolina, I have dibs on her black cashmere shawl."

On Deck 10, Carolina and Eula Mae found half a dozen couples, dressed in country club casual, dancing to big band music played by the ship's six-piece band. Others milled around a small buffet table covered with an assortment of cheeses, cold meats, bread, and desserts. While Eula Mae selected a slice of melon and a handful of grapes from an enormous fruit platter, Carolina located the dessert table and piled half a dozen chocolate éclairs on her plate. A young attractive steward followed them to a table for two and poured them cups of jasmine green tea.

"Does madam require a larger plate?" he asked.

Carolina discreetly licked a chocolate smudge off her thumb. "Thanks, but I think I can manage." He shrugged and turned away.

Eula Mae stirred a little bit of sugar into her tea. "Carolina, I know how much you love chocolate éclairs, but please don't feel obligated to eat as many as they put on the table."

"You know we rarely see a chocolate éclair at the Villas. The chef considers them unhealthy." Carolina studied her plate of luscious fats and carbs. "Your problem, Eula Mae, is that you're uptight. Too stuffy. You need some excitement in your life."

"I have quite enough excitement in my life, thanks to you. Stowaways, assassins, super agents, and smugglers. How much more do you think I can handle?"

"I'm glad you're getting into the spirit of things, Eula Mae. And to think when I first met you at the Villas, I thought you were boring."

Eula Mae shook her head. "How can you take this so lightly? Do you realize that if Colleen is right, there is a smuggling ring operating on this ship? I don't like that one bit. Maybe we should get off in Nassau and fly home before something bad happens."

"Now who's overreacting?"

Eula Mae sighed. "Yeah, I'm starting to sound like you, aren't I?"

Carolina finished the last chocolate éclair, wiping the last crumbs off the plate with her finger. "Mmm. Yum." She licked her lips and sighed, again. Sometimes Eula Mae made Carolina feel like she had a rock around her neck. Earlier, when the famous bridge guru bailed and nothing much was going on, Carolina could have been talked into flying home. But not now. Things were finally starting to get exciting. Somehow, Carolina decided, she needed to calm her friend down. "Leaving the cruise now is awfully extreme, don't you think? We're not the ones in trouble here. It's the stowaway. At any moment Colleen could be found and returned to her parents, or worse. If we leave the ship, who will look out for her with Mr. Greene and Mr. Smith out to nab her?"

Eula Mae pushed a slice of watermelon to the side and sighed. "That's true, but—"

"Aren't you having fun with your male admirers? Everyone at the Villas would be quite jealous to see you hanging out with a good-looking ship's officer and a magazine writer, a.k.a., Mr. Hunky Spy."

"Oh piffle," Eula Mae squealed. "Ron Dunten has his eye on you, and Yasuko is throwing herself all over the lieutenant. Not to mention both men are too young for me. They look like they're 50-something—not 70-something."

"Lots of men out there like older women. Nothing wrong with that."

Eula Mae sat up straight and stared at Carolina. "Peter's nice, but he certainly wouldn't have anything to do with an old woman like me. Besides, he is quite keen on Yasuko."

Carolina congratulated herself on accomplishing her goal. Eula Mae was no longer thinking about leaving the ship in Nassau. Nope, now she was annoyed at the mention of a possible relationship between herself and Peter.

"We're shipboard acquaintances only."

"Sorry, my mistake. I won't mention it, again. Should we pack our suitcases?" Carolina closed her eyes, crossed her fingers, and held her breath.

Eula Mae relaxed and leaned back into her comfortable chair and chewed thoughtfully on a strawberry. "I guess that won't be necessary yet."

"Yes!" Carolina said. "I doubt if we'd get a refund jumping ship now. Not to mention we'd have to pay to fly back to Jacksonville to get the car."

"However," and Eula Mae wagged her finger at Carolina, "if I feel at any point that anyone of us is in danger, then we're off this ship. Got it?"

Carolina nodded and congratulated herself on diverting Eula Mae from making a bad decision. "Eula Mae?"

"What?"

"If there were a smuggling ring operating on this ship, what do you think they could be smuggling?"

"Lordy, Lordy, Carolina. How should I know? Something valuable, I guess. Something illegal, obviously. Something like drugs—dope, heroin, cocaine. It's on the news all the time. Cruise ship passengers hide drugs any place they'll fit. Then drug-sniffing dogs can smell it in their luggage or other belongings."

Carolina had to agree with Eula Mae on that. Newscasters were always talking about the national opioid crisis, and how drug enforcement agents were arresting drug smugglers entering the country and confiscating their booty. Agents could even find drugs hidden in body cavities or drugs packed in small plastic bags swallowed by smugglers. Carolina remembered seeing on TV women arrested for smuggling drugs surgically implanted in their abdomens.

"If smuggled drugs are so easy to find with drug-sniffing dogs, why bother smuggling that stuff into the U.S.?" Carolina asked. "Why not diamonds or gold or government secrets or ancient antiquities or something that dogs can't smell?"

Eula Mae shook her head. "No, it has to be drugs. Nearly every night on ABC news they report some drug bust at an airport or border crossing. You didn't hear David Muir's special report last week? He said cocaine and heroin are moving from South America, through the Caribbean to the Carolinas and Georgia and further north."

"Just because you're 16 years older than me doesn't always make you right. You're wrong this time." Carolina stretched and stood up. "I think I need one more chocolate éclair for the road."

"Hmph! I don't know why you aren't 4 feet wide in the butt, what with all the sweets you eat."

"I have special brown fat. It burns up the calories." Carolina winked at Eula Mae and headed back to the buffet tables. Out of the corner of her eye, she caught a glimpse of Peter exiting a staff-only door behind the bar and walking out of Horizons. Pondering this unexpected occurrence, Carolina piled two chocolate éclairs on her plate and returned to Eula Mae.

"Didn't you say Peter went to bed?" Carolina asked as casually as she could.

"Yes," said Eula Mae, watching an older couple jitterbugging the night away. "He has to be on the bridge at 4 o'clock this morning, why?"

Carolina glanced back toward the back of the lounge. "Oh, no reason."

Day Two – Saved teenage stowaway from Purser, again; she fled before providing answers.

Overheard Purser and another man plotting to kill someone; pursued by Purser; saved by Peter; Purser says conversation about TV show; told Peter about two run-ins with the stowaway.

At Captain's cocktail party, Ron and Peter meet; Purser introduces scary friend, Mr. Smith.

Explained to Ron about stowaway and incident with Purser and Mr. Smith.

Ron joins us for dinner; Peter supports Purser, and asks for motive to kill stowaway.

Eula Mae says stowaway must know something bad about Purser. Could Purser be double-agent being blackmailed by stowaway?

Discovered stowaway (Colleen Burgess) in cabin after dinner; she is onboard to find out about ship's officer lost at sea,

her sister Garland, and believes her sister was murdered for knowing too much about smuggling ring operating on ship; Ron searches cabin for Colleen, but she escapes.

Ron tries to get information from me about Colleen.

At midnight buffet, I spot Peter, who was supposed to be asleep because he had to be on the Bridge at 4 a.m.

Questions: Why does Purser want stowaway dead? Why did Peter lie about going to bed? Why is Ron determined to talk to stowaway? What could the bad guys be smuggling?

After hiding her spy journal, Carolina settled into bed with her latest Craycraft spy thriller, *Spy on a String*. She started thinking about tomorrow's port of call. "What should we do in Nassau tomorrow?"

"It's already tomorrow," mumbled Eula Mae. "Go to sleep."

"Are we going snorkeling?" Carolina could be persistent when it was necessary.

"You know we're too old to snorkel. We'd be nothing but shark bait."

"It's what people do when they go to Nassau. It's the fun thing to do. Arthur and I used to go snorkeling in the Keys every summer. What else is there to do in Nassau except shop or visit the casinos?"

"No," Eula Mae said vehemently. "No gambling or shopping! Old folks like us don't need more stuff. All you talked about your first week at the Villas was how awful it was to downsize and get rid of stuff. Don't forget how you poked fun at poor Lilly when you discovered her bathtub and dishwasher provided storage for stuff she couldn't give up. And did you not whine and complain about Charter and Caitlyn refusing to take anything? Even their own stuff?"

"Yeah, don't remind me." Carolina remembered feeling guilty and sad to haul away carloads of stuff she and Arthur had accumulated during their married years—souvenirs from many vacations abroad, thank-you gifts from Arthur's many international students, handmade Mother's Day and Father's Day cards from Charter and Caitlyn when they were little, and furniture and stuff they'd inherited when their own parents had passed on. All that stuff that no one wanted.

"However, I read there's an interesting native market in Nassau full of handmade arts and crafts," Eula Mae said.

"What? Didn't you just say that we didn't need—" Caroline stopped mid-sentence at the sound of a soft shuffle outside the cabin door. Getting out of bed and tiptoeing to the door, she yanked it open and found a startled Mr. Gallenkemp crouched down outside. Ah hah! Now here was a person of interest, she thought. "What are you doing?"

The cabin steward slowly stood and handed Carolina a sheet of paper. "Port-of-call information, madam. I'm slipping one under everybody's door this evening."

"Oh? Well, thanks." Carolina shrugged, shut the door, and crawled back into her bed. "Such an odd little man. Do you think he's up to something sinister?"

Eula Mae propped herself up on her elbow. "Sinister as in being outside our door?"

"Doesn't it seem that something sinister is always going on outside our door?"

Eula Mae stared intently at Carolina. "Sinister as in everyone who passes our door is either a stowaway or a smuggler?"

"Okay, I'll keep an open mind as far as Mr. Gallenkemp is concerned. Good night, Eula Mae." As Carolina turned out the light, the phone rang. She turned the light back on and picked up the receiver. "Hello?"

"Mrs. Cunningham?" a deep bass voice asked.

"Yes?" Carolina looked at Eula Mae and shrugged.

"Make sure your deadbolt is on before you go to bed." The line went dead.

Carolina put down the receiver. She felt a chill run down her back.

"Who was that?" Eula Mae asked.

Carolina pulled up the covers and turned out the light. She was afraid if she told Eula Mae what the caller said, they'd be packing suitcases. Carolina yawned loudly. "Wrong number."

Chapter Nine
Something's Afoot

The native market in Nassau was easy to find. Carolina, Eula Mae, and Yasuko followed other tourists down Bay Street until they found dozens of brightly clothed Bahamian women sitting in stalls, weaving, plaiting, and braiding straw strips.

While Eula Mae and Yasuko walked from one stall to another, admiring the native women's handiwork, Carolina couldn't help thinking about last night's mysterious phone call. The voice hadn't sounded familiar. She leaned over, picked up a handmade straw hat, and decided that such a hat might be a good purchase. Every time she went in for her dermatology checkup, all she heard was "use sunblock" and "wear a wide-brim sun hat." Then her doctor would freeze off a suspicious spot or two. "How much?" she asked a young woman sitting nearby.

The woman, whose colorful head scarf matched her loose-fitting, sleeveless dress, kept on working. Without looking up, she said, "Twenty U.S. dollars."

Carolina stared at the woman, whose ebony face glistened under the Caribbean heat. Carolina glanced at the straw hat in her hand. She realized it was handmade and all, but that seemed like a lot of money for a little bit of straw.

"You're supposed to haggle with her," a voice whispered in her ear.

Carolina turned to see an older Asian man standing beside her, stroking a small white Manchu beard on his chin. She couldn't see his upper face because he wore a khaki sun hat with a wide brim.

"Offer her ten dollars," he said softly. "Tell her you don't have twenty dollars."

Carolina did as he suggested.

The woman stopped working and looked up. "I made that hat

myself. It is excellent workmanship."

Carolina started to feel like a dirty dog. This poor woman probably had six kids to feed and lived in a hut with dirt floors and no air-conditioning.

"But I make you good price. I sell you hat for fifteen, if you buy straw bag for fifteen. Thirty dollars for both. A great deal. You take?"

Carolina spluttered. "But I don't need a straw bag!"

The Asian man shrugged. "But it's quite a bargain, really. And you'll be helping the economy of a third world country. This woman works hard to put beans and rice on the table for her children. You should do the right thing." He gestured his head toward the woman, who had returned to her weaving work.

"What are you? The head of her marketing department?" When the man laughed out loud at her question, his entire face seemed to light up like one big smile. "Fine," said Carolina. She pulled out her wallet and handed the woman thirty U.S. dollars. Then she slapped the straw hat on her head and picked out a straw bag with a palm tree woven into its side. The weaver immediately returned to her work and did not even thank Carolina for her purchases.

Carolina looked at the lunch bag Dominic had given her at breakfast. No need to carry a bag in each hand, she decided, and stuffed the food in her new straw bag.

"That was your good deed for the day, madam." The man followed Carolina over to a table where Bahamian men were carving delicate boxes and puzzles from wood, and making shell jewelry. "Please, allow me to introduce myself. I'm Charlie Chan."

Carolina stopped in her tracks. "What? Charlie Chan? You have to be joking? No one would ever name their child after an old film detective. What was that actor's name? Sidney Toler?"

"Ah so! Impressive! Not many people living today could come up with Sidney Toler's name."

"Why not? He did star in twenty-two Charlie Chan movies. More than the sixteen Charlie Chan movies made by Swedish actor Werner Oland. Was your mother a Charlie Chan fan or something?"

"Hardly. However, my grandmother was. She had a dream that her grandson would become a world-famous detective. Therefore, she insisted I needed an appropriate name."

"Why not Sherlock Holmes?"

He threw up his hands. "Come on! Look at this face and these eyes, and tell me I'm a clone for Sherlock."

Carolina grimaced. "Okay, I see your point, Mr. Charlie Chan."

"Carolina!" Eula Mae yelled from behind her. Carolina turned away from Mr. Chan. "You have to come see this." She and Yasuko seemed excited over whatever they had discovered.

"All right, but first you should meet Charlie Chan." But when Carolina turned back around, he was gone.

"I don't see anyone," Eula Mae said, looking confused.

"Did you say Charlie Chan? Like that old Chinese detective series?" asked Yasuko. "Who would name their son that?"

Carolina shook her head. "It's a long story. What is it that you want to show me?" Confused by the disappearance of Mr. Chan, Carolina followed Eula Mae across the market to a woman wearing a red, orange, and purple tropical-print dress. The woman's gaunt ebony face glistened with perspiration. Long bony fingers worked rapidly, weaving golden strips of straw to form the body of a doll.

The stall was full of straw dolls in multiple sizes. Eula Mae picked up one that was about 2-feet tall with a straw basket full of straw fruit on its straw head.

"Isn't it great?" she asked. "I love it! I have to have it."

"Wait just a minute," Carolina protested. "Didn't you tell me that none of us needed any more stuff? That we all had too much stuff?"

Yasuko grabbed Carolina's straw bag and held it up in the air? "And this isn't more stuff that you bought?"

"There's a difference here. Straw bags and hats are useful. They serve a purpose. What purpose does a straw doll have?"

"To put a smile on my face and make me happy," said Eula Mae. She turned to the dollmaker. "How much?"

The woman plucked at her head kerchief, which matched her loose and flowing dress. "Twenty dollah."

"Bahamian dollars?" Eula Mae asked.

The dollmaker continued working and didn't look up. "Twenty dollah U Hess A."

Carolina couldn't hide her smile at Eula Mae's frustration.

"I thought everything was cheap here," she muttered under her breath.

The dollmaker grunted. "Take close look. I spend all evening making. Is full of superior workmanship. Not easy to make. You think you make one that good?" She grunted, again, and resumed her work.

Carolina pulled Eula Mae away from the dollmaker. "Charlie Chan said you're supposed to haggle. Let me try." She picked up the doll Eula Mae wanted. "How much?"

The woman glanced up at Carolina. "Special price just for you. Twenty dollah."

Carolina turned the doll over and examined it carefully. She shook her head as sadly as she could and put the doll down. "Too bad. I would have been willing to pay five."

The woman muttered something under her breath. "Twenty dollah."

"Eight dollars."

The woman shook her head. "Twenty dollah."

Carolina smiled and turned to leave, nudging Eula Mae along and speaking in a loud voice. "You don't really want that one, do you? It's not worth twenty dollars. I saw a better selection of dolls over there, and the prices are much more reasonable." Carolina winked and grabbed Eula Mae's arm. Yasuko followed.

"What are you doing?" Eula Mae hissed.

How could someone so smart be so clueless? Carolina wondered. "Shh, she'll call us back, if she thinks she might miss the sale."

The woman grunted. "Last and final offer. Twenty dollah."

"Carolina, I really want that doll." Eula Mae grabbed her shoulder.

Carolina sighed. This haggling was not as easy as she thought it would be.

"What are you whispering about? Can I be a part of the conspiracy?" asked Ron Dunten, coming from behind the women with an SLR digital camera.

"Mr. Dunten," Carolina greeted him coolly.

Ron grinned. "Come on, Carolina, you can do better than that."

Eula Mae frowned. "Carolina can't get that poor woman to reduce the price of her doll. I'm afraid if we keep hounding her, she'll end up asking more."

Ron looked at the dolls. "Which one?"

"The one in the red dress with a brown basket full of fruit on her head." Eula Mae pointed at the doll she wanted.

"That's a nice little doll. How much are you willing to pay for it?"

"Is 10 dollars too little?"

"Hold on and I'll see." Ron sauntered lazily over to the stall and started taking pictures of the dollmaker. He looked over the dolls casually and spoke to the woman. He smiled and handed her money. Then he wrote something on a piece of paper and gave that to her, too. The dollmaker tied the slip of paper to the doll and gave Ron a big toothless smile.

Ron walked back over to the waiting women. "The doll will be delivered to my cabin before the ship sails tonight."

"Thank you," said Eula Mae.

"My pleasure," Ron said. "I owe it all to my pleasant personality."

"That's not what I hear," Carolina said.

Ron's smile faded. "What do you hear?"

"Nothing, I'm sure," said Eula Mae. "So how much did the doll cost?"

Ron tugged on his ear. "She was one tough cookie. Ten dollars didn't work for her."

"What did work for her?" Carolina asked. "Fifteen?"

"Nah, a little bit more. Special price for me. Twenty-five dollah."

Carolina laughed so hard, her straw hat nearly fell off.

Eula Mae shook her head and gave Carolina a playful shove. "Come along, Champion Haggler. Let's see what else is on this island."

"Did anyone remember to bring the map?" asked Yasuko.

Ron's face turned serious. "You three aren't searching for trouble, are you?"

"No trouble," Carolina said. "We're doing what tourists do—shopping and seeing the sights."

"Maybe I should come along and keep you out of trouble?"

Carolina shook her head negatively. "Absolutely not!"

"We would be glad to have you tagalong," Eula Mae said. "Your company would perk up my day".

"I vote with Eula Mae on this," said Yasuko.

"Then it will be my pleasure." He turned around and looked at Carolina. "What's that in your straw bag?"

"Dominic packed us a small lunch," Carolina explained. "A very, very small lunch."

Ron reached into her bag with both hands and pulled out the lunch. "From the size of it, I'd say Dominic packed enough for four."

Carolina snatched the bag out of his hands. "Possibly, but if I get really hungry, there won't be enough for you."

Ron laughed. "No worries. I can always pick up a snack somewhere." He replaced the lens cap on his camera. "Seriously, Carolina, would my company spoil your day?" His blue eyes locked with hers.

Carolina felt her cheeks begin to warm. She was still a little bit miffed after his behavior last night. Still, she rationalized, if he stayed with the three of them, she wouldn't have to wonder what he was doing. "I suppose not."

"Yay!" chorused Yasuko and Eula Mae.

"All right then, ladies. Let's go. Our destiny awaits us."

Ron offered his left elbow to Eula and his right to Yasuko. Carolina ignored them all and walked ahead of the group. They walked through Parliament Square, saw the marble statue of Queen Victoria, the government buildings, and the charming Georgian structures built of coral limestone. They walked down Bay Street, looked in shop windows, and stopped in front of a jewelry store to admire tortoise shell jewelry in the window.

Suddenly, in the reflection of the shop window, Carolina caught a glimpse of a large, dark-complexioned man watching them intently. Could he be a spy, she wondered, or an assassin or merely an ordinary pickpocket? As the foursome continued down the street, browsing in one store window after another, the man stayed behind them. "See that man?" Carolina quietly asked Ron.

Ron glanced behind them casually. "Nothing to worry about. Follow my lead." Then he spoke in a voice loud enough to be heard by the man. "Say, would everyone like to see the Queen's Staircase?" Ron turned the women around, and led them past the very startled man.

Carolina had to give Ron points for the great maneuver. Foreign agent caught off-guard by Mr. Hunky Spy. Agent Craycraft would love it.

At the foot of Bennett's Hill, where the staircase began, Carolina looked behind them. "He's still there, Ron." She was starting to worry.

"Ignore him," Ron instructed them. "When we reach the top of the staircase, you three head for Fort Fincastle. No need to rush. There's a great view of the ship from the top. Meanwhile, I'll circle around the Water Tower. From the fort, you should take the path down from the castle. Do not go back down the staircase. Head in the direction of the ship, and I'll meet you by Victoria's statue. Got it?"

"Got it." What a great plan, Carolina thought. Her heart rate quickened, and she no longer felt like a victim.

In a voice loud enough for the man to hear, Ron said, "The Queen's Staircase has 65 steps carved out of limestone cliffs in 1795, to provide easy access to the fort."

Carolina paused at the bottom of the staircase. It looked like a long way to the top for three older women like them, she thought. She always tried to avoid steps because of the osteoarthritis in her knees. Surely Eula Mae would balk at climbing up that many steps, too.

"Really? 65 steps? I'll count." Eula Mae started up the steps.

Carolina grunted, grabbed the handrail, and started up, followed by Yasuko and Ron. The foreign agent followed them at a distance.

Continuing to speak loudly, Ron provided a little history. "If you inspect the steps closely, you can see traces of the pickaxes used by slave laborers. The staircase honors the reign of Queen Victoria."

At the top of the staircase, the foursome paused to catch their breath. "All those steps made me hungry," said Eula Mae. "I'm surprised Carolina hasn't stopped to nibble on our lunch. Why don't we stop here in the shade and eat?"

Ron put his arm around her shoulders and whispered in her ear. "This gentleman coming up the steps is following us. Lunch can wait. Tell Yasuko to follow Carolina. We have a plan." He pushed Eula Mae playfully away in Yasuko's direction. "Okay," he said loudly, "Last one to the fort forfeits their share of lunch to me!"

The three women grabbed hands and headed toward the fort at a brisk pace; Ron veered left around the Water Tower. The foreign agent paused long enough to watch Ron ambling in a different direction from Carolina, Eula Mae, and Yasuko, before following the women.

Even when the three women heard a howl of surprise and the sound of a scuffle behind them, they didn't stop or slow down. From the top of Ft. Fincastle, they spent a minute enjoying the view of the *Emerald Dream* before heading down to Elisabeth Avenue and in the direction of their ship. When they reached Queen Victoria's statue, they collapsed on a bench, sweaty and out of breath.

"What's going on?" Eula Mae gasped for air. "I'm a feeble old woman. Before I keel over from a major coronary, I'd really like to know what I died for."

Carolina wiped her dripping face with tissue and handed extra ones to Eula Mae and Yasuko. "Looks like that man following us was not after Ron—he was following the three of us."

Eula Mae wiped the moisture from her upper lip. "Does he think we'll lead him to Colleen?"

"But we don't know where she is," Yasuko protested.

"He doesn't know that, Yasuko," Carolina explained.

Eula Mae shook her head. "None of this makes any sense to me." She pulled a bottle of water out of her bag and took a long swig.

"I know. Nothing makes sense to me, either." Carolina bent over in an effort to calm her breathing. "You know, I'm a much stronger old woman from never missing exercise class, but my body can't take any more punishment unless it gets fed."

"I'm not hungry now," Eula Mae said. "I lost my appetite."

"Let's break out the food anyway." When Carolina turned around, she saw Ron standing in front of them, holding a handkerchief to his jaw.

Eula Mae stood up. "What happened? Are you all right?"

"Just a scratch." Ron shifted his jaw and bent his neck. "The other person looks much worse."

"You look pretty banged up to me." Relieved that Ron had escaped an untimely end, Carolina suddenly understood why Ron split away from her, Eula Mae, and Yasuko. He knew the man was following them. Ron had circled around to grab the stalker from behind. Just like any good agent would do. "Who threw the first punch?"

"If anyone asks, I tripped running down the staircase."

Eula Mae examined Ron's jaw. "Did the other guy trip, too?"

Ron winked. "You know, I think he did. Right after I politely suggested he not follow us. Then I asked why he was doing it."

Carolina stifled a laugh. "What'd he say?"

"To see where you went and what you did."

"That makes no sense," Yasuko said.

"That was my thinking, too," Ron said.

Unless he really hoped we'd lead him to Colleen, Carolina thought. "Who told him to follow us?" She bet it was the purser or Mr. Smith.

"He said he didn't know."

"How convenient," Carolina said, her hands inside her straw bag. "Oh no!"

Eula Mae looked at her. "Oh, no, what?"

"It's gone."

Ron frowned. "What's gone?"

"Our lunch! I lost our lunch!" Carolina cried out. "What will we do?"

Ron began to laugh. "Is that all? I thought you'd lost your passport or your wallet."

"This isn't funny to her, Ron," Eula Mae explained. "No lunch means no chocolate éclairs."

Ron laughed harder. "I'm sorry, Carolina. How about we return to the ship and have a real lunch in the dining room?"

Carolina collapsed against the bench back. "Any minute I may pass out." All the adventure and excitement had eaten up her carbs and energy.

Eula Mae gave Carolina a shove. "The faster we get back to the ship, the sooner you get to eat."

Carolina stood and sighed. "I guess a late lunch is better than no lunch." Maybe, she considered the possibility, Dominic might have tucked away a few chocolate éclairs in the galley.

When they returned to their suite, it was *deja vu*. The door was ajar, but this time when they entered, they found their suite in shambles. Clothes were thrown everywhere. Drawers were emptied. Mattresses pulled from the frames. And on the vanity mirror—written with Eula Mae's cranberry-orange lipstick—was a message: *U R 2 nosy.*

Chapter Ten
More Questions, No Answers

Mr. Gallenkemp stood in the doorway, sighing and wringing his hands. "I'm so sorry, madams. I made your beds this morning and straightened up. Everything was tiptop when I left." Again, he sighed and wrung his hands.

Eula Mae picked up the pants suit she bought for the cruise and hung it back in the closet. "That's it. We're going to see the Captain."

Mr. Gallenkemp shook his head. "Oh, no, madam. You can't."

"Why not?" Eula Mae asked.

Carolina cringed. In the short time she'd known Eula Mae, she'd learned quickly that when her septuagenarian friend was totally pissed, you didn't tell her "no, you can't."

Mr. Gallenkemp started to stammer and turned to Carolina. "Madam, please, don't get me in trouble with the Captain. Please go to lunch. Allow me to clean up your room and notify the Captain myself. I'll take care of everything."

Carolina glanced from the poor groveling cabin steward to a steamed Eula Mae and held her breath. She wasn't sure if going to the Captain was a good plan. The Captain might be "one of them." Unless he wasn't. There was also the possibility that Mr. Gallenkemp was protecting the smuggler or spy who messed up their suite.

Eula Mae stared at Mr. Gallenkemp. Carolina saw that she was wavering. "Eula Mae, you know it isn't his fault our suite was tossed," she said.

"Lordy, Lordy, such a mess, but you're right." Eula Mae straightened up and nodded.

Mr. Gallenkemp licked his lips. "Before you leave, could you please look around and make sure no valuables are missing?"

"Our valuables are locked in the safe," Yasuko said.

"Yes, that's right," agreed Eula Mae. "Our passports, jewelry, and money."

"Very good, madams. May I suggest you head to the main dining room before they close," Mr. Gallenkamp said.

"Lunch sounds good." Eula Mae opened the door and walked out of the suite, followed by Yasuko.

Mr. Gallenkemp relaxed and sighed with relief. Then he bent over, picked up a lipstick tube with his handkerchief, and put it in his jacket pocket.

"What are you doing?" Carolina asked. It seemed to her like a strange thing for him to do.

"I'll give it to security, madam. There might be fingerprints on it."

"Of course," Carolina agreed. Shades of "C.S.I." She left the suite, closing the door behind her. But she couldn't help wondering about ship's security being able to process fingerprints. There must be more crimes committed on cruise ships than she thought.

Ron was shocked to hear about the women's suite being vandalized. "Must be a warning for you to mind your own business."

Carolina swallowed a bite of sausage pizza. "The purser is responsible. I'm sure of it."

"Do you have solid proof you could take to court?" Ron asked.

"No, but I bet we could get some." she sipped her Zero Coke. "What do you think, Eula Mae?"

Eula Mae looked at Carolina, Yasuko, and Ron and their empty plates. Her lunch—asparagus soup and a fruit plate—had not been touched. "I don't understand. We've been threatened, followed, spied upon, our belongings violated, and yet you can still eat?"

Ron smiled at her outburst, then wiped his smile away with his napkin. "Even the condemned get a last meal before being executed."

Carolina reached out her fork toward Eula Mae's plate. "Can I have your kiwi and papaya if you're not going to eat it?" It was rare when something bothered her appetite.

Eula Mae sighed and pushed the fruit plate in Carolina's direction. "Take all of it." Then she turned to Ron. "What are we going to do?"

"Nothing," said Ron.

Eula Mae looked dumbfounded. "What do you mean nothing?"

"Our personal belongings were violated," Yasuko joined in. "Why would we do nothing?"

"Trust me on this. It's best if the three of you continue to act like normal cruise ship passengers. Swim in the pool, play ping pong, take in a movie, go to the arts and crafts session, whatever. But don't snoop around."

Carolina leaned toward Ron, quivering with excitement. "I get it. We want people to think we're just passengers having fun, right?"

"You got it!" Ron nodded.

Carolina frowned. "But what will we really be doing?"

"Nothing!" Ron stood up. "Unless you hear from the stowaway, again."

"And if we do?" asked Carolina.

"Let me know immediately. Now if you'll excuse me, I have an interview and a story to write. Stay out of trouble."

After lunch, the three women were relieved to see that true to his word, Mr. Gallenkemp had their suite cleaned up. Yasuko announced that she was going to play mahjong in the game room. Eula Mae stretched out on her re-made bed for a nap. Carolina sat down and began writing in her spy journal:

Day Three – Toured Nassau on foot; followed by foreign agent who was beaten by super spy Dunten.

Cabin searched and turned upside down; lipstick message— U R nosy—left on mirror; cabin steward removed lipstick tube for fingerprinting by security. Also, last night, received phone call warning about locking door.

Questions: Who was foreign agent working for? Was the person who vandalized our room searching for something or only wanting to scare us? Why would cabin steward be blamed for someone tossing suite? Why does Ron want us not to report being followed?

After hiding her journal, Carolina finished her espionage thriller, *Mrs. Craycraft's Adirondack Adventure,* and sighed happily. Perfect ending. She gazed at her sleeping friend. "I'm going to the library for another book. Eula Mae, can I get you anything?" No response. Carolina sat up, yawned, and slipped on her sandals. "I'll be right back. You won't even know I left."

Carolina tiptoed out of the suite, shutting the door quietly behind her. At the elevator, she pressed the UP button. The doors opened. A steward inside the elevator smiled, as she pressed the button for the Promenade Deck.

"You're Carolina Cunningham, aren't you, madam?" he asked with a British accent.

"How did you know?" Carolina backed away from him to the other side of the elevator.

"Everyone knows about you, madam. How you saved the stowaway from Alvin Greene."

Oh, great. Just what she needed—a reputation. "Where did you hear that? And who are you?"

"I'm Jimi, madam. Here's your stop—Promenade Deck."

The doors opened, and Carolina smiled at the steward. "Thanks for the ride, Jimi."

"My pleasure, madam."

Carolina walked toward the stern of the ship, past the hair salon, the barber shop, and other shops, which were closed while the ship was in port. This end of the ship was deserted, since most passengers were either exploring Nassau and Paradise Island or in their cabins napping like Eula Mae or sunning around the pool or playing mahjong like Yasuko.

As Carolina searched the shelves in the library for another Craycraft spy thriller, she heard someone come up behind her.

"What are you doing?"

Startled, Carolina dropped the book she was holding. "Omigosh, Peter, scare me to death, won't you? Are you on duty? Don't they ever let you off the ship?"

"I could ask you the same thing. You're supposed to be on shore having a good time."

"I'm having my good time here." What was it to him anyway?

"Where are your two friends?"

He was certainly being awfully nosy, Carolina thought. "Eula Mae is taking a nap; Yasuko is playing mahjong. Why aren't you on the island?"

"I'm on duty. What about you?"

"We toured Nassau this morning, but this foreign agent kept following us and making us uncomfortable. So we ate lunch on the ship, and we're not going back ashore."

Peter motioned her to a sofa and sat down. "What foreign agent are you talking about?"

Carolina told Peter about the man that had followed them, and how Ron convinced him to leave them alone.

"How did Ron do that?"

Carolina stood up and pulled an old worn Sherlock Holmes book off the shelf. "I'm not sure. Eula Mae, Yasuko, and I were behind the fort and didn't see."

Peter frowned. "You were lucky Ron was with you."

"I suppose, but while we were in Nassau, someone ransacked our suite." Carolina glanced furtively over her shoulder to check his reaction.

Peter jumped to his feet. "What? That's never happened on this ship before. Did they steal anything?"

"Nothing was missing, but they left a threatening message on our mirror." Carolina finally spotted a Mrs. Craycraft book – *Patagonia Adventure* – and re-shelved Sherlock Holmes. "Ron thinks we should stop snooping around."

"He has a point. You should follow his advice."

"Not as long as I suspect the purser is up to something." After all, she reasoned, would Mrs. Craycraft be thwarted by a little lipstick?

"My advice to the three of you is not to stir up trouble."

"It's too late for that." Clutching the Mrs. Craycraft book, Carolina headed out the library door. "See you at dinner? I have to get back to the suite before Eula Mae wakes up."

"Walk with me and we'll talk more."

"Where're you headed?" Carolina asked.

"To meet someone."

"A ship's officer?" Now she was the one being nosy.

"Yes," he said, seeming to hesitate. "One of the crew has discovered a problem with the wiring. I need to check it out."

Was that beads of sweat forming on his upper lip? They walked in silence for a few minutes, passing darkened shops and continuing toward the ship's bow. They even walked through the closed casino. It looked more exciting in the evening with the multi-colored lights flickering, the one-armed bandits dinging, and the lucky winners squealing.

Carolina stopped in front of the last elevator before the bow. "I need to return to my suite. Will you be at dinner?"

"Yes, of course," said Peter, giving her a slight salute with his fingers, as he continued forward.

When she reached for the DOWN button, Carolina heard whispers and turned around. In the shadows, she could see a little old lady with white hair, resting on a padded bench, talking to a stuffed white bulldog in her lap.

The woman smiled, which lifted up half of her sagging face. 'Dearie, I don't think that elevator is working."

The bell dinged and the elevator doors opened. Carolina walked into the empty lift, smiling back at the little old lady. "Looks okay to me." She pressed the button for D Deck.

The old woman shook her head and petted her bulldog. The elevator doors shut. As the elevator jerked and began to rise, Carolina heard the woman's voice. "We tried to warn her, didn't we, Napoleon?"

What a character, Carolina thought. But when the lift suddenly jolted and stopped between decks, she wondered if the old woman knew what she was talking about. Carolina frowned and pressed the D Deck button, again. Nothing. That wasn't good. She pressed the red emergency button, but heard no bells or alarms. Not that she'd been stuck in a lot of elevators, but surely something was supposed to happen when you hit the red emergency button. It worked that way at the Villas.

Last month Carolina had been in the elevator with four other women headed down to dinner when it stopped on the third floor. The doors opened and Calvin Sinclair, who weighed at least 400 pounds, squeezed into the elevator. The doors shut, the elevator groaned, and suddenly dropped and jerked to a stop between floors. Everyone shrieked and squealed, even Carolina. Then Calvin sighed and pressed the alarm button, which sounded loudly. Within minutes, the Villas maintenance man rescued everyone and admonished Calvin about overloading the elevator, again.

But the ship's alarm did not seem to be working. "This is not my day," Carolina muttered out loud and beat on the doors with her fists. "Help! Help! Anyone out there?"

A little quiver of concern started behind Carolina's belly button. She sighed, gripped the elevator rails, and slowly lowered herself to the floor. No need to stand and fret, when it could be a long wait for help. Maybe the alarm was silent and someone would arrive any moment. She opened the Mrs. Craycraft book and started to read. Without warning, the lights went out, and a thud sounded over her head. Thank goodness, she thought. Someone was coming to rescue her. "Hello? Is anyone up there?" She grabbed the elevator rail and pulled herself to her feet.

No response except strange sounds and scrapings. This was followed by screeching sounds overhead—like sounds of the hatch opening. Carolina saw a pale sliver of light and heard heavy breathing.

"Who's there?" Carolina called out, feeling the hairs on her arms and neck stand on end. In the semi-darkness, she became aware of someone dropping down into the elevator. Feeling a physical presence close to her, she backed up against the wall. She could smell the muskiness of his body odor and feel the warmth from his body next to hers.

"Who are you?" A chill went down Carolina's spine. If he had come to rescue her, she reasoned, he should say so. But not a word was uttered. Instead, a pair of strong hands gripped her shoulders roughly. She screamed, jabbed out with her knee and connected with his tender spot. Mrs. Craycraft would have been proud. The intruder howled, loosened his grip, and yelled words Carolina hadn't heard since Arthur dropped his bowling ball on her brother's foot. Carolina kicked and beat the foreign assassin with her fists, screaming shrilly, until he pinned her down on the floor. His knee pressed firmly into the center of her chest. She couldn't breathe. The elevator bumped and dropped, but Carolina did not feel a thing.

Chapter Eleven
Rescued

When Carolina opened her eyes, the woman with the stuffed bulldog was standing over her, and Ron was kneeling beside her, looking worried, and rubbing her hands.

"Carolina?" he asked.

Carolina pulled her hands back and tried to sit up, but the walls whirled around her. She fell back, holding her head. She didn't know what had happened to her or why Ron was holding her hands.

The old lady smiled broadly. "Napoleon wouldn't want to be trapped in a lift all by himself, would you, Snookums?" She kissed the stuffed dog on its black plastic nose.

Carolina's brain felt oozy, and she thought she might throw up. Making another attempt to sit up, she tried to sort out what had happened.

"You're all right, Carolina, but you certainly gave us a scare," Ron said.

Carolina breathed deeply. "My chest hurts." Then she started to remember. "Someone tried to kill me," she croaked. For all she knew, it might have been Ron. She glared at him suspiciously.

Ron frowned, and his eyes narrowed. "What do you mean?"

"Somebody pressed their knee into my chest, and I couldn't breathe." A tear ran down her cheek. Omigosh! She had not cried since Arthur's memorial service. For goodness sakes, Carolina, get a grip. Mrs. Craycraft never became hysterical because somebody tried to kill her. But she couldn't help it. After all, nobody was paying her big bucks to be stoic. A sob escaped from her throat.

Ron put his arm around her. "You're going to be okay." He talked soothingly to her, and patted her shoulder. Even though she'd never admit it to anyone, this made her feel warm and fuzzy all over. "You should have listened to Mrs. Coolhardy and taken another elevator," Ron said, bringing an end to the special moment.

"That's right, dearie. I told you the lift was broken. Isn't that right, Napoleon?" The old lady wagged the dog's tail and woofed.

Carolina pushed back from Ron indignantly. "It's my fault somebody tried to kill me?" She looked at Ron warily. How did she know it wasn't Ron? After all, he was in the elevator holding her hand when she came to.

Ron pulled a handkerchief from his pocket and handed it to Carolina, who wiped her eyes and blew her nose. "When the elevator doors opened, you were the only person inside," Ron said.

"He dropped out of the ceiling, Ron. He must have left the same way."

"It was a man?"

"Most definitely. I kneed him in his—"

Mrs. Coolhardy covered her stuffed dog's ears.

"Carolina, would you recognize him if you saw him, again?"

"The lights were out, Ron. It was dark."

"Did you recognize his voice?"

"He didn't say anything, but he did scream and use really foul language when I kneed him in his—"

"You know what?" Ron rubbed Carolina's arm. "I think when the elevator stopped between floors and the lights went out, you had a panic attack and hyperventilated. Maybe you fainted, fell down, and hit your head in the dark."

Carolina wiped her eyes and blew her nose, again. "You think I hallucinated that someone tried to kill me?"

Ron looked at her, unsmiling. "No, not at all. Getting trapped in an elevator is scary at best. A highly imaginative person—"

"That's it. I'm out of here." Carolina tried to stand, but she didn't have the strength in her thighs and knees to do it. She knew—thanks to her hours of yoga classes—she could always roll over into the downward dog position and scoot herself up, but that would be embarrassing. "Are you sure you're ready to stand up?"

Before she could open her mouth, Ron swiftly pulled her to her feet.

Carolina grabbed Ron's upper arm to steady herself and marveled at the muscle mass she felt. She had thought he was in his late fifties, but after feeling his arm, she decided he was early fifties and worked out with a personal trainer.

"Let me help you to your suite," Ron offered.

"No, I'm okay." Carolina took a step, but her knees buckled.

Without hesitation, Ron picked her up in his arms and carried her down the corridor. She realized she had not been picked up in a man's arms since Arthur carried her over the threshold of their home at the end of their honeymoon. Feeling too woozy to protest, Carolina looked over her shoulder at Mrs. Coolhardy who was snuggling her stuffed dog.

"Holey moley, Napoleon," Mrs. Coolhardy said. "This is going to be a fun cruise after all."

"Lordy, Lordy! What happened to her?" Eula Mae asked, as Ron carried Carolina into their suite.

"Is she going to be all right?" asked Yasuko.

"She should be fine," said Ron. "She got stuck in one of the elevators. Thinks someone tried to kill her. That's all." He sat her on the bed.

Eula Mae turned pale and sat down next to her. "Carolina, is that true?" She wrung her hands.

Carolina rubbed her fingers over a sore spot on her neck. "The stupid elevator stopped between floors," she said. "When I pressed the red alarm button, nothing happened. Then the lights went out, and this man came down from the ceiling." An unexpected sob escaped from her throat.

"How awful!" Yasuko exclaimed.

"That sounds unbelievable," Eula Mae said.

"I know it sounds crazy, but it's true." Why didn't anyone believe someone was out to harm her? Carolina took a deep breath. "This man—obviously up to no good—sat on me." She swallowed hard, closed her eyes, and pictured Mrs. Craycraft stuck in an elevator with an assassin. One hand chop to his throat and the killer would drop senseless to the floor. The thought was calming.

Eula Mae reached over and hugged Carolina. "I can't believe everything that is happening to us."

"Me, either," agreed Yasuko. "It's like we're caught up in the middle of a horror movie or something."

Funny, thought Carolina, feeling the same thing. She wiggled out of the "touchy-feely" moment and looked up at Ron. Now that her head had stopped swirling, Carolina's brain started to function. "How did you find me, Ron? I thought you were working on your magazine story?"

"I took a break to deliver Eula Mae's doll." Ron indicated the straw doll on the desk. "She was worried because you were gone when she woke up. She thought you might have gone to the library. When I went to look for you, I met this elderly woman with her stuffed dog, squawking about some woman, who fit your description, stuck and screaming on the broken elevator."

"It didn't seem broken to me."

"Apparently it was. Luckily, after I pressed the call button, the elevator moved down. When the doors opened, you were lying on the floor."

Carolina frowned. If what Ron said was true, then he'd foiled the killer. She shuddered and looked up at Ron in surprise. "You saved my life."

"Some credit goes to Eula Mae for worrying and to Mrs. Coolhardy for cluing me in about the elevator. Anyway, it's all over now. Try not to think about it." He knelt down beside her. "You should see the ship's doctor."

He stood and turned to Eula Mae. "Keep her quiet and in bed. I need to talk to the Captain about this."

Carolina sat up. "But it's tea time," she protested.

Yasuko grabbed Ron's arm. "We were waiting on Carolina, so all of us could go to tea."

"I seriously doubt if you three will starve, if you miss one tea," Ron said.

Eula Mae and Yasuko blocked the door to prevent Ron from leaving. They gave him the evil eye.

Ron rolled his eyes. "Fine. I'll tell Mr. Gallenkemp to bring you a tea tray with lots of goodies."

Carolina cleared her throat and stared at Ron.

"With lots of chocolate éclairs." He reached into his jacket pocket. "Before I forget, I think this is yours." He handed Carolina the Craycraft book. "Ever thought of switching to a different genre?"

Carolina snatched the book out of his hand and pushed it under her pillow. "No."

After Ron left, Eula Mae clasped Carolina's arm. "I knew we should have flown home this morning. This whole thing is escalating. We could still get an evening flight."

"I tell you I'm fine. Ron is probably right. Sitting in a hot, dark, stuffy elevator could make even a strong person imagine things. I nearly scared myself to death and passed out."

"I don't want to go now," Yasuko butted in. "This holiday is just starting to get interesting. You won't believe who played mahjong with me!"

"I don't know." Eula Mae shook her head.

"I'm clueless," said Carolina.

Yasuko giggled like a teenage girl. "Charlie Chan!"

"The invisible haggler in the straw market?" asked Eula Mae.

"Yes!" Yasuko said, excitedly. "He taught me mahjong-winning strategy."

"Well, bless his pea-pickin' little heart for that," said Eula Mae. "I'm mighty happy for you, but I still think we need to pack up and fly home tonight."

Carolina decided it was time to distract her, again. "Ron says your doll came? Let's look at her."

"What? Oh." Eula Mae picked up the doll and handed it to Carolina. "It doesn't look all that great to me now. I can't believe I paid $25 for it. Like I needed it."

"It's called impulse buying." Carolina turned the doll over in her hands, running her fingers over the small pieces of straw fruit in the basket. Then she hefted the doll in her left hand. "That's strange."

"What?" Eula Mae asked.

"This doll feels heavier than I remember."

"What are you talking about? Hand it here." Eula Mae grabbed the doll, but Carolina didn't let go.

"Carolina, give it to me."

"I'm not through looking at it."

As they both tugged on the doll, its head tore away from the body. A black drawstring bag fell to the floor with a muffled clunk.

Yasuko grabbed it off the floor. "What's this?

"That's what I'd like to know." Eula Mae snatched the bag out of her hand, untied the string, and fingered open the top. She peered into the bag.

"What's in it?" Carolina asked, trying to peer over Eula Mae's shoulder.

Eula Mae poured the contents onto the bed. "Lordy, Lordy! It's just three pieces of green glass. Looks like a broken Sprite bottle."

Carolina examined the biggest piece of glass, rolling it between her fingers. A beautiful, dark green in color, the piece was smaller in diameter than her little finger and about an inch long. It was shaped like the quartz crystal earrings Arthur had given her one Christmas. The base of the green crystal was embedded in some sort of rock. "Mmm."

"What do you mean, "Mmm?" asked Yasuko.

Carolina ran her fingers over the green crystals. Smooth as glass, except for their gray-rock bases. "This reminds me of a Craycraft book—*The Columbian Emeralds Adventure*."

"Emeralds?"

Carolina held the biggest crystal up to the light. "Yes, the best and most expensive emeralds in the world are mined in Columbia. They are highly valued for their deep green color and their purity."

"Purity?" Yasuko asked. "What does that mean?"

"Look at this one?" Carolina handed it to Yasuko, who put on her glasses and looked at it. "See? It's almost flawless. Very little cracks or fissures."

"How do you know all this?" Eula Mae asked.

"Because Mrs. Craycraft got mixed up with emerald smugglers, and she learned all about emeralds."

Eula Mae edged closer to Carolina and picked up one of the crystals. "You really think these are emeralds? Seriously?" She frowned. "I don't know, Yasuko's emerald ring doesn't look anything like this."

"That's because these are raw and uncut. Right out of the mine. These emerald crystals have to be carefully removed from their rock host with chisels and hammers." Carolina considered the possibility that she could be wrong. After all, her information did come from a fiction book, but it sounded good coming from Mrs. Craycraft.

"Uncut emeralds? Not a broken Sprite bottle?" Eula Mae took the three green crystals over to the bedside lamp and held them under the light. "Why would someone put emeralds in my doll?"

"How would they know it was your doll? Ron bought it and sent it to his cabin, remember?" Carolina leaned forward. "Unless Ron put the crystals in the doll himself."

Eula Mae looked at Carolina in surprise. "That's highly unlikely."

"Is that any crazier to believe than what else is going on around here?" pointed out Yasuko.

"But Ron stopped that man from following us in Nassau?" Eula Mae said. "And didn't he rescue you from the elevator?"

"Or was it the nutty old lady with the dog?" Carolina asked. "Maybe Ron was the one in the elevator with his knee in my chest."

Eula Mae and Yasuko sat down on the bed next to Carolina. Eula Mae still held the crystals in her hands. "But Ron said he was going to talk to the Captain."

Carolina nodded. "But what if the Captain is one of <u>them</u>." She pulled her spy journal out of the bedside drawer and thumbed through the pages, checking her notes. "Ron told us to stop snooping. And doesn't he want us to turn Colleen over to him?"

Eula Mae dropped the crystals on the bed. "But I like Ron. Don't you?"

"He's okay, I guess," admitted Carolina. She wasn't going to admit that in spite of her doubts, she did have feelings for him.

"I like Ron," said Yasuko. "But I like Peter better."

"Only because he wears a uniform," pointed out Eula Mae. "We've all noticed how shamelessly you flirt with him." She locked eyes with Carolina. "As for you, Carolina, I don't understand why you are hesitant about your feelings for Ron? Do you think he's bad?"

"I didn't say he was a bad guy. Although it is a possibility. But we don't have enough facts to know for sure, so we have to be objective. Spies and agents always get into trouble when their emotions take over."

Eula Mae gave Carolina a gentle shove. "You and your spies. Tell me what you honestly think about him."

Carolina blinked. Her gut instinct screamed that Ron was one of the good spies, but she didn't want to tell Eula Mae about her true feelings for him.

Their conversation was interrupted by a knock on the door. Eula Mae stood up, leaving the crystals on the bed. "Who's there?"

"Mr. Gallenkamp with tea. Requested by Mr. Dunten."

Carolina smiled and wondered if he'd remembered the chocolate éclairs.

Mr. Gallenkamp entered the suite, glancing briefly at the crystals on the bed. He watched out of the corner of his eyes, as Carolina gathered up the crystals and dropped them into the black bag.

Mr. Gallenkamp noticeably stiffened. Then he looked away, put down the tray—which did include chocolate éclairs—and left without another word.

Carolina grabbed a chocolate éclair. "Now there goes a man of few words." She poured herself a cup of tea. "Actually, on second thought, a man of no words."

Yasuko poured herself a cup of tea and politely placed a scone with clotted cream and a strawberry tart on her plate.

Eula Mae shook her head when Carolina offered to share her chocolate éclairs. "I wish that dang stowaway would come back and tell us what's going on."

Carolina licked the cream out of her éclair. "I'm worried about her."

Eula Mae finally gave in and selected a small cup of chocolate mousse. "I'm worried about all of us."

Carolina swallowed the last bite of éclair. "Yes, I am, too. We have too many questions and not enough answers." Yasuko and Eula Mae moved over to Carolina as she reached for her cell phone. "Let's check in with Lilly. Maybe she can help." Carolina called up the WhatsApp and touched on the video icon. In mere seconds, Lilly's smiling face appeared.

"Good afternoon, Carolina! Oh, and you, too, Yasuko and Eula Mae. Everyone has been asking about you. Are you having fun? Aren't you in Nassau today?"

Eula Mae peered over Carolina's shoulder. "Yes, and we saw the straw market, the Queen's Staircase and—"

Yasuko grabbed the phone. "And we were accosted by a foreign agent and—"

Carolina snatched the phone back. "And I was nearly killed in the ship's elevator."

"Unbelievable," squealed Lilly.

"We're not making this up," shouted Eula Mae.

"Please tell all," Lilly said. "This sounds really exciting! What an adventure!"

Not leaving out a single detail, Carolina—with Yasuko and Eula Mae putting in a word or two along the way—filled Lilly in on how their day had gone so far.

"Nothing has happened here to compare with that," said Lilly. She paused as though in thought. "Except Ruthie Ann's issue with Beulah Mae came to a head yesterday."

"What do you mean?" asked Carolina, picturing prim and proper Ruthie Ann Dunlap in her mind. Some folks referred to her as the "hat lady" because she always wore a suit with a frilly blouse, large pearl necklace, and a fancy brimmed hat. "What happened?"

Lilly held the phone closer to her face and spoke softly. "You know how she is always complaining at the association meeting about residents not cleaning up the dog poop off the grounds and sidewalks?"

"Who can forget that?" Yasuko said. "Especially after that one time she stepped in a pile of poop."

"Well, she finally figured out the guilty party was Beulah Mae and her King Charles Spaniel Lovey. For weeks, Ruthie Ann started picking up Lovey's poop and saving it. Then late last night, she dumped all of it in front of Beulah Mae's door. This morning when Beulah Mae headed out to walk the dog, she stepped in the poop pile and slid down to the floor on her ass. Such a ruckus!"

Everyone laughed. Ruthie Ann was not the only resident at the Villas who at one time or another had stepped in Lovey's poop. She just complained the loudest and decided to take matters into her own hands. Carolina could relate to that.

"By the way, Lilly," said Carolina. "Before we hang up and head to dinner, could you please use your talented fingers to help us?"

"Whatever you need."

"Could you please see what you can find online about a ship's officer on the *Emerald Dream* lost overboard earlier this year?"

"Sure thing. Anything else?"

"One more thing. See if you can find out anything about emerald smuggling involving cruise ships."

"What? What's up with that?"

"Look at this." Carolina reversed the phone camera and turned it to focus on the crystals. "See if you can find any images of emerald crystals that look like these."

"Wow! Cool!" exclaimed Lilly. "Can you shoot me a photo?"

"Not a problem," Carolina replied. "Thanks, Lilly! Good night!"

Peter, Carolina, Eula Mae, and Yasuko placed their dinner orders without Ron, who barely arrived in time for the main course.

"Sorry I'm late, but deadlines have a higher priority," he said, glancing at Carolina's plate. "That looks good. What is it?"

"Lamb curry, Singapore-style. It's delicious."

Ron pointed at her curry. "Dominic, I'll have some of that."

Dominic did an about-face and left for the kitchen. "Be right back."

Ron spread his white linen napkin across his lap. "By the way, ladies, the Captain has invited us to visit him in his wardroom for after-dinner drinks."

Peter strangled on his iced tea and fell just short of spewing it all over the table. "What a privilege!" he said, wiping his mouth with his napkin. "It's most unusual for the Captain to entertain passengers in his wardroom. What's the occasion?"

"I bet he wants to hear how I nearly died in the elevator today," Carolina guessed.

"What?" questioned Peter, who seemed visibly concerned. "I heard someone was stuck in a lift, but I had no idea it was you. How bloody awful! You weren't hurt, were you?"

"Oh, nothing serious like that. Somebody just tried to kill me."

"I do not understand your American humor. What really happened?"

Peter listened without interruption, as Carolina re-told her elevator incident story. "You three ladies aren't having a good cruise," he said. "First you get followed in Nassau. Then someone ransacks your suite, and now Carolina gets assaulted in a lift. Terrible things like that never happen to passengers or crew on this ship," he said.

"At least not since the ship's officer fell overboard, you mean?" Ron asked.

"Occasionally accidents do happen on cruise ships. People fall overboard, individuals get stuck in lifts, but we don't broadcast it among the passengers," Peter said.

"Why not?" Yasuko asked.

"It doesn't take much to upset passengers. We have to handle them with kid gloves. If they thought passengers were being trapped and nearly getting killed in the lifts, there would be ship-wide panic. Besides that, it's not good publicity. Next thing you know, it will be viral on

Facebook or YouTube." Peter stood up. "Now if you'll excuse me, I have to return to my station before we drop the lines and push back. Good evening."

Surprised by his sudden departure, the rest of the group watched Peter leave the dining room. Dominic handed Carolina a plate of chocolate éclairs, as she watched Peter disappear.

"It would have been better if you hadn't mentioned the elevator incident," Ron said.

"He said he'd already heard about it." Geez, what was Ron's problem, Carolina wondered.

"It was just a matter of time before he found out it was Carolina," Eula Mae said.

"Still, we don't know who can be trusted," said Ron.

Carolina licked the chocolate off the top of the éclair. "We don't even know if we can trust you."

Ron raised his right eyebrow. "You're right, Carolina. Sometimes you don't know who your friends really are."

Carolina bit into the éclair and savored the chilled cream that oozed out into her mouth. "And even if we find out, it might be too late."

The Captain ushered the group into his wardroom and shook their hands. "Good to see you again, Eula Mae Davis. Carolina Cunningham. Yasuko Crane. And, of course, Ron Dunten. resident writer, correct? Please be seated. May I offer you something to drink?"

A steward entered with a tray and passed around glasses of white wine. After the drinks were served, the Captain turned to Carolina. "Mrs. Cunningham, I have a report indicating you were stranded in one of our lifts this afternoon—in the dark. I daresay it was a terrible experience. Mr. Dunten says you believe someone dropped down into the lift and assaulted you. Is that true?"

Carolina swallowed a sip of wine and closed her eyes. Goose bumps broke out on her arm as she remembered. "Yes, that's right." She opened her eyes. The Captain stared at her intently. "At first, I thought he was coming to rescue me. Instead, he grabbed me, threw me to the floor, and pressed his knee into my chest until I couldn't breathe."

The Captain shook his head. He slammed his fist down angrily on his desk. "How bloody awful. I find it quite shocking that this could happen on my ship." He pulled out paper and pen. "We need to investigate this horrific incident immediately. I've already notified our security officer. This should be resolved as quickly as possible."

"I certainly hope so," Eula Mae said. "You have a lot of retired folks on this cruise. If they don't feel safe, they won't be back."

Yasuko, who had been sitting quietly on the side, set down her wine glass. "Who investigates crimes on cruise ships anyway? The FBI?"

"The International Maritime Law is the governing law in international waters. Of course, the FBI has the authority to investigate and prosecute crimes involving Americans anywhere in the world. Once a passenger reports a crime, an investigation takes place, a report is made of the findings, and the evidence is shared with the appropriate law enforcement authorities. But first, we must have the facts."

The Captain turned to Carolina. "Mrs. Cunningham, could you please describe your assailant to me?"

"Sir, the lights were out in the elevator. I couldn't see his face."

"I see. What did he say to you? Did he threaten you in any way?"

"No, sir, he just grabbed me. He did say a lot of bad words when I kneed him in his—"

Ron cleared his throat.

"Is it possible that you were so frightened you fainted?" the Captain asked.

"When he grabbed me, I kneed him in his—"

The Captain waved his hand. "Uh, yes, yes, I understand. Then what?"

"That's when he started screaming and saying the bad words."

"I'm sure he did. Then what?"

Carolina closed her eyes and rubbed her forehead, trying to remember. "It's sort of hazy. We struggled. He pushed me to the floor and tried to kill me. I don't remember anything after that."

"Are you sure he tried to kill you?"

Eula Mae looked agitated. "Captain, if Carolina says someone tried to kill her, then someone tried to kill her."

"Please, Mrs. Davis, I'm only doing my duty. I need facts for my report. I'm sure Mrs. Cunningham believes someone tried to kill her, but I have to ask questions to make sure an actual crime was committed. This is my responsibility."

The Captain's eyes gazed intently at Carolina. "I have a report from maintenance that a crew member entered an elevator for repairs this afternoon. A female passenger stood between him and the control box. When he tried to move her out of his way, she attacked him with kicks and punches and screamed bloody murder. They fell to the floor at which point he literally had to sit on her to prevent her from doing him further bodily harm."

Carolina jumped to her feet, her face burning. What was this? Was she now a hysterical old woman with dementia? Was her perception of the events faulty? Did she overreact to the situation? "Sir, I know what happened to me. If he really was a repairman, wouldn't he have said so and brought a flashlight?" Carolina headed for the door.

"Mrs. Cunningham, please return to your seat," the Captain called out, rubbing the bridge of his nose.

Carolina slowed, but didn't stop.

"Please?"

"Carolina!" Eula Mae called out.

"Please, Carolina," Yasuko said.

Carolina turned at the door and wondered if that was a hint of a smile on Ron's lips.

"I did not say I don't believe your version of events in the elevator, Mrs. Cunningham. I'm merely trying to get the facts. I need to know if what happened to you was a coincidence or if it was intentionally directed at you. Can you think of any reason why someone would want to frighten you?"

She looked at Ron, Eula Mae, and Yasuko, then back to the Captain. "I don't know, sir."

"Maybe she knows too much," Eula Mae speculated.

"What does she know?" the Captain asked.

Carolina stood tall—at least as tall as she was able, considering that she was getting shorter at each annual checkup—and lifted her chin. "First of all, I know about the stowaway."

The Captain tugged on his ear. "My dear, half the people on this ship know about the stowaway."

"The purser doesn't like me."

Ron frowned.

Eula Mae grimaced.

Yasuko covered her face with her hands.

The Captain smiled.

Carolina seethed. Were she and the stowaway the only two people on the *Emerald Dream* who believed the purser was bad news?

"What does Alvin Greene have to do with this?" the Captain asked.

"I overheard him and Mr. Smith plotting to kill someone, and if the someone isn't the stowaway, then it has to be me."

The Captain frowned. "Now why does that sound familiar?" He searched through a short stack of papers on his desk. "Ahh, yes, here's a report from the purser about a passenger named Carolina Cunningham who became hysterical when he approached her to return a book she had dropped."

"That wasn't the way it was at all."

"No? Why don't you tell me your version?" The Captain held out his wine glass, and the steward refilled it.

"He chased after me because he thought I overheard something."

Eula Mae cleared her throat. "Don't forget, someone trashed our suite and left a threatening message on the mirror."

Carolina slid to the edge of her seat. "Oh, and something else. Someone followed us in Nassau today. Isn't that right, Ron?"

"That's right, Captain. I asked him to stop following us, and he was more than agreeable."

The Captain jotted down a few notes. "Do you have any more incidents to report? Because the more information I have, the quicker we can bring about a resolution to this horrid affair."

"How about the black bag that fell out of your straw doll, Eula Mae?" Carolina pointed out.

Ron frowned. "What's this?"

Eula Mae looked at Ron. "You know the doll you bought at the straw market? A bag full of green crystals fell out of it."

"Not just any crystals, Eula Mae. Raw emeralds," Carolina explained.

Ron and the Captain snapped to attention. "Emeralds?" asked the Captain.

"Carolina, what are you talking about?" Ron asked.

"We were going to tell you later," explained Eula Mae. "We thought maybe you put the crystals in the doll."

Ron stood up. "Where's the bag now?"

Carolina rose to her feet. "Back in the doll. Why?"

The Captain stood up. "I want to see this doll."

The doll wasn't in the closet. The women checked every shelf and every drawer. The doll was gone.

"But I left it right here before dinner." Carolina ran her hand over the empty spot on the closet shelf and shook her head. "I don't understand what happened to it."

"She's telling the truth," Eula Mae said.

"Yes, I saw her put it there," confirmed Yasuko.

The Captain looked at the three women. "I'm astounded. Unbelievably, you three ladies seem to be involved with questionable people and activities on my ship—a stowaway, a possible murderer, and emerald smuggling. Did I miss anything? What else?"

"Well—" Carolina hesitated. Should she tell him about the stowaway's sister? But what if Colleen was right? What if the Captain was "one of them"?

Eula Mae interrupted her thoughts. "Captain, is it possible that whoever took that doll, also hid the bag in the doll, and attacked Carolina in the elevator?"

Carolina nodded. "I think the stowaway figures into all of this, too."

The Captain turned to Ron. "Mr. Dunten?"

Ron, who was carefully examining the closet, slid the doors shut and faced the Captain. "I believe everything is connected, but we're missing vital pieces of the puzzle." He looked at Carolina and raised his right eyebrow. "However, we do know that for reasons unknown, certain parties are trying to scare these three women."

Chapter Twelve
And More Questions

Carolina, Eula Mae, and Yasuko were awakened by a light tapping on their cabin door. Carolina's cell phone indicated it was 5:58 a.m. She sat up in bed and listened; the tapping continued.

"Carolina, did you hear that?" Eula Mae whispered

"What is it?" Yasuko asked.

The tapping became louder. Carolina left her bed and tiptoed to the door. "Who is it?" she whispered.

"Colleen."

Carolina flung open the door and pulled her inside. "Where have you been? I've been worried sick." She locked the door behind her.

Colleen sat down on the desk chair. "I found an empty cabin on one of the lower decks."

"The cabin steward doesn't suspect anything?" asked Yasuko from her sofa bed.

"Few passengers stay on that deck. Mostly crew cabins or entertainers only onboard for a few days. The steward rarely goes down there. My biggest problem has been getting something to eat. The purser is always watching for me in the café and around open buffets on the pool deck. I don't know if I'll get fed today or not."

Eula Mae threw her legs over the side of her bed and stood. "Is this the infamous stowaway?"

Carolina jumped. She'd forgotten Eula Mae and Yasuko had not met the stowaway. "Eula Mae, this is Colleen Burgess."

Yasuko waved from her bed. "I'm Yasuko Crane."

"Hello, Colleen." Eula Mae reached out and shook her hand. "I've never met a stowaway before."

"I've never been one before."

"Excuse me for not getting up, but I'm tired," Yasuko called out.

"Sorry to barge in at such an early hour, but I'm feeling desperate." Colleen's head fell forward, her face in her hands.

"It's all right," Eula Mae said. "With everything happening to Carolina, we don't sleep much anyway."

"Did you hear that someone attacked her in the elevator?" Yasuko asked, as she pulled herself out of bed.

Colleen's eyes widened. "No, what happened?"

The four of them sat together on Carolina's bed. After hearing the details, Colleen shook her head. "I told you that purser is a bad person."

Carolina squeezed Colleen's shoulder. "I wish we had more information to convince the Captain of that."

Colleen shrugged. "I told you everything I know."

"Do you know when your sister first suspected a smuggling ring was operating on this ship?" Carolina asked.

"During the last cruise." Colleen chewed her lower lip. "She went down below to get more prizes for games and contests, and noticed the hatch to the ship's hold was open."

Eula Mae leaned closer to her. "Was that unusual?"

"Most certainly. It's supposed to remain locked at all times, except in port. Then she overheard one of the ship's officers and the purser talking about getting something through U.S. Customs."

"Who was he talking to?" Carolina asked, making notes in her spy journal.

Colleen shook her head. "Unfortunately, room in the storage hole was tight. When she tried to move, she overturned a box in the hole, and the purser saw her."

"What happened?" Yasuko asked.

"She said she greeted the purser as calmly as she could and reminded him to lock the hatch when he finished. She didn't think he suspected anything. That was our last phone conversation. I never heard from her, again."

"How awful," Carolina said. "She didn't know what they were smuggling?"

"No, but it has to be drugs," Colleen said. "What else do they smuggle on cruises?"

"How about emeralds?" Eula Mae asked.

"Emeralds?" Colleen frowned. "Why emeralds?"

Carolina stood up and started to pace. "We found a bag of green crystals stuffed into a doll we bought in the straw market. We think they might be raw emeralds."

Colleen gasped. "Emeralds? I don't know." She tugged on her braid. "I was so sure it was drugs."

"Well, it is practically all you ever hear about being smuggled," pointed out Yasuko. "That and diamonds."

"Antiquities," suggested Eula Mae. "There seems to be a big demand for them, too."

They sat in silence for a moment, then Carolina told Colleen about Ron. "We need more help to figure this out. A freelance writer onboard wants to talk to you."

Colleen's eyes widened. "Me? Why?"

"For his magazine article about the *Emerald Dream*. He wants to help you, too." Eula Mae said.

Colleen wrapped her arms around herself. "I don't know. Do you trust him?"

Carolina placed a hand on Colleen's arm. "It's better not to ask questions like that."

Eula Mae rolled her eyes. "What Carolina means is—"

Yasuko finished her sentence. "We're not sure."

Colleen frowned. "Why not?"

Carolina opened her spy journal. "It's complicated. Some things about him don't add up." She thumbed through the pages and stopped at her last written notes. "Take last night for instance. We met with the Captain, and Ron seemed awfully friendly with him. Don't you find that a little strange? Especially if the Captain is one of <u>them</u>."

Colleen twisted the end of her braid around her finger. "But if he's writing a feature article about the ship, then the Captain needs to be sucking up to him so he'll write something nice."

"Yes, that's true," Eula Mae said.

"Don't forget," added Yasuko, "that Ron did get rid of that horrid man following us in Nassau."

"You don't have to keep bringing that up. It's here in my notes, and

I'm not forgetting it. However, he did make light of the whole thing to the Captain."

"Perhaps he's a humble person?" Colleen suggested.

"He did beat that guy up," Eula Mae insisted.

"Did he now?" Carolina questioned. "We didn't see them actually fighting, did we? Ron inferred that they had. And let's not forget he was in the elevator with me when I came to. We simply have no proof he is who he says he is."

"We could check him out?" Colleen suggested. "Google him or send an e-mail message to that magazine he writes for?"

"We could, if we knew which magazine it was." Carolina agreed.

"He never told us, now that I think about it," Eula Mae said. "Let's ask him at breakfast."

Carolina threw her hands in the air. "What else can we do?"

"Pretend we're tourists having a good time on a cruise ship?" Eula Mae suggested.

"What about the straw dolls?" Colleen asked. "If your doll had a bag of something in it, maybe someone else's doll does, too."

"Do they make and sell dolls in Grenada?" Yasuko asked. That was their next port of call. "If anyone buys a doll, we can check it for green crystals."

Carolina grimaced. "How would we know who buys a straw doll?"

"Someone could stand near the security entrance to see what purchases are delivered to the ship," Colleen suggested. "Everything has to be screened."

"I could buy another doll," Eula Mae said. "Only I'm not sure I want another one. I paid $25 for that last one and it's gone."

"Maybe it isn't always a straw doll," Carolina said.

Colleen's eyes narrowed.

Eula Mae frowned. "What do you mean?"

Carolina lowered her voice. "What if the emeralds are placed at random in souvenirs purchased ashore that are large enough to hold the emeralds?"

Colleen jumped off the bed excitedly. "Carolina, I think you have it! The native dollmaker didn't put in the emeralds."

"It was someone onboard the ship," Eula Mae finished.

"Who would do that?" asked Yasuko.

Carolina smiled. Things were clicking into place. "A member of the crew or an officer? Anyone who comes in contact with purchases delivered to the ship."

Eula Mae's eyes widened. "Mr. Gallenkamp?"

Carolina scowled. "He does seem to snoop around our door a lot. I know he saw the emeralds yesterday before we could put them away."

"He has access to a lot of cabins," Eula Mae reminded them.

"True," agreed Colleen. "But he rarely gets off the deck where he works."

"Yes," agreed Yasuko. "It has to be someone higher up in the chain of command."

"The purser!" everyone said at once.

How funny, Carolina thought, that everything keeps coming back to him. "Obviously we all agree the purser fits into this somehow."

"That man is lower than a snake's belly in a wagon rut," Eula Mae pointed out.

"That may be true, but we need more facts in order to prove it. We need to go ashore and observe."

"What if something goes wrong on Grenada?" Yasuko asked.

"Are you forgetting that we're only tourists out for a good time?" Carolina reminded them. "How could anything go wrong?"

"Well," Eula Mae said, "if it's possible for anything to go wrong, it certainly will if it involves us."

Carolina clapped her hands. "I have an idea. Let's disguise Colleen so she can go with us."

Colleen looked incredulous. "How?"

"The purser is looking for someone with long brown hair, so we'll cut yours short, and I'll loan you more of my clothes. What do you say?"

"Cool! But how will I get past security going on and off the ship?"

Carolina bit her lower lip thoughtfully. "We'll figure it out when the time is right."

An hour later, Colleen fingered her two inches of funky, spiky hair in front of the mirror. She turned right and left to see how she looked in Carolina's stretch jeans with an elastic waist and a plaid green and white blouse. "I feel kind of old-lady frumpy," she said.

"Bite your tongue and mind your manners, young lady." Eula Mae handed her a pair of green polka-dotted sunglasses and a slime-green bucket sunhat. "Here, try these."

"Yuck!" exclaimed Colleen, putting on the glasses and hat. "Yikes! Not even my own mother would recognize me now."

Carolina frowned. "One problem solved, but how will Colleen get through security without an ID card?"

Colleen pulled off the sunglasses. "I might be able to slip out through the kitchen galley. When the ship is in port, a hatch is open to off-load garbage and take on grocery supplies and other deliveries."

"That sounds risky," Eula Mae said.

"Maybe Dominic could help?" Carolina thought out loud.

"Dominic?" A smile spread across Colleen's face. "He was one of my sister's favorite crew members. I met him once when my family cruised on this ship. I didn't know he was working this cruise."

A noise sounded outside their door, and the ship's daily program of events appeared underneath. Carolina bent over and picked it up. "Ahh, Mr. Gallenkemp at work."

Colleen glanced at herself in the mirror one more time. "What time is it?"

"My stomach says it's time for breakfast," Carolina said.

"Stomachs never lie," Yasuko said.

Eula Mae looked at her watch. "It's nearly 8 o'clock."

Colleen backed toward the door. "Why don't you three go to breakfast and bring me back something to eat. I'll be on G Deck in room 208. Knock once and I'll let you in."

"Don't leave yet," Eula Mae warned. "Mr. Gallenkemp will see you."

"But you said this was a disguise. I've gotten this far, let's give it a try." When she opened the door, Mr. Gallenkemp was standing right outside. She stepped into the corridor, flashed a big smile at him, and turned back to us. "Bye, guys! See you after breakfast."

The women watched her saunter down the corridor. Mr. Gallenkemp didn't give her a second glance.

Ron was drinking a cup of coffee when Carolina, Eula Mae, and Yasuko were seated for breakfast. "Thought you three had fallen overboard."

Dominic spread a napkin across Carolina's lap. "If we had, you'd be the first to know," she replied.

Dominic smiled and handed out breakfast menus. "A beautiful morning, my dear ladies. Calm seas and lots of sunshine. What else could you ask for?"

"I'd like to start with some fresh fruit. Maybe strawberries and sliced bananas. Are the bananas any riper than yesterday?"

"A little bit," he confessed.

"I hope so. How about a stack of blueberry pancakes and sausage?" Carolina asked.

"For you, the best blueberry pancakes and sausage onboard." He turned to Eula Mae. "Anything for you, beautiful lady?"

"Scrambled eggs and a croissant, please."

"And you Mrs. Crane? Do you feel like eating something this morning?"

Yasuko ran her finger down the menu and stopped at the egg choices. "Two poached eggs and an English muffin, please."

Carolina handed Dominic the menu. "Could you please wrap up some sweet rolls and fruit for me to take back to my room?"

"No sooner said than done, my dear lady." He headed for the galley.

Ron finished his cup of coffee. "Carolina, you're a walking, bottomless pit."

"I simply like good food."

"Nothing wrong with that," he said. "What plans do you three have for today?"

"We might watch the water volleyball competition at the main pool," Eula Mae answered. "Or we could attend that lecture on the history of Grenada."

Ron nodded his approval. "Those are both excellent choices and should keep you out of trouble. I'll be in my cabin working on my article. Deadline's coming up."

Eula Mae took a sip of orange juice. "That sounds too much like work, Ron. You're on a cruise, after all."

"Trust me, I'm not on vacation. I'm working. My editor reminds me every day."

Dominic returned with breakfast for everyone and left for the galley.

"How sad for you," Carolina said. "By the way, which magazine do you work for?"

"I freelance, so I write for many travel magazines. Please pass the jam."

Carolina paused with the fork halfway to her mouth, when she saw Eula Mae push the jam tray in Ron's direction. But when he reached for it, Eula Mae snatched it back. "What IS the name of the publication you're currently writing for?"

"Are you really interested, Eula Mae?" He half rose from his seat, reached across the table, dug his spoon into the blackberry jam pot, and sat down to spread it on his English muffin.

"Would I ask if I wasn't?"

Ron nodded and shrugged. "Okay, why not? *Travel the World*. A magazine for the socially elite." He reached into a portfolio on the floor beside him and pulled out a copy. "Here. I have an article on page 36."

Carolina leaned over Eula Mae's shoulder as she turned to page 36. Together they read the headline— "The Great Gobi Desert: Hot Spot of Your Travels" —which ran across two pages. Ron Dunten's byline ran underneath.

Ron grinned annoyingly, bit into his English muffin, chewed, and swallowed. "Why do you look so surprised? Keep the magazine as a gesture of goodwill, if you like." He wiped his mouth on his napkin and stood up. "I have to get back to work. See you at lunch. Stay out of trouble."

Eula Mae agreed to deliver the breakfast rolls to Colleen, so Carolina could take care of something else. "What are you up to Carolina?"

Carolina watched Eula Mae and Yasuko step into the elevator. "I'll explain later." She turned and took the stairs down to the Computer Room, which was larger than she thought it would be: three rows of desks with four computers on each row. Several passengers hovered on the side, waiting for a chance to check their e-mail.

By the time Carolina signed her name and suite number in the log book, a number of computers freed up, and she claimed one. In a matter of minutes, she found the website for *Traveling the World* magazine and the e-mail address of the managing editor, Luke DuBois.

"Dear Mr. DuBois," she typed. "Do you know a writer named Ron Dunten? If so, is he currently on assignment in the Caribbean? Most urgent that I hear from you soon. Lives could be in danger. Thanks, Agent Carolina Cunningham"

Carolina smiled with satisfaction, clicked "send" and logged off.

Chapter Thirteen
Incident on Grenada

When Carolina caught up with Eula Mae, Yasuko, and Colleen on the Lido Pool Deck, they were seated in lounge chairs in the shade, watching young bikini-clad women dive into the small salt-water pool for teaspoons. Here in the center of the deck was located the main pool and two hot tubs, surrounded by dozens and dozens of chaise lounges. Here was the great outdoors—blue sky and sunshine on good days or wind, cold temps, and rain on bad days. Here passengers could leave their cramped cabins to breathe the ocean air, sip drinks from the bar, read a good book, take a nap, or soak up the sun.

Carolina joined her friends as a buxom blonde surfaced from the water with a mouthful of spoons. One boob plopped out of her red near-nothing string bikini. No one seemed to notice. The unabashed cruise director counted 18 spoons and declared her the winner.

"My gosh! It looks like the entire ship is here watching this spectacle," shouted Carolina above the roar of an enthusiastic cheering crowd.

"Lordy, Lordy, you missed the swattin' contest," Eula Mae yelled back. "All those near-naked fillies sitting on the shoulders of hunky stud muffins."

"Oh yeah!" Yasuko, holding a pink drink topped with paper umbrella and cherry on a swizzle stick, leaned towards Carolina's ear. "The girls were beating each other with Styrofoam tubes and trying to knock each other off."

"And the men were just a grinnin' like Cheshire Cats," Eula Mae explained.

Carolina looked around nervously. "That sounds entertaining, but what if somebody recognizes Colleen?" She didn't see anyone looking their way. In fact, everyone seemed to be focused on an extra-fluffy-around-the edges twenty-something with fire-engine-red hair. She was flaunting a leopard-print thong bikini. "Eeeee-yew and double yuck!" Carolina mumbled under her breath, wishing she could un-see what she just saw.

Eula Mae turned a page in her book: *Evenings with Cary Grant*. "Relax, Carolina. No one is going to recognize Colleen. Not with her great disguise. Besides, this place is too crowded."

Colleen suddenly slumped in her chaise lounge. "Don't look now, but here comes the purser," she hissed.

Carolina couldn't resist checking for herself. Sure enough, there he was, Saint Alvin Greene, only 30 feet away—smiling and talking to passengers as he passed through the pool area. His gaze wandered in their direction and froze. He scowled.

"He sees me!" Colleen squealed.

"Don't panic. He's looking at Carolina," Eula Mae said, not looking up from her book.

Eula Mae was right. If looks could kill, Carolina knew she'd be convulsing in the midst of death throes. But the purser turned his gaze away when Mrs. Coolhardy—with the stuffed-excuse for a dog—tugged on his sleeve. Was it only her imagination, wondered Carolina, or did that little old lady wink at her? With his attention focused on Mrs. Coolhardy, the four women left their seats and slipped away through the throng of happy, sweaty passengers.

The next morning, her adrenaline pumping, Carolina waited with Eula Mae and Yasuko on the pier at St. George, Grenada. All three women were covered in sunscreen and wearing sun hats. Carolina's dermatologist always fussed if he detected even the slightest hint of a tan. This was frustrating to her. She thought older men and women looked better with a little bit of color. Pasty-white old folks always looked like they were in bad health—as in circling the drain.

In the shade of the ship, Carolina dutifully checked her wide-brimmed sun hat, adjusted her sunglasses, and looked around for

Colleen. From their vantage point—next to a frenzied group of taxi drivers and tour guides—the women could see everyone disembarking the ship for a day on the island. At the bottom of the gangway, a ship's photographer snapped photos of giddy passengers in front of a "Welcome to Grenada" sign. Many passengers, like Carolina and her entourage, avoided being pulled over for a photo. Most of them were in a hurry to reach their tour bus and capture a good seat near the front.

Ship shore excursions offered not only tours of the port city, but also visits to attractions and destinations farther away—the best beach resort, snorkeling or sailing trips, off-road trips through rain forests. Also, as long as passengers were on one of the ship's shore excursions, they knew the ship would not sail without them should the tour bus return late. But, according to Carolina's thinking, there was something to be said for taking a map and meandering on foot through a town to check out the sights, sounds, and culture.

The pier was a frenzy of activity. In addition to hordes of passengers boarding buses, the ship was being serviced. Huge hoses sucked out waste water, while other hoses took on fresh water. Pallets of bagged recycle material, like cardboard, drink cans, bottles, and paper, were taken out of the ship by forklift. But the three women were primarily interested in a busy hatch in the lower bow where crew members unloaded boxes of fresh fruit and vegetables—bananas, mangoes, papaya, melons, lettuce—from small vans. Other crew members worked a forklift to carry endless pallets of bottled water into the ship.

The familiar face of their table steward Dominic caught Carolina's attention. After glancing up and down the pier, he pushed a large wheeled cart—piled high with black plastic trash bags—over to a stack of wooden crates filled with produce and came to a halt. Lifting several bags on top, Dominic rearranged other bags, while the cart rocked gently from side to side. He grinned at Carolina, Eula Mae, and Yasuko, and waved. As he pushed the cart beyond the crates and toward a large blue trash bin, Carolina noticed a woman in a wide-brimmed straw hat leaning over a box of lettuce. She straightened up, turned around, and smiled.

Carolina blinked. "Colleen!"

"Hey, you guys!" She grinned and crossed through a stream of passengers to reach them.

"You did it!" Carolina was relieved that Colleen had been able to bypass security and get off the ship. Carolina, Eula Mae, and Yasuko gave her a group hug.

Posing like a diva, Colleen said, "Call me Miss Can-Do. I'm so excited to get off that ship! Are we ready to explore this Island of Spice?"

"Let's get moving before anyone we know sees us," Eula Mae suggested.

"Wait, Colleen, you need to see this." Carolina opened her denim tote bag. "Dominic packed us a lunch, again. We don't have to return to the ship to eat. Wasn't that nice of him?"

Colleen nodded. "I wouldn't be standing here with you now without his help and the garbage cart. Do I smell?"

Carolina stepped back from her and grimaced. "Are you what stinks?"

"I have a small spray bottle of Febreze in my bag," offered Yasuko.

"Lordy, Lordy, why do you have that?" Eula Mae asked.

"We're visiting third world countries," Yasuko explained. "You never know when you'll stumble across an offensive odor."

"Yes, like the stench of rotting bodies," Carolina offered.

"Exactly," Yasuko said.

Eula Mae shook her head. "All right, that's enough, everybody. Colleen, get out your map and let's move it."

Colleen unfolded and studied her map. She looked around and pointed. "This way." The group marched down the pier, through the cruise terminal, past the souvenir hawkers, and into the streets of St. George.

"Wow," Carolina exclaimed. "Compared to Nassau, Grenada is way less developed."

"Mercy me, it really is different," agreed Eula Mae. "Small pastel-painted houses. No monster-size concrete hotels. No gambling casinos. And I hear the island has beautiful beaches."

Colleen halted at a street corner, studied her map some more, and looked up. "Where's Ron? I thought he was coming this morning?"

"Eula Mae told him we were shopping for lingerie," Yasuko said. "He said on second thought, he would work on his story this morning."

Eula Mae shrugged. "We're going sightseeing with him this afternoon."

"Guess I can meet him then, if I choose to do so," Colleen said.

"It's a good thing he's not here," Carolina said. "This gives us an opportunity to look for anything suspicious without him hanging around."

From Grenada's cruise terminal, the women headed in the direction of the market on Granby Street. Along the way, Carolina paused to take photos of the quaint shops they passed and the homes that stair-stepped up the hillsides. Obviously, she decided, the folks who lived in St. George had really strong legs from walking up and down the steep roads. When they reached Granby Street, Carolina arranged everyone for a group-selfie photo with the market in the background. She used her WhatsApp to send it to Lilly and followed Eula Mae, Yasuko, and Colleen into the noisy, chaotic, market place, where dozens of rainbow-colored umbrellas shaded crude wooden tables and native Grenadians, who pushed their wares to hordes of cruise ship passengers.

The pungent smells of spices, vegetables, fruit, and other produce were mixed with the stench of sweat. The market was crowded, and the women found it difficult at times to keep together. They trolled along narrow areas between stands, searching for dolls or anything else that could conceal a bag of emeralds. Instead, they saw stands of spices, fresh fruit and vegetables, bolts of brightly colored cloth, hundreds of large conchs, and straw hats and bags.

"Do you see any dolls?" Carolina asked, pausing to wipe the sweat from her face and take a swig of water. Island time was approaching noon, and the day was heating up.

Eula Mae's shoulders slumped. "Maybe they don't make them on Grenada."

Colleen sighed. "Maybe this island's too small for smugglers."

"Maybe nobody on this island knows how to make dolls," Yasuko said.

The women wandered around for another hour and saw absolutely nothing sinister or suspicious. Zero. Nada. Zilch. "Tomorrow we'll anchor at Barbados," Carolina said. "Maybe they make straw dolls." She tried to think positively.

Colleen sighed, again. This time louder than before. "I just hate to wait that long to find out anything."

"What are we going to do in the meantime?" Carolina asked. "Is anyone hungry?" She opened the denim bag.

Eula Mae looked over Colleen's shoulder at the map. "I think I see a grove of trees on the other side of the Carenage. Maybe a park? We could eat our picnic lunch there."

"Yes, lunch in a nice shady spot. Close the bag, Carolina. No eating until we get there," Eula Mae said.

"We know how you are," Yasuko spoke up. "By the time we're ready to eat, most of the food will be gone."

Carolina closed the bag and fell in step with Colleen. "I'm sorry this has turned out to be a total bust."

"Don't worry about it," she said. "After all, we're supposed to be tourists, aren't we?"

Carolina nodded. "As long as it doesn't interfere with our plans."

"I think this afternoon I'll try to get into the ship's hold. See if I can find anything suspicious," Colleen said casually. "My sister must have seen something down there that put her life in jeopardy. I want to know what it was."

"Maybe I can sneak away from Eula Mae and Yasuko during their afternoon naps and go with you." She glanced at Eula Mae to see if she were listening.

"I heard that," Eula Mae said. "And I don't like what I heard."

Carolina shrugged. "Then stop listening."

"I'm playing mahjong with Charlie Chan, again. I don't care what you do," Yasuko said.

Eula Mae stopped so abruptly that Colleen and Carolina piled into her from the rear. She spun around, hands on hips. "What if the wrong people see you? You could be in danger. No one would hear you scream in the bowels of the ship."

"I think we can take care of ourselves." Carolina spoke confidently, but found it difficult without a special agent gun to back her up. Eula Mae could be so annoying, she thought. Just because she was 16 years older did not make her the boss here.

"Help!" Yasuko's voice sounded from the middle of a multitude of aggressive native women selling brightly colored skirts and dresses. The three women hurried over to rescue her, but soon found themselves standing back to back in the middle of excited native women screaming "Twenty U.S. dollah" and shoving brightly colored clothing in their faces. Carolina felt like a CIA agent surrounded by terrorists.

"Now what?" Eula Mae yelled.

Eula Mae pushed a parrot-decorated sun dress out of her face. "Anybody need to buy a sultry, sexy dress for Island Night?"

A thoughtful expression crossed Carolina's face. She closed her hand around an earth-green island dress and felt the material. Soft cotton. She took a closer look at the seams. Well-made, she thought. Someone had carefully and skillfully sewn the dress together.

"Twenty-dollah!" yelled the woman holding the other end of the dress. "Special price for you!" The woman grinned, flashing several gold teeth. Her head was covered with an orange, yellow, and green bandana, which was creatively tied in a knot on top. Sweat rolled down the sides of her ebony complexion.

Carolina laughed. Was everything in the Caribbean on sale for the special price of twenty dollah? "You have a deal." She didn't care what Charlie Chan said. She wasn't going to haggle. Unzipping her denim bag, Carolina reached under Dominic's lunch for her wallet and handed over a twenty-dollar bill. "Did you make this dress yourself?"

The woman nodded, and folded and rolled up the dress before handing it to Carolina, who stuffed it and her wallet back in her bag. She made sure the lunch was on top and easily accessible—should she get hungry.

"Are you buying that one?" asked Yasuko, who was standing next to Eula Mae. They were surrounded by four native women eagerly showing them one dress after another.

Carolina nodded. "The dress I purchased appears to be well-made. I've seen lesser quality goods on sale at Walmart." She was trying to make her way over to Eula Mae, when a car horn sounded behind them. The sea of native women parted for a black limousine that drove up and stopped a few feet away from Carolina.

Curious to see such a fancy car on this small island, Carolina watched as driver and passenger doors swung open. She expected a local celebrity or politician to step out of the car. Instead, two men in jeans, sporting tropical shirts, jumped out and stared directly at her. A stout, muscular man with an ebony complexion and shaved head waved at her. "Come, pretty lady. We take you and your friends on tour of our beautiful island. Only five-dollah a piece to see spice farm and banana trees."

"No, thank you," Eula Mae said.

The man took a step closer. "We take you to see tropical rain forest and jungle waterfall. You have a good day. What you say?"

"Thanks, but no thanks," Carolina said and turned around, but the man grabbed her from behind. "Hey, let me go!" she screamed and wished, again, she had signed up for that self-defense class at the Y.

"Sweet lady, come for ride with me," he said, dragging Carolina toward the limo. "Jorell," he shouted over his shoulder, "Grab the girl."

"Hey!" yelled the woman who had sold Carolina the dress. "Don't you mess with my good customer, Bastian."

"What do you think you're doing?" Yasuko yelled at the men.

Eula Mae pushed forward, trying to elbow her way through the native women, but in their determination to sell their merchandise, they had her completely hemmed in.

Carolina quickly realized she desperately needed a plan of action. Once this Bastian guy maneuvered her into the limo, she might be done for. How would Agent Craycraft handle this situation?

A second man, tall and lanky with dreadlocks and wearing a bright red, blue and yellow Caribbean shirt, forced his way through the frenzy of indignant native women and dresses, and grabbed Colleen's wrist. She screamed and kicked him in the shins, but he would not release his grip.

Carolina felt like her heart was trying to leap out of her chest. She found it difficult to breathe and think.

In the meantime, Eula Mae, screaming like she was being gutted, managed to break free from the native women. She came up behind Carolina's captor Bastian and started beating him in the back with her fists. Jorell, with a kicking, screaming Colleen thrown over his shoulder, grabbed Eula Mae with his free hand and pulled her off Bastian's back.

Just as Esmeralda and two other native women joined the fray to rescue their customers, Carolina thought of a plan. And these women would be part of it. Carolina screamed as loudly as she could. "How much for six sun dresses?"

Instantly the mob of native women—pulling Yasuko along with them—surged around Esmeralda, Carolina, and Eula Mae, shouting and waving dresses. Anxious to sell their wares to these American tourists, they scrambled over the hood of the limo and shoved into Carolina, Eula Mae, Colleen, and two shocked men, who lost their balance and toppled backward onto the ground. Taking advantage of the situation, Carolina and Colleen wrenched free of Bastian and Jorell, and fled from the screaming women. The would-be kidnappers struggled to get up, but were trampled on the ground in the process.

Frantically searching for Eula Mae and Yasuko, Colleen and Carolina saw their heads in an undulating sea of tangled bodies and brightly colored dresses and skirts. Panting and sweating, the four women joined hands. Like a locomotive, Colleen pulled the women in the direction of the ship, slowing only when someone stumbled. They didn't stop until they reached the ship, where they collapsed on top of wooden crates near the bow line.

A ship's officer rushed over to them. "Are you all right?" They turned their heads in his direction and recognized Peter, but were too breathless to respond verbally. He pointed past them to the native women across the way, who were kicking out the limo's windows. Sirens sounded in the distance. "I say, it bloody well looks like a riot!"

"Yeah, the result of getting between a customer and a potential sale." Carolina said gasping, still winded from running. This was why she had given up jogging and 5K runs. The orthopedist said she was killing her knees. Her family doctor said she wasn't as young as she used to be. They both suggested she take up water aerobics for older women with osteoarthritis. But no way was she going to put her saggy, wrinkled body into a swimsuit and wear it in public.

Returning to the ship, Mrs. Coolhardy and her stuffed dog paused and looked back at the commotion. "See, Napoleon," she said, patting him on his head, "I told you we were returning to the ship too soon. We could be over there vandalizing that car with the others."

A short fat man, sporting bright yellow walking shorts and three cameras around his neck, rushed over to Carolina. "Say, didn't you just come from over there? What happened?"

Frowning, Peter focused on Carolina, who took a deep breath and shrugged. "Not sure, but those women are pissed about something. Maybe somebody dissed their sundresses."

"Excuse me," Peter said. "I need to check into this in case it involves any of our passengers."

As Peter ran off, a woman twice the size of the man waddled over. She was wearing red short shorts, which from the rear exposed two large jiggly cheeks. "What's going on Sweet Pea?"

"A riot of some sort." The fat man looked back at Carolina. "Baby Dumplin' and I were goin' over that way, but I guess now we better not." He turned back to Baby Dumplin' and kissed her forehead. "Come my love, let's take a ride in a glass-bottom boat instead."

As the opulent couple walked off arm in arm, Eula Mae leaned forward and whispered. "Think we should talk to the police?"

"Definitely not," said Colleen.

Eula Mae looked indignant. "But those men tried to kidnap us. They should be arrested."

"This isn't the United States," Yasuko said.

"So what?" asked Eula Mae.

"Carolina, can you please explain to Eula Mae why we shouldn't talk to the police?"

"If you're worried about justice, Eula Mae, I think those women may have given them all the justice they deserve." Carolina looked at the flashing blue and red lights. "Besides, if we go back over there and get mixed up in that mess, we might get stuck at the police station and miss our sailing time. Would you want to get stuck on this island with those guys?"

Colleen nodded in agreement. "This island is part of the Commonwealth. They'll probably be in jail very soon."

We could always hope, Carolina thought. She didn't understand why they tried to kidnap four American women. She thought in the Caribbean it only happened to family members of prominent or rich men. Carolina stood up and watched passengers disembarking and heading into St. George. "Uh-oh!"

"Uh-oh what?" asked Eula Mae.

"It's your writer friend," Colleen said, after seeing Ron. "I don't feel like meeting him. Before he gets any closer, I better scoot. I see Dominic. I'll disguise myself as a crate of papaya for the return trip onboard. See you later."

As Ron approached the three women, his eyes followed the departing Colleen. "Who's your friend? Did I run her off?"

"Oh, uh, we just bumped into her. She's on spring break from Michigan State," Carolina said, looking down at her denim bag. Was it her imagination that the bag looked smaller? "Didn't get her name."

"Is that right, Eula Mae?" Ron looked her straight in the eye, but she didn't reply. He watched Colleen disappear behind crates full of fruits and vegetables. He turned back to the women. "Have you had lunch?"

Ron was speaking Carolina's language. Now that her body was calming down, she was getting hungry. "We were talking about a picnic in a shady spot. Maybe in a small park." Carolina opened her bag and pulled out the sundress she had purchased and her wallet, but no lunch was in the bag. "Oh no, not again."

Ron's eyes narrowed. "Not again, what?"

Carolina felt like such an idiot. "Our lunch is gone."

"Gone?" Eula Mae asked.

"How did you manage that?" Ron asked.

Carolina pointed in the direction of the lingering crowd and the limousine. "In all that ruckus, I guess."

Ron looked over his shoulder at the crowd of women still milling around the far side of the Carenage. "What sort of ruckus?"

"We have no idea," Eula Mae quickly answered. "Some disagreement between native vendors, I reckon. You know how a crowd can turn into a mob of wet hens."

Ron watched the native women and rubbed his chin thoughtfully. "Yes, I do know." He stared back at Carolina for a few seconds. "Say, I have an idea —why don't we take a taxi to Grand Anse Beach, and I'll treat you ladies to lunch at La Belle Creole?"

"Fresh seafood?" Carolina asked.

"The best restaurant on Grenada. It has a great view of the bay.

After lunch, we'll take a little sail around the island and finish the afternoon off with a walk on the beach."

"Eula Mae? Yasuko?" asked Carolina.

"Count me in," Yasuko said

"I'll go on one condition," Eula Mae said.

Ron crossed his arms across his chest. "I'm listening."

"We will not discuss stowaways, smugglers, assassins, or secret agents."

Ron's mouth slowly widened into a grin. "Agreed."

"Carolina?" Eula Mae looked at her expectantly.

Carolina shrugged. "Sure." After all, she didn't say she couldn't think about them.

Chapter Fourteen
An Uneasy Feeling

Yasuko and Eula Mae started talking about getting ready for dinner around 6 o'clock. But Carolina, still stuffed from their big lunch at La Belle Creole, was not the least bit interested in eating, again. Also, she was anxious about receiving a response from the magazine editor, Luke DuBois, concerning his travel writer, Ron Dunten.

"I need to run a quick errand," Carolina said, crossing in front of Yasuko and Eula Mae to reach the door.

Eula Mae, comparing two pants tops, didn't even glance at Carolina. "Don't be gone too long.".

"Yes, we don't want to be late," Yasuko added, as she pawed through a travel pouch full of jewelry.

Carolina opened the door and looked over her shoulder. "I'll only be gone as long as it takes to check my email. No longer." Carolina heard Eula Mae grunt unhappily, as she shut the door behind her.

Fortunately, the computer room was empty. Most likely because everyone was getting dressed for dinner, Carolina figured, sitting at the first computer and signing into her account. She scrolled through her email quickly and held her breath as she clicked on a message from Luke DuBois. A short message immediately popped up on the monitor:

Dear Agent Cunningham,

Writer Ron Dunten is currently on assignment in Alaska. Do you know who is trying to steal our writer's identity?

Regards, Luke DuBois, Managing Editor, Traveling the World.

"Omigosh!" Carolina read and re-read the message. Ron was an imposter. Even though she had suspected as much, she really didn't want to believe it. She printed out the message and hurried back to the suite, where Eula Mae and Yasuko were still dressing for dinner.

"Put a rush on it, Carolina, or we'll be late."

"I'm ready," Yasuko said, blotting her lipstick on a tissue. "Where have you been?"

Carolina held out the printed message. "Checking my email."

"What's that?" Eula Mae snatched the paper from Carolina's hand.

"I sent an e-mail to the managing editor of *Traveling the World* and asked about Ron Dunten. That's his answer."

"I don't understand." Eula Mae unfolded the paper and read the message. She gasped and handed it to Yasuko. "He isn't Ron Dunten?"

Carolina shook her head.

"Then who is he?" asked Yasuko, reading the message.

Carolina sat down on her twin bed. "I don't know. One of the smugglers? One of <u>them</u>?"

"Whoever he is, he's definitely not Ron Dunten." Eula Mae plopped down on the bed next to Carolina.

Yasuko pulled the chair out from the desk, sat down, and looked at Carolina and Eula Mae. "At least not the travel writer, Ron Dunten."

"Maybe a secret agent? Or a professional assassin?" The possibilities were endless. Carolina strained her brain searching for pieces of information and clues that would provide an answer.

"What should we do now?" Eula Mae asked.

Carolina sighed. "We could ask him who he really is."

Eula Mae stood up and gave Carolina a you-have-to-be-out-of-your-mind look. "Lordy, Lordy, you've got to be kidding!"

"You're crazy!" Yasuko said. "He'll just lie to us."

Or, Carolina thought, he could throw all of us overboard.

Peter and faux-Ron were already at the table, when Dominic seated the three women for dinner. "Did you ladies have a nice day?" Dominic asked.

"Yes, we did. We walked all over the island and ate a delicious lunch at La Belle Creole," Eula Mae said, looking up from the menu.

Carolina kicked Eula Mae's foot.

Dominic turned to Carolina. "But Mrs. Cunningham, what about the lovely picnic lunch I made for you?"

"Oh … well … what I mean is …" Carolina blushed.

Everyone at the table, except Carolina, laughed.

"She lost it," Eula Mae said.

Dominic frowned. "You lost my lunch, again?"

Carolina hung her head and nodded.

"You don't like my lunches, tell me."

"I'm sorry, Dominic. I dropped it during the riot."

"The fiasco by the Carenage?" Peter asked.

Before Carolina could respond, Eula Mae cleared her throat and shot a warning glance in her direction.

"Maybe the tail end of it, why?" Carolina asked. "Did you find out what happened?"

"The local officials say three American women tried to hijack an island taxi."

Carolina's cheeks began to burn. "What? That's not—" Eula Mae kicked her leg.

Ron leaned over toward Carolina. "That's not what?"

Carolina reached under the table and rubbed her leg, wondering what Eula Mae's problem was. "That's not what I heard."

"Peter's story sounds exciting," Eula Mae said. "Tell us more."

Peter leaned back in his chair. "Two male passengers in the taxi managed to fight off the hijackers. Fortunately, no one was hurt."

"Very interesting, Peter," interrupted Ron. "But I want to hear Carolina's version."

Carolina glared at Eula Mae and shifted her legs to be safe. "I heard the men in the taxi were trying to rob the women or kidnap them or worse."

Ron smiled. "Who was the source of your story, Peter?"

"Local police."

"And you, Carolina?"

"A passerby."

Peter nodded his head. "Aren't you glad you weren't mixed up in that bloody mess?"

"Very much," Eula Mae agreed.

"Definitely," Yasuko added.

"Yes," Carolina said. "Like you said, Peter. It was fortunate no one was hurt."

After dinner, Peter and Ron joined Carolina, Eula Mae, and Yasuko in the Tropic Room to watch the illusionist, the Amazing Hygate. Tables and chairs were arranged in a horseshoe shape and stair-stepped slightly down to a circular area with a wood floor that served as a dance floor and stage. In the very back of the performing area, the ship's small band provided music for dancing and stage shows. Throughout the cruise, whenever the ship reached a port, performers and entertainers would disembark to other ships, and new ones would come onboard. Carolina couldn't imagine such a nomadic life, moving from cruise ship to cruise ship all over the world.

After Amazing Hygate performed a few simple illusions with cards and disappearing flowers, a passenger from the audience was volunteered by his family to help the illusionist with his show. Bubba Brown from Hiram, Georgia—who claimed to be an expert marksman—was handed a rifle and told to aim and fire the weapon at Hygate's mouth. After the illusionist caught the bullet between his teeth, the audience went wild, and two stage assistants helped a pale Bubba back to his seat. As a finale, the illusionist lifted a table with his mind and floated it off stage.

As Hygate made his exit, the small band began to play, again. Ron rose from his seat and hovered over Eula Mae. "Eula Mae, would you care to dance?"

Carolina was shocked and surprised. And something more. Was it a little bit of jealousy she felt because Ron had asked Eula Mae to dance instead of her? After all, wasn't Eula Mae at least 20 years older than Ron? It was bound to be a disaster. Surely Eula Mae couldn't dance. She would step on Ron's toes and make a big fool of herself. Carolina smiled. There was no way that Eula Mae would dance with Ron. Then she watched in disbelief as Eula Mae placed her hand in Ron's and stood up.

"Thank you, Mr. Dunten. I'd love to dance with you."

Faux-Ron, a.k.a Hunky Spy or possible drug lord, led Eula Mae to the dance floor and drew her close. Too close, thought Carolina. They slowly danced across the floor, through the Tropic Room doorway and outside onto the deck—out of sight. Carolina fought down the urge to run after them and save her friend from possibly being thrown overboard.

In the meantime, Peter shook his head and stood up. "Excuse me, Carolina and Yasuko, but I need to get back to my duties. Have a good evening."

Carolina didn't see how she could have a good evening when Eula Mae was outside with Faux-Ron. She turned to Yasuko for help in rescuing their friend, when an Asian man sporting a Manchu beard walked up. "Good evening, ladies," he greeted. He looked at Carolina. "Well, hello, I believe I know you from the market place in Nassau."

"Oh, yes," Carolina spluttered. "Charlie Chan. How could I forget a famous name like that." She pointed to Yasuko, who was already on her feet and gushing. "And I believe you know my friend Yasuko from the mahjong sessions."

Charlie smiled and nodded. "Yes, I do remember Yasuko. I never forget a cutthroat mahjong player."

Yasuko offered Charlie her hand. The next thing Carolina knew, he was leading her onto the dance floor. Before they took their first dance step, Carolina hastily slipped through the heavy wooden doors to the outside deck. She walked past a line of empty lounge chairs. In the morning, passengers would be fighting to see who would be sitting, relaxing, reading, and enjoying life on deck.

Carolina heard Eula Mae and faux-Ron talking and laughing before she saw them dancing on deck without music. Carolina hid in the shadows behind a steel beam support and watched. When Ron pulled Eula Mae over next to the rail, Carolina prepared herself to scream bloody murder and jump on top of Ron, if he tried to harm her friend.

"Shouldn't we go back inside?" Eula Mae asked Ron. "Carolina, Yasuko, and Peter might worry." Eula Mae stepped toward the doorway, but Ron grabbed her wrist and pulled her back.

"What's your hurry, Mrs. Davis? Are you afraid I'll throw you overboard?"

Carolina's stomach twisted. Was now the time to scream and go on the attack? She could run for help, but faux-Ron could throw Eula Mae overboard before she found anyone to listen to her. So, what was her plan? What would Agent Craycraft do? She decided to wait for further developments.

"Of course, I'm not afraid of you," Eula Mae said. "Should I be?"

"Not at all. I'm completely trustworthy." He let go of her hand. "Would you feel comfortable going with me somewhere to talk privately?"

Carolina closed her eyes and silently pleaded, "Say 'no,' Eula Mae."

"I ... uh ..." Eula Mae hesitated.

Since Ron's back was to her, Carolina poked her head out of her hiding place to catch Eula Mae's attention. Carolina frowned at her and shook her head. Then she ducked back out of sight.

Faux-Ron took a step back from Eula Mae. "I thought you weren't afraid of me?"

Eula Mae glanced back in Carolina's direction. "No, I'm not afraid of you, Ron. Sure, I'll be glad to talk to you 'til the cows come home."

Ron chuckled. "I think we'll be finished with our conversation long before then. Shall we amble?"

Carolina gritted her teeth and followed them inside—at a discreet distance. Mrs. Craycraft would have been proud.

Ron took Eula Mae back to his cabin. Once the door shut behind them, Carolina listened at the door. Mrs. Craycraft would have surely bugged his room, she thought, but she didn't have access to all of that high-techie spy stuff. Fortunately, she could hear Ron's booming bass voice perfectly. Carolina knew what she was doing was outright snooping and eavesdropping, but since she didn't know who faux-Ron really was, she felt any secret agent would do the same.

"See," she heard Ron's deep voice through the door, "no tortuous devises and no restraining chains."

Eula Mae replied with a failed attempt to be witty. "You probably keep them hidden so you won't upset the cabin steward."

"You have found me out, Mrs. Davis. Please, have a seat."

"Where's your computer?" Eula Mae asked.

"Under the bed, why?"

Carolina pressed her ear closer to the door and wondered why Eula Mae had asked him that. Her stomach knotted, as she envisioned Eula Mae looking under the bed. A few seconds of silence ticked by. The sweat started to trickle down Carolina's back.

"You look surprised to see my laptop, Mrs. Davis. Did you think I was lying? I showed you my article in the magazine. Wasn't that enough proof for you?"

Carolina gasped. "Oh no! Don't say it," she whispered. "Don't do it." But she knew Eula Mae would.

"The real Ron Dunten—the travel writer—is in Alaska on assignment," Eula Mae said.

Carolina closed her eyes and slid down onto the carpeted floor. She waited for the sound of a muffled gunshot, but it didn't come. Maybe, she thought, he used a silencer or maybe he planned to slit her throat or choke her to death. Carolina opened her mouth and prepared herself to scream.

"That's what I wanted you to think," said Ron.

Carolina opened her eyes wide and closed her mouth. Huh?

"What do you mean?" Eula Mae asked, and it sounded like she had moved closer to the door.

"Don't you think that when the managing editor received Carolina's e-mail, he immediately called me to find out what was going on?"

Carolina bit down on her knuckle. No, that couldn't be true. He was only saying that to cover his ass like any secret agent would.

"He did?" Eula Mae asked.

Dang it all. That woman could be so gullible, Carolina thought.

"Of course, he did. He and I decided it would be a great joke to write Carolina and tell her Ron Dunten was in Alaska."

"I think you're making that up," Eula Mae said. "You're not the real Ron Dunten, and we're going to prove it."

The next few seconds were a blur. Eula Mae bolted out of Ron's cabin, tripping over a crouched Carolina and falling into Mr. Gallenkemp, who was standing behind Carolina. Everyone went sprawling to the floor like a line of dominos.

"My, my, my. What have we here?" Ron stood in his doorway, looking down at Eula Mae, Carolina, and Mr. Gallenkemp. He stepped forward and helped Eula Mae to her feet. "Mrs. Davis, are you all right? You don't want to break a hip or shoulder on this cruise."

Mr. Gallenkemp stood and helped Carolina to her feet. "Pardon me, Mrs. Cunningham ... Mrs. Davis. I am so sorry. Thank goodness no one was hurt."

"Thank you, I'm fine. No problem." Carolina glared at Ron and looked at Eula Mae. "Are you sure you're okay?" she asked, realizing that any broken bones at Eula Mae's age could be the beginning of the end. She thought about her cousin Ashley who went to the beach on vacation, fell in the parking lot, and broke her hip. Four days later she was dead.

Eula Mae straightened herself upright and shook her shoulders. "Yes, I think so," she mumbled. "My bone density test last month showed I have strong bones. No osteoporosis."

Carolina gave her friend a hard look. Eula Mae might have strong bones, she thought, but she looked shaky and confused.

Mr. Gallenkemp glanced at Ron. "Sir, if everything's all right, I need to finish my evening turndown and chocolate distribution. Sorry for the collision, ladies."

"Everything's fine, Mr. Gallenkemp," Ron said.

Carolina put her arm around Eula Mae's waist and began leading her in the direction of their suite.

"Wait, don't go," Ron called after them. "Please?"

Carolina looked at him over her shoulder. "You're not serious."

He gestured with his head toward his cabin door. "Dead serious, Carolina. We need to talk and get some things straight without you crouched down outside my door listening to private conversations." He reached out to Eula Mae. "Please, Mrs. Davis. You will want to hear what I have to say."

Eula Mae looked from Ron to Carolina. Then with her head high and her chin up, she walked slowly through Ron's cabin door.

Ron raised his right eyebrow at Carolina. "Well, Mrs. Cunningham, the ball's in your court. Are you coming in or do you plan to stay in the hall and listen at the door?"

Carolina didn't think it was a good idea to go into Ron's cabin, but she felt obligated to protect Eula Mae. She gritted her teeth and trudged past Ron into his cabin. He closed the door behind her. This time, she didn't hear the lock click.

"Both of you. Please sit," Ron commanded. Carolina and Eula Mae backed up and sat on the sofa. Ron crossed his arms one over the other and looked at the women in silence for a few seconds. "Okay, listen up. I can't explain everything to you right now, but believe me when I say that I am not an assassin or a spy or a smuggler. This nonsense has gone on long enough. Now go back to your suite and think about what I said."

Carolina could not believe that was all Ron had to say. She wanted to smack him good. His mama had not raised him right. She pulled Eula Mae toward the door, but stopped halfway. She had to get in the last word. "Don't tell me what to do, Mr. Dunten or whatever your name is."

Ron's eyes narrowed. "I'm telling you two this for your own good. Carolina, you need to leave the detecting to the heroines in your books and to the real professionals. Eula Mae, you need to keep your friend out of trouble." Ron opened the door.

Eula Mae surprised Carolina by walking right into Ron's personal space. "Is that what you are, Ron, or whatever your name is? Are you a real professional?"

"What if I am?" he asked.

"Well I s'wanee, if you aren't the turd in the punchbowl," Eula Mae said.

Carolina cringed and gasped. "Eula Mae, let's go." She grabbed her arm and pulled her into the hallway. She could not believe what Eula Mae said to Ron's face, and she could not help but smile at her gutsy friend for saying it.

Looking grim, Ron stood by the door and shook his head. "Good night, ladies. If you go ashore tomorrow, be very careful. Stay with the crowds and be wary of any natives driving limousines." He shut the door firmly.

As they returned to their suite, Carolina fumed in silence, wondering if faux-Ron was exhibiting a genuine concern or issuing a veiled threat.

Day Four – Colleen awakened us early; She met Eula Mae and Yasuko; we talked about everything that happened yesterday.

We changed Colleen's appearance so she could leave the ship with Dominic's help.

In St. George, we were nearly kidnapped by two foreign agent types disguised as locals; we were able to escape with help of Native women.

Magazine editor replied that real Ron Dunten was working in Alaska, but when Eula Mae confronted him, Ron said he told his editor to say that.

Questions: Were foreign agents in St. George working for the purser? Were they only trying to scare us? Who is Ron really? Is he lying or telling the truth?

Just as Carolina put her spy journal away, the WhatsApp chirped on her cell phone. It was Lilly wanting to do a video chat. Carolina hit the "accept" icon and Lilly's face appeared on her phone. Yasuko and Eula Mae sat on either side of Carolina on her bed.

"I'm glad you haven't gone to bed yet. I wanted to touch base with you and tell you what I found out about Colleen's sister Garland," Lilly said.

Eula Mae, Yasuko, and Carolina huddled over the cell phone. "What did you find out?" Carolina asked.

"Not very much. Based on a few news stories, I found that passengers saw her fall off the *Emerald Dream* into the water about 20 miles southwest of St. Thomas. A Coast Guard airplane, an HC-144 Ocean Sentry, searched more than 1,800 square miles of ocean for her to no avail. Nothing mentioned about how she fell overboard. Sorry, that's it."

"That's a bummer," said Carolina. "Anything on the emeralds?"

"Still working on it. From what I've uncovered so far, the best emeralds are mined in Columbia in the Andes mountains."

"Columbia?" questioned Carolina. "That's a long way from here."

"Columbia produces the best quality of emeralds. Their emeralds are highly prized because of their dark green color and purity." Lilly paused to catch her breath. "Because of supply and demand, emeralds are by far the most expensive of the beryl crystals."

"So, the emeralds found in Columbia are the absolute best?" Carolina asked.

"Yes, that's right," Lilly answered. "South America is the world's most emerald-rich continent, and Columbia alone produces about 60 percent of the world's emeralds."

Yasuko fingered the small emerald hanging around her neck. "The emerald crystals we found had pieces of ugly rock stuck to them. Why is that?"

"When the miners dig the emeralds out of the earth, they are encased in chunks of rock called the matrix. The rock matrix could be calcite or quartz or carbonate or black calcite," explained Lilly.

"Carolina said the emeralds had to be carefully and tediously extracted from the rocks," said Eula Mae.

"Which only adds to the cost of emeralds," explained Lilly. "Do you have your emeralds nearby? I can look at them and tell you what type of matrix they are attached to."

"That's not going to happen," said Carolina, quickly explaining how Eula Mae's doll and the emeralds were stolen.

"I'm so sorry. That's really scary," Lilly said. "Is there anything else

I can tell you?"

"Let's get to the smuggling part," said Eula Mae.

Lilly laughed. "Always wanting the nitty-gritty quickly?"

"Bet your sweet ass," Eula Mae admitted. "because we're right in the middle of it."

Lilly looked at her computer screen and scrolled down. "I hope you won't be too disappointed, Carolina, but so far I've found no mention of trench-coated international spies smuggling emeralds."

"What?" Carolina brought the cell phone closer to her face. "Seriously?"

"I'm afraid so. Looks like the real smugglers are the "mules" or miners, mine owners, members of the military and rebel groups, who carry the stones from the mines, through the mountains—by foot, horseback or motor scooter—to gem brokers in bordering countries, who sell to international buyers, who in turn smuggle the emeralds into other countries."

"That's a lot of middle men," said Yasuko.

"And that's before they are cut into beautiful gemstones and made into jewelry," pointed out Carolina.

"Here's the part I don't fully understand," Lilly said, "Gem smuggling is not a high-profile problem like drug smuggling because illegal gems don't hurt anyone. However, if gem smuggling can be linked to terrorism, money laundering, drug smuggling, or organized crime, then it's a whole new ball game."

"I don't understand," said Eula Mae.

"Me, either," piped in Yasuko.

"Stop and think about this," Carolina said thoughtfully. "We went in those shops in Nassau. You saw the prices on the emeralds. Rings that cost $10,000 and up. Remember that one necklace priced at over $100,000?"

"Phooey!" Eula Mae said. "We're talking about smuggling raw emeralds that haven't even been faceted or made into jewelry."

Lilly cleared her throat. "Yes, and as raw emeralds, U.S. Customs isn't that concerned about them being smuggled into the states. But once the green crystals are cut into beautiful, flawless gemstones, then they become good investments for anyone involved in illegal activities. They're small and easy to hide. One gem stone worth $10 million could fit in your hand, making emeralds an excellent investment vehicle for non-detectable and easily kept assets. Perfect for terrorists, money laundering, drug smugglers, and organized crime syndicates. But enough about emeralds today. What's the news on your end?"

Eula Mae elbowed Yasuko. "Yasuko met a new fellow."

Lilly grinned. "Really? Tell all."

Yasuko shook her head. "Nothing to tell. He loves to play mahjong. He's a good dancer, and we enjoy sitting and talking, and enjoying the moment."

"His name is Charlie Chan," Eula Mae said with a laugh.

Carolina stood up. "Okay, that's it for today, Lilly. We have to get to bed. We have a long day ahead of us in Barbados tomorrow. We'll tell you all about our adventures later. Tell everyone we said 'hello' from the *Emerald Dream*." Carolina pressed the red icon. No one would have to rock her to sleep tonight.

"Are we ready, ladies?" asked Carolina the next morning. They had finished breakfast and returned to their suite to get ready to disembark in Barbados. "Let's do this. Ready or not, Barbados, here we come!"

With Dominic's help, again, Colleen joined Carolina, Eula Mae, and Yasuko on shore in Bridgetown, Barbados. With another box lunch tucked into Carolina's denim bag, the trio headed down the pier to the cruise terminal, which contained lots of small duty-free shops. Yasuko had to be dragged away from the Harley Davidson Store, but not before Carolina agreed to take a photo of her astride a display bike. The photo was immediately sent to Lilly to show everyone in the Villas.

In the terminal, the trio checked out every shop in the complex, but found no dolls. Yasuko was the only person to purchase anything—a set of plastic dominoes with Barbados painted on the back of each tile. The tiles were stored in a small box with hinged top and handle. She said they reminded her of her mahjong tiles back at the Villas.

Frustrated, the women exited the terminal and caught a shuttle to downtown to see the Careenage, Trafalgar Square with the Dolphin Fountain, and statue of Lord Nelson. Along the way they watched vessels unloading cargos of bananas, plantains, and mangoes. They saw shrimp boats, fishing boats, sailboats, and schooners. At Trafalgar Square they took pictures of the fountain that commemorates the introduction of piped water to the island. After all, Carolina reminded everyone, they were tourists, and as such, they needed to take touristy photos.

From Trafalgar Square, they headed for the shops on Broad Street. They walked up and down Broad Street and Prince William Henry Street, but found nothing suspicious. No smugglers. No assassins. No secret agents. The streets were swarming with so many cruise ship passengers, it was hard to tell if anyone was following them, but Carolina did make sure there were no black limos in sight.

Suddenly Colleen came to halt, causing Eula Mae and Carolina to stumble into Yasuko.

"What's wrong?" Carolina asked, checking the lunch. It would look bad if she lost their lunch, again.

"Look, in the doorway of that dusty little shop," Colleen hissed. "The one with the strange-looking rugs hanging from the doorway."

"I see Baby Dumplin' and her husband. What about them?" Carolina asked, not understanding the significance of this. Today the voluptuous redhead was wearing a bright orange halter and matching scooter skirt. Her husband had on a red tank top and red polka-dotted shorts. No, not red dots. Make that red ants, Carolina soon realized, once she took a closer look.

Eula Mae took a step in their direction. "Yes, but look what they have in their hands."

Carolina and Yasuko took a closer look. Two stuffed dolls.

The women hurried over to the shop, where they found a large assortment of handmade dolls on display. Their black cotton bodies were stuffed with what felt like wadded paper. The faces were crudely painted. Each doll was clothed in a bright, colorful dress and white apron, and sported large gold-colored loop earrings and a head basket full of painted paper fruit.

They were the ugliest dolls Carolina had ever seen. Even uglier than the straw dolls. They looked like they'd been made by a child. Did people really buy these things?

"What do you think?" Colleen asked.

"They're not as large as the straw dolls, but I guess if you took out some of the stuffing, there would be room for a bag of crystals," Eula Mae said. "Carolina?"

"I certainly wouldn't buy one. Now can we eat?"

Eula Mae sighed a loud aggravated, martyr sigh. "You're completely hopeless." She turned to Colleen. "Let's talk to them."

Eula Mae walked up to Baby Dumplin's husband, who was paying for two dolls. "Hello! Remember us from Grenada?"

The man looked up and smiled. "Yes, of course. The riot. Remember, Honey?"

Baby Dumplin' grinned and nodded.

"Are you buying dolls?" Eula Mae asked.

"Yep," he said, accepting his change from a native woman, who was dressed in a green and yellow muumuu. "Baby Dumplin' is crazy over dolls. Aren't you, Honey?" She nodded and tittered.

Carolina rolled her eyes. "Are you enjoying your cruise?" she asked Baby Dumplin'. Leaning over, she watched the man sign his name, the name of the ship, and his cabin number, so the dolls could be delivered to the *Emerald Dream*. She looked up and smiled. "It was nice seeing you two, again. Have a good day."

As the four women walked away from the shop, they could hear Baby Dumplin' chortling behind them.

Carolina leaned over close to Eula Mae's ear. "His name is Felix Ferdinand, cabin 7400."

Colleen rubbed her hands together. "Tonight, we should drop by and borrow the dolls."

"What makes you think they would loan us the dolls?" Eula Mae asked.

"We tell them we want to show them to a friend who collects valuable dolls," Colleen suggested.

Carolina spotted a bench in the shade and herded the other three women in that direction. "Let's eat before our lunch gets lost, again." Once seated, Carolina distributed bottles of water, napkins, potato chips, ham and cheese sandwiches on whole wheat, and chocolate éclairs. At the bottom of the bag was a container of strawberries and bananas. Carolina picked up one of the bananas. "Look, the bananas are now quite ripe. Perfect to eat."

"By the time we reach our last port of call, they will be too ripe to eat," offered Yasuko.

"Make that too rotten," muttered Eula Mae.

Half an hour later, Colleen, Eula Mae, and Yasuko watched Carolina finish the last of the chocolate éclairs. "Mmm." She licked a smidgen of chocolate off the back of her hand. "That should hold me until tea-time."

Eula Mae shook her head and turned to Colleen. "Did you find anything in the ship's hold?"

"No, everything was sealed tight. I struck out. Sounds like you didn't do much better. I can't believe Ron's editor told him about Carolina's e-mail."

"Nothing is what it seems, as far as Mr. Dunten goes," said Yasuko. "He's like opening a Japanese puzzle box."

"How's that?" asked Colleen.

Yasuko looked surprised. "You know there's something inside the box, but you don't see any way to open it. You turn it over in your hand and feel all of the sides, pushing and pulling until something gives. If you push and pull in the right places long enough, the box slowly opens and the contents are exposed."

Eula Mae shook her head and stuffed all traces of their picnic lunch into an overflowing trash can next to the bench. "What I can't believe is that the editor told Carolina the real Ron was on assignment in Alaska."

"Yeah, what an awful thing to do. Guess the joke's on you," Colleen said. "We seem to be coming up empty-handed. We need to do something. Time is running out, and the cruise is almost over."

Eula Mae shrugged. "I don't know what to do."

"Don't look at me," said Yasuko. "Seems like all we do is try to avoid getting kidnapped or worse. Yet we keep attracting the wrong kind of attention no matter what we do."

"I know my daughter Georgia wouldn't be happy if she knew what was going on," pointed out Eula Mae. "Carolina, you know Caitlyn and Charter wouldn't be thrilled either. Why aren't you saying anything?"

Everyone looked at Carolina.

Carolina chewed on her lower lip thoughtfully. "I have nothing to say. I'm thinking. I'm going over bits and pieces of information in my mind. I don't like what it all adds up to."

"Which is what?" asked Eula Mae.

"That maybe Ron was lying about the editor to throw us off the trail."

Colleen gasped. Eula Mae's jaw dropped. Yasuko's face remained inscrutable.

"But," she continued, "my gut instincts say Ron is trustworthy." And Agent Craycraft always says to rely on your gut instinct, she remembered. "I'm thinking we should sit down with Ron and tell him everything."

"What?" Colleen choked.

"Could be risky," Yasuko said.

"Lordy, Lordy," Eula Mae said. "I don't know about spilling our guts."

"If you didn't care what I thought, you shouldn't have asked." Carolina scowled at her friends. Were they attempting a mutiny? Guess she needed a different approach. "Okay, okay, how about this? Why don't we invite Ron to our suite for a civil discussion?"

"What if he gets all huffy and ugly and mean?" asked Eula Mae.

Carolina threw her hands up. "Goodness gracious! There are four of us and only one of him."

Yasuko went down into a martial arts stance and chopped the air with her hands. "I have this covered."

Carolina rolled her eyes upward and sighed. "Are we in agreement on this?"

Eula Mae and Yasuko nodded.

Colleen frowned. "But what if we find rocks in Baby Dumplin's dolls? I don't think we should tell him everything." Her dark eyes flashed as she spoke.

"Agreed," Carolina said. Just in case her gut instincts were wrong.

Their great plan sputtered and died when neither Ron nor Peter made it to dinner. "The lieutenant has shore leave this evening," explained Dominic. "Mr. Dunten sends his apologies, but he has an article to finish before the ship sails tonight."

Carolina, Eula Mae, and Yasuko sat at the table in silence. Carolina wondered if Ron really was in his cabin writing. She seriously doubted it, and she was getting an uneasy feeling in the pit of her stomach, again. She had no appetite, but she ordered a fruit salad with strawberries and perfectly ripe bananas, poached salmon, and Charleston grits to keep up her strength. She managed to eat half of it, but passed on dessert.

"Are you not feeling well tonight?" asked a concerned Dominic. "How about some strawberries to go?"

Carolina pushed her chair back from the table and stood up. "No, thanks."

Eula Mae and Yasuko followed Carolina from the table. "You're scaring me," Eula Mae said as they exited the dining room. "What's wrong?"

"I'm not sure. I feel uneasy. Like something bad is going to happen."

Chapter Fifteen
Real Smugglers

Baby Dumplin' answered Carolina's knock.

"If it's all right, I'd like to borrow your two dolls for a few minutes to show a friend," Carolina said and smiled.

Baby Dumplin' giggled. Her massive bosom bounced and jiggled. "You sure can." She grabbed the dolls off her vanity and handed them to Carolina.

"Thanks, I'll bring them back within the hour." With a doll in each hand, Carolina hurried back to the suite, where Colleen, Yasuko, and Eula Mae were waiting to examine them.

"Ouch!" Eula Mae yelled, trying to remove one of the dresses. "Be careful, they're put together with pins." She sucked her wounded finger.

"Let's make sure we don't destroy them," Carolina said. "I like the Ferdinands, and they are expecting the dolls back in the same condition as when I borrowed them."

Colleen took the doll away from Eula Mae. "You know what? This doll is heavier than the other one." Cautiously she removed a pin from the back seam.

"Will you hurry," Carolina said, looking over her shoulder. "The suspense is killing me."

"Don't rush me. Do you want me to stick myself? Do you want to see me bleed?" Colleen removed the last pin, spread open the seam, and pulled out a small wad of newspaper. "Got it!" she yelled, grabbing a small black bag from underneath. She opened the bag and pulled out a rock matrix with two small emerald crystals embedded in it.

"Wow!" exclaimed Yasuko. The emeralds were a gorgeous, dark green color with no cloudiness or imperfections that they could see. Everyone smiled.

Carolina rubbed her fingers over the glassy emeralds. "How much do you think they're worth? Let's see if Lilly has been able to come up with anything." She pressed the WhatsApp on her cell phone and was soon connected to Lilly's smiling face.

"Lilly! We found more emerald crystals in another doll today," Carolina told her.

"That's great. I was thinking about calling you," Lilly said. "I have a little bit of information on your emeralds and smuggling." She shuffled through a stack of paper to the side. "Raw emeralds can be worth thousands and thousands of dollars."

Eula Mae rubbed one of the green crystals with her finger. "Are you sure?"

"I don't see how," mumbled Yaskuo.

Carolina reversed her cell phone camera. "Take a look at what we found. Do they look like they're worth a lot of money?"

"Hard to tell at this point," Lilly said, her face pressed into the phone to see the emeralds better. "I feel pretty confident that they are Columbian emeralds. They appear to have excellent color and transparency."

"I still say they look like pieces of Sprite bottles." Eula Mae said.

"They definitely aren't that," Yasuko said.

"You're right about that," Lilly said. "I also found out that even if the emeralds are illegally smuggled out of Columbia, they can legally be brought into the U.S., simply by declaring them in U.S. Customs. No import duties are charged—even on loose gemstones," said Lilly.

"Then why go to the trouble to smuggle them into the U.S." asked Eula Mae.

"Because the emerald-producing country is being bled dry of profits. Their government wants to end the illegal export of emeralds. The smuggling continues because it is cheaper, easier, and less risky than exporting through legal channels. There's widespread corruption everywhere with officials being paid to look the other way."

"And unless the gem-smuggling money is being used to support terrorists or organized crime, then it has a low priority," Carolina reminded everyone.

"You got it. Oops. Sorry to end this conversation," Lilly said, "But bingo starts in five minutes, and I don't want to be late."

"Thanks for your help, Lilly. Tell Archie to keep exercising his new knee and get stronger," said Carolina, pressing the red icon to end the call.

A noise sounded outside the cabin door.

"Shhh!" Carolina said and held her breath.

The sound of paper rustling could be heard, and someone slid something under the door.

Eula Mae sat down on the bed. "It's only Mr. Gallenkemp and the daily program."

"Strange we always hear him leave, but we never hear him arrive," Carolina said. "How many times have we opened that door and found him outside? He crept up behind me last night when I was listening outside Ron's door."

"Sounds suspicious," Colleen said. "We better keep an eye on him."

Yasuko tossed the raw emeralds from one hand to the other. "What are we going to do with these?"

Eula Mae picked up the phone and pressed zero. "Hello. This is Eula Mae Davis. I need to speak to the Captain immediately. Uh-huh. I see. It's urgent that I reach him." She sighed. "Yes, I understand. Thanks." She dropped the receiver into its cradle. "The Captain is unavailable. He's greeting passengers in the Blue Room."

Carolina took the emeralds from Yasuko and returned them to the black bag. "Eula Mae, pin Baby Dumplin's dolls back together—stuff in more paper if you need to—and give them back to her. I'll take these emeralds to the Captain."

"I don't feel comfortable with you running around the ship with those," Eula Mae said.

"For goodness, sakes, Eula Mae! I'll be walking in public places. People are crawling all over this ship."

Yasuko stood next to Carolina. "No one will know she has the emeralds."

Eula Mae hesitated. "Well, if I had my druthers, we'd invite the Captain to come to our suite and pick them up." She sniffed.

Carolina put the bag in her pants pocket. "I'll be all right."

"Oh, okay." Eula Mae handed one of the dolls to Colleen. "Here, you pin the dolls back together and return them to the Ferdinands. I'll go with Carolina."

Colleen shook her head. "Uh-uh!"

"But I need to go with her," Eula Mae said. "We can both talk to the Captain together."

"I want to go, too," Yasuko said.

"No," Carolina insisted. "I appreciate your offers to help, but it's best I do this alone. The Captain already thinks I'm a demented troublemaker."

"Don't say a word to him about me," Colleen said.

Carolina walked over to the door, patting the bag of rocks concealed in her pocket. "Not until you're ready." She opened the door, glanced up and down the hallway, and slipped out. She headed down the corridor to the elevator, trying to shake the feeling that someone was watching her. She pressed the UP button and waited.

When the doors slid open, the elevator hung about six inches higher than the floor. Goose bumps broke out on Carolina's arms. She backed away. No way was she taking a chance on getting stuck in the elevator, again. Instead, she walked up four flights of stairs to the Promenade deck, passing several much younger passengers bouncing down the stairs. They're probably wondering what an older woman is doing walking up the stairs, she thought. More likely, they're thinking she might keel over any moment from a major coronary.

Exhausted, Carolina paused on the next landing to gasp and catch her breath. She heard the elevator doors open behind her and caught a blur of movement. Then she felt hands against the middle of her back and found herself hurtling through space. Her arms and hands flew out defensively, as her body hit the carpeted steps, tumbling and rolling. She sprawled to a stop on the landing, halfway down to the next deck.

Uncertain how long she had been face down on the landing—had she lost consciousness?—Carolina tried to prop herself up on her elbow. Now she knew how it felt to be run over by a Mack truck. Dizziness turned to queasiness. The stairs seemed to run up and down like escalators, and the walls were not behaving like walls, either. She felt for the familiar bulge of the black bag in her pocket, but it was gone. She blacked out.

Sometime later, Carolina became aware of a sharp pain in her hip. She groaned out loud at the pain and worried that a broken hip at her age would be the beginning of the end. Life in assisted living or a nursing home. Sitting, drooling in a wheelchair. Definitely, no more high seas adventures.

Carolina felt a comforting hand on her arm and heard the voices of a man and a woman beside her. She opened her eyes and saw a worried and concerned middle-age woman looking down at her. Carolina opened her mouth to ask if the woman had seen her black bag, but the words didn't come out.

The woman patted Carolina's hand. "Don't worry, dear, Howie has gone for help. You're going to be all right."

I can only hope, Carolina thought, and passed out, again.

Chapter Sixteen
Martinique Experience

Carolina opened her eyes under bright lights with a man's smiling face looming over her. "Ah, you're awake. I'm Dr. Sigman, the ship's doctor. I say, nasty fall you had there. How do you feel?"

She felt like someone had thrown her down the stairs. And this man looked very happy about it. Calm down, Carolina, she told herself. He's only the doctor. The cruise company obviously pays him big bucks to keep that smile plastered on his face. Carolina took a deep breath. "Woozy. Light-headed. My body hurts all over. Will I live? Anything broken?" She tried to raise herself off the pillow. Big mistake.

Dr. Sigman laughed merrily. "I say, no broken bones, just lots of bruises and a possible concussion. You can count yourself lucky for a woman your age. Those steps are carpeted, but that's concrete underneath. Let me just say that old bones can be quite brittle."

Somehow Carolina didn't feel so lucky. Could she have tripped? No, she remembered, someone pushed her down those steps, but who? And why? "My black bag is gone! Where is it?"

Old Smiley Face frowned. "Mrs. Cunningham, let me assure you that you came in here with only your suite key card in your pocket. That's how we know who you are. We're trying to locate your friends now. Meantime, you need to stay in bed and rest. You've been through quite an ordeal. Most passengers who take a fall on those steps fracture a wrist or break an arm or leg. Don't worry, you'll be fine by the time we reach St. Thomas."

Carolina's eyes popped wide open, and she tried to sit up, again. St. Thomas was two days away. She couldn't stay in bed that long. She was on a mission.

"No, no, no, Mrs. Cunningham." Dr. Sigman pushed her gently back onto the bed. "Lie there and rest. Someone is waiting outside to see you.

Ten minutes." He disappeared from view.

Carolina turned toward the door, expecting to see Eula Mae. Instead, Ron walked in. His mouth was smiling, but his eyes weren't. "The doc says you must have been running thirty miles an hour when you hit those steps."

Carolina avoided Ron's intense gaze. She didn't need this interrogation. Where was Eula Mae? "Guess I was going too fast for road conditions. Sort of stupid of me to fall down like that. Makes me feel like an old lady."

"Yeah, it's so stupid I don't believe for one minute that's what happened," Ron said. "Who threw you down the steps?" He pulled a chair over to her bed, sat down, and waited.

"You think my fall wasn't an accident?"

"That's correct."

Carolina knew there was only one way to end this conversation. "Guess we're even. I don't think you're really Ron Dunten."

Ron slapped his hand on the chair arm.

Was he agitated with her? Carolina certainly hoped so.

"Carolina, if you weren't lying in that bed, I'd ... I'd ..."

"You'd what?" Carolina fought down the angry words struggling to get out. Now wasn't the time for a good agent to lose her cool. The doctor would return any second. She just needed to stall for time. "Let's call a truce. I'll tell you everything you want to know—how I was nearly abducted, all about smuggled emeralds, and everything I know about my accident tonight. I'll even arrange for you to meet the stowaway."

Ron leaned forward in his chair. "It's about time you came to your senses." He leaned even closer and placed his hand on hers. "Do you feel like talking now."

Carolina slipped her hand out from under his. She nodded, stifling a yawn. "Just tell me one thing."

"One thing?" He looked suspicious. "Like what?"

"Who are you—really?" Carolina fought to keep her eyes open, but suddenly she was feeling woozy.

Ron grabbed her arm. "What do I have to say or do to get through to you?"

Carolina cried out. "Stop, you're hurting me."

Ron released his hold and stood up. "Sorry. You're really annoying me."

Dr. Sigman ran into the room. "What's going on in here, Mr. Dunten? Your time is up. Mrs. Cunningham needs to rest."

"Five more minutes," he insisted.

"Not tonight." The doctor guided Ron to the door. "You can talk more tomorrow."

Yeah, you tell him, doc, Carolina thought, and attempted to smile at Ron as he left.

The next morning, when Dr. Sigman walked into her room in sick bay, Carolina was shoveling in a mouthful of scrambled eggs.

"How do you feel this morning?" he asked.

She swallowed the eggs before answering. "Very sore." She finished a glass of fresh-squeezed orange juice.

He smiled. "You banged yourself up pretty good, so you'll be sore for a few days, believe me. By the way, your friends are outside to take you back to your suite."

Carolina wiped her mouth with her napkin. "Thank goodness. We're going to check out Martinique today."

"No."

"No, what?"

"Since you might have a mild concussion, you will remain in bed the rest of the day."

"But—"

"No buts. If you feel good this afternoon, you can go to dinner. Now this is the part where you say, 'Yes, doctor, anything you say.'"

Carolina crossed her fingers underneath the sheet. "Yes, doctor, anything you say."

"For the last time, Carolina, I'm not leaving you here alone," Eula Mae said.

Yasuko, checking to make sure she had her ship's ID card, credit cards, and cash, said, "I will be going ashore to keep Colleen out of trouble."

Carolina grimaced. She felt fine. Her head felt a little achy, but otherwise, she was good to go. "You're being ridiculous, Eula Mae. You said you wanted to visit Martinique and practice your French."

"What if I leave you onboard all alone and something happens to you? How will I explain that to Charter and Caitlyn? If they knew what was going on here, they would fly down and drag you back to the Villas."

"Nothing is going to happen to me. I'm confined to bed."

"I'll stay here and keep her company, Eula Mae," Colleen said. She had been sitting quietly on the corner of Carolina's bed listening to the debate. "Mr. Gallenkemp will bring us lunch, and tea and chocolate éclairs in the afternoon. That way you and Yasuko can go ashore. We'll be fine."

"Well—" Eula Mae's eyes narrowed as she considered this.

Carolina watched Eula Mae falter. "You know you want to see Mount Pelee and the city the volcano destroyed, St. Pierre. You can snap lots of photos to send to Lilly."

Eula Mae rubbed her forehead. "I would like to see the statue of Empress Josephine. Did you know she was born on Martinique?" She threw her hands in the air. "What am I saying? Yasuko and I can't go by ourselves."

"Take Ron with you," Carolina suggested. "That way he won't be around to bother me."

"Absolutely not!"

"How about the half-day shore excursion?" Colleen said.

"Perfect!" Carolina agreed, pointing at the port-of-call information sheet. "Says here the last one leaves the pier at 10 o'clock, so get moving."

Eula Mae looked at her watch. "Yikes! It's 9:45 now. We better skedaddle. Okay, I'm going, but you better stay in this suite with the door locked until I return."

"Of course, we wouldn't dream of leaving." Carolina looked at Colleen and grinned. But if we did leave, she promised, we wouldn't be gone long.

After lunch in the suite, Carolina was feeling antsy. She had finished her newest spy thriller, and was ready for a little action. "Colleen!"

"What?" Colleen jumped out of her seat. "Something wrong?"

Carolina swung her legs over the edge of the bed and put her feet on the floor. "No, I feel great."

"Then what are you doing? You're confined to bed, remember?"

"I can't lie here any longer. I'll get bed sores on my bottom."

Colleen made an attempt to push Carolina back into bed. "This is not a good idea. Falling down those steps really banged you up and knocked you cuckoo."

"Out of my way." Carolina stood up, grabbed a pair of blue denim capris and stepped into them, buttoning and zipping them up. She couldn't believe how her shoulders and hip ached. "Man, am I sore. Like an arthritic old woman."

"I can't imagine why."

"I see you're wearing my favorite Tigger shirt. You better not damage it." Carolina pulled off her pajama top and tugged a short-sleeved white top over her head, groaning in the process. "Okay, now let's check out the hold."

"Not a good idea." Colleen glared at her. "First of all, you're not supposed to be out of bed, and secondly, the hold is probably still locked."

Carolina slipped into practical walking sandals for older women and ran a comb through her Einstein-wiry hair. She ignored Colleen just like she would Eula Mae. "Maybe so, but at least I'll feel like we're doing something. Whoever threw me down the stairs took the black bag. We're losing the race. Ready?" Carolina headed for the door with a reluctant Colleen following.

No one was loitering near the hold and everything seemed secure.

"See, I told you it would be locked," said Colleen, annoyed. "The smugglers must be somewhere else."

Carolina leaned over and rested her forehead and forearms against the cool, metal bulkhead. It was a minor setback, of course, but at least they had tried. She straightened up and looked at Colleen. "They have to stuff the emeralds into the dolls some place."

Colleen rubbed the back of her neck and tilted her head to one side. "Hmmm ... well ..."

Carolina gave Colleen a few moments to think, since she herself didn't have a plan. Surely Colleen could come up with something. She wasn't disappointed.

"All on-shore purchases sent to the ship are unloaded on D deck for sorting and cabin delivery. We could hang out there and look for something unusual," Colleen said.

"Or sinister or suspicious!" Carolina gave Colleen a hug. "Let's go!"

Carolina and Colleen settled down on a stiff, institutional-looking sofa not designed for comfort or napping. From their seats, they could observe the hatch and the stewards as they unloaded launches from the island. While two stewards sorted through the packages, other stewards delivered them to cabins. Perfume and liquor were coming onboard by the gallons. Carolina couldn't think of a way that smugglers could hide emeralds in those bottles. They waited like secret agents on an international stake-out, while pretending to read books.

"I don't see a doll anywhere," Carolina said half an hour later. "Could they stuff the emeralds in something else?"

"Probably just about anything. Maybe even that." Colleen pointed to a box labeled Omega clock.

The women watched the steward pick up the box and glance around, before walking off. "Let's follow him," Carolina said, already out of her seat.

Colleen nodded, and fell in step behind her.

Like sneaky secret agents, they followed the steward and watched him deliver the box to cabin 8253. Carolina shrugged. Disappointed, they returned to Deck D.

Six large packages and six false alarms later, they collapsed onto the sofa, feeling discouraged. Carolina glanced at her watch. "It's nearly teatime."

"It's also time for Yasuko and Eula Mae to return from their shore excursion and for the doctor to check on you. We should return to the suite."

Carolina nodded, but then she noticed a steward pick up a huge package and walk away. She had a really good feeling about this one. "Okay, but let's follow one last package." They took off after him.

The steward walked down the corridor at a fast pace. Suddenly he turned around and looked at them. Carolina and Colleen stopped at the elevator and pushed the UP button. When they looked back, he had disappeared.

"He's gone." Carolina could not believe it. One second he was there and then "poof" he was gone. They walked down the corridor to where they had seen him last. "The only place he could have gone is through this door. Where does it go?"

"Down to the luggage room." Colleen hesitated. "But that would be the perfect place to do something illegal."

Carefully and quietly, like good spies—Mrs. Craycraft would be so proud—they crept down the stairs to the luggage room door, which stood ajar. "This room is very large," Colleen whispered. "Runs the width of the ship."

As silently as possible, Carolina and Colleen slipped through the door, crouched down and slithered around pieces of stored luggage. Their adrenaline was pumping. Then Carolina heard something and motioned for Colleen to stop and listen. What was that sound? Paper rustling? Slowly and cautiously they moved toward the noise, their excitement growing. Yes, Carolina realized, this was what made spying such a thrill.

Edging around a support girder, Carolina caught a glimpse of the steward. She and Colleen hid in the shadows and watched him remove a large wrapped item from a box. He cut away layers of tissue paper, revealing a large porcelain vase. From a nearby trunk, he removed a black drawstring bag and dropped it into the vase. Then he stuffed wadded-up paper into the vase, carefully re-wrapped it, and returned it to the box.

Carolina motioned Colleen to make their exit before the steward left or they would be at risk of getting locked in. Colleen must have shared her concerns, for she hurried toward the exit and disappeared through the door. Moments later, as Carolina reached the door, a man pushed his way into the room, shoving her aside. She gasped in terror as strong hands grabbed her shoulders and pulled her into the corridor.

"Carolina, what are you doing here?" thundered a familiar voice.

Relief flooded through her. "Peter?" she gasped. "You nearly scared me to death. I thought you were one of <u>them</u>."

"You mean 'one of them' as in an assassin or a smuggler or a kidnapper?"

Carolina tried to pull back from him, but Peter wouldn't release his grip on her shoulders. She felt a quiver of fear in her abdomen. "Peter, let go of me."

"What are you doing down here?" he hissed. "This deck is off limits to passengers."

Carolina's stomach twisted into an icy knot. This was not the smiling, pleasant, courteous Peter who ate dinner with them. This Peter was obviously one of them.

Chapter Seventeen
What's the Truth?

While Carolina tried to comprehend this new revelation, the steward stepped out of the luggage room with the large box in tow. He hesitated; his eyes widened. "Lieutenant Lieberson. Is something wrong, sir?"

Peter never took his eyes off of Carolina's. "No, Swanson, everything is taken care of. Go about your business."

"Yes, sir. Thank you, sir."

The steward looked at Carolina curiously, but he walked down the corridor without a backward glance.

Carolina swallowed hard and wondered if the steward would remember seeing her should she disappear off the *Emerald Dream*. Omigosh! Peter really was one of <u>them</u>. She was sure of it now. How could she have been so blind? Her chin began to tremble. Carolina Cunningham, she fussed at herself. Don't go and get all old lady sappy. Think about Agent Craycraft. Would she wring her hands and cry? Of course not. Even if he threw her overboard, Carolina knew she needed to be strong like Agent Craycraft. But she also needed a plan.

Peter glared at her. "One more time, Mrs. Cunningham. What are you doing down here?"

Carolina stood dumbfounded. Speechless. Until his fingers dug into her shoulder. Then she yelled, "Ouch, that hurts."

He dropped his hands and stepped back, sucking in a deep breath, and letting it out in a loud swoosh. "I'm sorry, Mrs. Cunningham." He rubbed the back of his neck. "Look, I'm not the bad guy here. I'm only looking out for your interests. You and your friends are my very favorite passengers." He smiled at Carolina as though they were best friends. "But the Captain would be furious if he knew you were down here." He rubbed the back of his neck, again. "The Captain has the power to make you and your suite mates leave the ship. You would have to pay for your own transportation home. Not to mention the problems you would have island-hopping to a major airport."

Carolina blinked. He wasn't going to slit her throat or throw her overboard? Peter wasn't one of <u>them</u> after all? He was only angry because the ship's hold was off-limits to passengers? But now there was a new worry. If they were thrown off the ship, she would not be able to solve the smuggling case or find out about Colleen's sister or learn Ron's true identity. Even worse, she would be sent back to the Villas in disgrace. Eula Mae and Yasuko would never forgive her, and Charter and Caitlyn would be furious. But if Peter was not one of <u>them</u>, would he be able to help?

Carolina put on her best "but-I'm-oh-so-innocent" face. The one she used when Charter thought something she wanted to do was risky behavior for an old lady—like hiking in the North Georgia mountains or whitewater rafting. "You can't let the Captain throw us off the ship. We know all about the emerald smuggling."

Peter's eyes narrowed and he grabbed Carolina's wrist. "What did you say?"

"We know what the smugglers do with the emeralds." Carolina could tell he was shocked. His fingers tightened around her wrist. She tried to pull herself loose.

Peter shook his head and released his grip. "What smugglers?"

Carolina noticed he was breathing faster. "The ones operating a smuggling ring on this ship. We saw the steward—you called him Swanson?—stuffing emeralds into a vase. You saw him carry it out of the luggage room. Don't you get it?" Carolina waved her arms about. "The passengers smuggle the emeralds through U.S. Customs, and they don't even know what they're doing." She paused to catch her breath.

Peter grabbed Carolina's shoulders and shook her. "You said 'we.' Who's 'we'? You couldn't be talking about Mrs. Davis. I saw her go ashore."

"Colleen. You know? The stowaway?"

"The stowaway?" His face paled.

"Yes, Colleen's sister, Garland Burgess, was the ship's officer who went overboard. Colleen snuck onboard to find out what really happened. We think Garland found out about the smugglers, and they had to shut her up."

"Bloody hell! How did you figure this out?" Peter rubbed the back of his neck.

Carolina couldn't help but notice that he looked blown away. Probably he was surprised that three older women and a teenage girl had uncovered what he didn't know existed.

"We found emeralds in Eula Mae's straw doll. But when the Captain asked to see them, they had disappeared. He thought we were lying. Then we found emeralds in another doll bought in Barbados, but I lost them on my way to show them to the Captain." She pointed up the stairs. "If you get that box from the steward, you'll find emeralds in the vase. Then the Captain will know I'm not crazy."

Carolina paused to catch her breath. She was excited about solving the case, and could see that Peter was overcome with admiration for her amazing ability to put together the puzzle. He stood there, wide-eyed, staring at her and muttering under his breath. A crimson blush crept out of the neck of his white shirt and spread upward over his face. Some strange noises sounded from his throat, as he put his face into her personal space.

Carolina stepped back when she realized that even though Peter's mouth was smiling, his eyes had narrowed and his right one was twitching. Really badly twitching. He backed her up against the wall. She sucked in her breath. Was he angry and jealous that she, Eula Mae, Yasuko, and Colleen had uncovered the smuggling ring?

"Carolina, there's something you should know. But first you must promise that everything I tell you remains between you and me."

Omigosh! Had she heard right? Was Peter taking her into his confidence? She couldn't believe it. She let out her breath in a rush. "I promise. Tell me."

"Good, I knew I could count on you. You see, you aren't the only one who knows about the smuggling ring."

Her ego deflated. "I'm not?"

"I've known for quite a while. In fact, I was one of the first to notice and report it to the proper authorities. U.S. Customs and the F.B.I. are already investigating." Peter glanced up the staircase and lowered his voice. "They think the Captain is the ringleader."

"What? No way!" Carolina thought about it for a second. Yeah, she guessed that made sense. But if that were true, was Ron working with the Captain? This would require more thought. "Are you sure?"

"Absolutely. Federal agents are onboard this ship now, watching every move the Captain makes. Everyone involved will soon be arrested."

Carolina felt hope. Maybe Ron was a federal agent. She brightened at the thought.

"I'll contact the unit leader and pass on your information. It might help the agents with their case." He smiled and gently squeezed her shoulder. "Remember, we did not have this conversation." He looked down at his bright, white shoes. "I'll—uh—have the F.B.I. put a bodyguard on you, your friends, and the stowaway—uh—Colleen." He looked Carolina straight in the eye. "For your own protection, of course."

Carolina felt good, but she noticed Peter didn't. She watched him wipe perspiration from his face. His hands were shaking. She guessed he felt responsible, and it was taking its toll. "Don't worry, I won't tell anyone. It's going to be okay, Peter." She gave him a reassuring smile— like the one she gave Charter when he thought she went to a movie with friends, but she really went kayaking down the Savannah River. "I'm relieved this is all over. I've been stressed out all week. Now I really can relax and enjoy being a tourist."

His shoulders relaxed and his eye stopped twitching.

"What about Colleen?" Carolina asked.

"What? Oh—uh—we better keep her hidden until the Captain is arrested. By the way, maybe you should tell me where she is? You know—uh—so I can have an agent keep an eye on her?" He looked at Carolina anxiously.

Peter was right, Carolina thought. Colleen's poor parents had already lost one daughter on this ship. It would be bad if something happened to her. "She stays in a vacant cabin on G Deck." Carolina looked at her watch. "I need to run. If the doctor doesn't find me in our suite, no telling what will happen. I might not get dinner." Carolina started up the stairs without looking back. She felt like a load of bricks had been lifted off her shoulders.

As soon as they heard the news, Eula Mae and Yasuko were relieved, too.

"You should've talked to Peter after you first talked to Colleen," Eula Mae said.

"Yeah, yeah, yeah." Carolina decided not to mention the part about following the steward into the luggage room and getting caught by an angry Peter. Fortunately, Colleen escaped before Peter came along.

Carolina searched for Colleen before dinner to tell her the good news, but couldn't find her. She figured she was hiding somewhere. Which seemed strange, thought Carolina, since she should be in the suite with everyone else talking about what they had discovered in the luggage room. Had something happened to Colleen?

Peter did not make it to dinner. Something about a small emergency in the engine room, according to Dominic.

"Is the ship in trouble of sinking?" Carolina asked. In the Craycraft book *Trouble on the High Seas*, the ship began sinking not long after the engineer made an emergency trip to the engine room.

Dominic laughed. "Oh, no, dear lady, probably just a screw loose."

Carolina looked across the table at Ron and gave him her broadest smile. It was her I-know-something-you-don't-know smile.

"How are you feeling tonight?" Ron asked pleasantly.

"Great, thank you," Carolina replied, as Dominic placed a plate of roasted Long Island duckling in front of her. She picked up her knife and fork, and easily sliced off a piece of duck, while trying to figure out how Ron fit in with the emerald smuggling.

"Glad to hear that. You ready to talk?" He looked at Carolina steadily.

"Anytime you're ready," she replied sweetly.

"How about a stroll around the deck after dinner?" he asked. He glanced over at Eula Mae and Yasuko. "Alone."

Eula Mae dropped her fork. "You want to take Carolina for a walk?"

Ron nodded.

Eula Mae rolled her eyes. "Sure, no problem. Don't mind me and Yasuko. We'll be as happy as two pigs in a pile of poop."

"Good. Carolina and I are overdue for an interesting chat," Ron said, plopping a piece of fried calamari into his mouth.

"Should be interesting all right." Carolina stared at Ron intently. Because she was ready to find out who he really was.

The reflections of a full moon simmered on a calm sea. Carolina stood at the rail, enjoying the moment as the ship steamed toward the U.S. Virgin Islands. St. Thomas would be the last port-of-call before returning to Jacksonville. And tonight, she hoped to get answers to her questions.

"Guess this is as good a spot as any to have our chat," Ron said, standing next to her on the deserted Games Deck by the children's paddle pool. Most passengers were finishing dinner or already conspiring to get good seats near the stage for the evening's Hollywood musical spectacular.

Carolina wondered if Ron had been assigned as her bodyguard or was her real bodyguard watching them from somewhere nearby? "If you insist."

"Shall we sit?" He pulled two deck chairs close to the rail.

Carolina sat on one chair. Ron took the other. A few seconds of silence passed.

"What are you thinking?" he asked.

Even though she wasn't looking at him, Carolina could feel his eyes on her. She pictured Agent Craycraft sitting with double-double-agent Monty Mongrove in *Middle East Misadventure*. Could Ron really be trusted? "I was thinking that in three days we'll be back in the Villas at Kensington Grove, and all of this will seem like a dream."

He spoke softly. "Or a nightmare."

Carolina finally looked up into his face. The dark shadows gave him a sinister look in the moonlight. "I like to think I'll only remember the good things. All the bad things are over."

"Are they?" He sounded incredulous.

"Isn't this case nearly wrapped up?" She watched his face for a reaction.

His eyes widened. "Carolina—"

A noise on the deck below distracted her. She looked down at the children's pool and saw a man dressed in black and a woman, wearing deck pants and tee, locked in an embrace. Ahh, shipboard romance. But then the woman struck the man in the face with her fist and kicked him. She was screaming, but her screams could barely be heard. These two were definitely not lovers. "Ron, look!"

Ron's gaze followed her pointing finger, and he jumped to his feet. "Hey!" he shouted. "What's going on down there?"

"Help!" the woman screamed.

Carolina watched in horror as the man grabbed her around the waist, lifted her up and threw her over the rail. Carolina screamed.

"Man overboard!" Ron yelled. He raced towards the emergency alarm.

"Man overboard!" Carolina screamed and threw a life ring and flare over the rail. Her heart pounding, she fought down a sick feeling in the pit of her stomach. Would the woman be able to find the life ring? Could the ship find her in the dark? The flare was already fading from view as the ship cruised away.

The ship's alarm sounded. Just like the tornado warning siren at home. Chaos followed. Crew members, officers, and passengers came running out on deck. The ship began to slow down. Too bad they couldn't simply throw on the brakes and put the ship in reverse, Carolina thought. But she knew that a 30,000-ton ship couldn't stop on a dime.

Eula Mae and Yasuko ran out on deck with the other passengers and found spots along the rail to see what was happening. Carolina joined them and told them what she saw. It took almost an hour for the ship to change course and return to where the flare floated in the sea.

"I was afraid something had happened to you." Eula Mae hugged Carolina tightly.

"She really thought Ron had thrown you overboard," Yasuko said with a laugh.

"Have you seen Colleen?" Eula Mae asked.

"No." And that began to worry Carolina. No, don't go there, she told herself. That couldn't have been Colleen. She chewed her lower lip and leaned over the rail. Absolutely impossible. Peter told her an agent would watch over Colleen. No way it could be her. Carolina focused on the lifeboat being lowered into the water and watched for a sign of the woman in the water. But all she could see was the flare.

The rescuers worked orderly and fast, searching in a grid pattern. Carolina wondered if they had a lot of practice searching for overboard passengers. Crew members searched the water in the area of the flare with the help of bright spotlights on top of the tender and the *Emerald Dream*. Suddenly a dark floating mass materialized in the lights, and two rescuers jumped into the water. Carefully, they pushed and pulled something over to the tender. Two crew men reached down from the tender and dragged a limp body into the boat.

"She's alive!" a crew member shouted from the boat.

Passengers and crew cheered. "Yes!" Carolina screamed. Caught up in the moment, Carolina, Eula Mae, and Yasuko hugged each other.

As the tender headed back to the ship, Carolina led Eula Mae and Yasuko down to the medical center. It was the logical place to take her, Carolina decided. They didn't have to wait long before three officers pushed a stretcher off the elevator and down the hall toward the medical center's door. As the stretcher passed them in the patient lobby, the woman's pale, wet face rolled into view. The three women gasped out loud. It was Colleen.

Chapter Eighteen
Kidnapped

Shock washed over Carolina. She froze, unable to move. Yasuko and Eula Mae stood silently a few feet from her.

"What are you doing down here?" a voice asked.

The three women turned around to face a grim-looking Ron. A tear rolled down Carolina's cheek. "It's Colleen." She could barely talk. "Someone tried to murder Colleen."

"I know." He put his arm around Carolina and hugged her against his chest.

Part of her wanted to shove him away, but another part of her felt comforted. Carolina also felt conflicted.

"We need to talk to the Captain," Ron spoke softly in her ear.

Carolina nodded. "I know," she agreed.

Ron dropped his arms and guided Carolina, Yasuko, and Eula Mae in the direction of the Captain's office.

While Ron and the Captain huddled and whispered in the corner, the three women sat together on a stiff office sofa. Not the most comfortable sofa to sit on, but acceptable. The kind of sofa you would expect to see in the Captain's office.

Carolina felt numb all over. It was like she only half-existed. Her brain kept running the image of Colleen's ashen face through her mind over and over—like a continuous loop of film.

Ron walked over, handed each of them a glass of water, and sat on a chair near the Captain's desk. Carolina sipped the water and tried to focus. Just when she thought everything was under control, it wasn't. What had happened? Something had gone terribly wrong.

Eula Mae reached over and squeezed Carolina's hand. She squeezed back and looked up at Ron. She could see that he was worried—and angry. Was he scowling at her or the situation?

The Captain, who stood beside Ron, cleared his throat. "Mrs. Cunningham, do I understand correctly that the young woman we rescued is Colleen Burgess, our stowaway? You and Mr. Dunten actually saw the man throw her overboard?" He crossed his arms across his chest.

"Yes." Carolina took another sip of water.

"It was intentional? Not an accident?"

The image of the man lifting Colleen and throwing her overboard went through Carolina's mind, again. She glanced at Ron.

Ron nodded his head. "Without a doubt, sir. He picked her up and tossed her over the rail like a sack of potatoes."

"Did either of you recognize the man?"

"No, it was too dark," Carolina said. But she knew it had to be Mr. Smith.

The Captain looked at Ron, who was studying Carolina. "Mr. Dunten?"

"No, sir. It happened too fast."

"I see. Did they appear to know each other?"

"I don't know," Ron said with a shrug.

"When I first saw them, they looked like they were embracing," Carolina remembered. "But then I realized Colleen was trying to get away from him. She will know who did it," she said hopefully. "She was right there, face to face with the murderer."

The Captain stood and walked around to the back of his desk. "Unfortunately, she's in critical condition and may not regain consciousness."

"Lordy, Lordy," exclaimed Eula Mae. "Gracious me. There are some mean, cruel people in this world."

"We need to find the connection between Colleen's sister falling overboard last month and someone trying to murder Colleen tonight. This is unbelievable," the Captain said.

"I tried to tell you someone was trying to murder me, but you thought that was unbelievable, too," Carolina said.

Ron cleared his throat and shook his head at Carolina.

A steward entered the office and whispered in the Captain's ear. The Captain cleared his throat. "It seems Colleen Burgess has regained consciousness. Let's talk to her."

Yes, thought Carolina, now they could find out who tried to kill her.

Colleen's face was pale against the white infirmary pillow. Her short hair was still damp from the ocean. Her eyes were closed, when Carolina took a chair by the bed and gave Colleen's hand a squeeze. "How are you feeling?"

Her red-rimmed eyes slowly opened. "Terrible," she said hoarsely. "What happened to me?"

"They fished you out of the ocean. Don't you remember? They had to turn the ship around and send out a rescue boat to find you."

Colleen frowned.

Carolina guessed her body was in shock, and her brain needed time to process this information.

Colleen closed her eyes and grimaced. "I can't remember," she choked out the words.

"It's all right, Miss Burgess" the Captain said, touching her shoulder. "What is the last thing you do remember?"

Colleen cleared her throat and sipped the water brought to her by the nurse. "I remember waiting in my cabin for everyone to finish dinner, so we could talk." She paused. Her eyes blinked open. "Someone slipped a message under my door that said I should meet Carolina and Ron at the children's pool."

Carolina glanced at Ron, who stood at the foot of the bed with Eula Mae and Yasuko, and back to Colleen. "I didn't send any message. So, you went?"

"I think so." She frowned and shook her head. "Yes, I did go. It was dark. I didn't see you. Then someone grabbed me from behind." She swallowed hard and wiped her nose with the back of her hand. "A man ... we struggled ... and he threw me ..." Her voice faded away. "I-I couldn't breathe. I kept kicking and trying to get to the surface." A sob escaped her throat. "I remember seeing a light floating on the water with a life ring nearby, but the ship left me." Colleen covered her mouth, as convulsive sobs racked her body.

Carolina sat down on the bed and put her arms around her. "It's okay. You're going to be all right."

"Who attacked you?" Ron stepped closer to the bed.

Colleen gasped. "What's he doing here?"

"It's all right." At least Carolina hoped it was all right. "He and the Captain know you're the stowaway." There was no turning back now.

Colleen glanced from Carolina to Ron and the Captain. "Do they know Garland was my sister?" she whispered.

Carolina nodded. "Yes. They are hoping you know who threw you overboard. Was it Mr. Smith?"

Colleen shook her head slowly. "I don't know." She frowned. Her eyebrows furrowed together. "It was dark, so I couldn't see his face clearly. My memory is fuzzy."

Uh-oh. That's not good, Carolina thought. Back to square one. Special spy Carolina thwarted, again. What was she going to do now? Wait for someone to throw her or Eula Mae or Yasuko overboard? Obviously, they couldn't count on the FBI to keep them safe.

"Time to let my patient get some rest," Dr. Sigman said, signaling for them to leave.

Ron leaned over Colleen. "Get some rest. We'll talk more later. Maybe you'll remember something else."

Colleen nodded and closed her eyes.

Carolina gave Colleen's hand another squeeze, and followed everyone out of the room and into the elevator.

The Captain sighed loudly. "It's most regrettable that Miss Burgess doesn't remember who attacked her."

"Not unusual after a traumatic life or death situation," Ron said.

The Captain ran his hand over his face. "Let's hope she remembers something soon." He turned to the three women. "You three do know that I'm responsible for everything that happens on this ship, right?"

"Yes," they answered at once.

"When a crime happens on a cruise ship at sea, I am the ultimate authority. It is up to me to discover the truth." He looked at them sternly. "It is also my responsibility to make sure there is no ship-wide panic among the passengers. I'm requesting that you not discuss this with anyone. May I count on your cooperation?"

The elevator stopped and the doors opened.

"Of course," Eula Mae and Yasuko chimed together.

"Not even Peter?" Carolina asked. She needed to know.

The Captain growled. "Especially not him."

Carolina's eyes widened in surprise. The wheels began to turn in her brain. Especially not with Peter? Did the Captain suspect Peter was working with the FBI?

Ron cleared his throat. "What the Captain means is that the officers and crew have already been warned about discussing tonight's rescue with any passengers."

The Captain grunted. "Mr. Dunten's right. Now may I have your word?"

"Absolutely," Carolina said.

"You can count on us," agreed Eula Mae.

"Me, too," said Yasuko.

"Thank you, ladies, and good evening," the Captain said.

Carolina thought she saw Ron wink as the elevator doors closed. Now what did that mean?

Dismissed, the women headed toward their cabin suite. Carolina shook her head. The Captain certainly didn't look or act like one of them, but how would he act if he were? She suddenly remembered a spy thriller she had read the month before in which this sweet old lady turned out to be an assassin with 87 kills to her credit. Maybe Ron was arresting the Captain right this very minute, providing Ron was who he claimed to be.

Eula Mae collapsed on her bed. "I can't believe Colleen doesn't remember who did it. Good thing you and Ron were there to sound the alarm." She shivered. "What if no one saw her go over the rail?"

"She'd be missing just like her sister," pointed out Yasuko.

Carolina started undressing for bed. "I don't understand where her bodyguard was. Peter said the FBI would assign one."

"Maybe they couldn't find her," suggested Eula Mae.

"Maybe." Carolina grabbed her toothbrush and started squeezing the toothpaste tube.

Eula Mae lay back on her bed. "Do you think they will arrest her for stowing away on the ship?"

Carolina spit in the sink and stuck her head out of the bathroom. "I seriously doubt it."

"I wouldn't count on that," Yasuko called out from her sofa bed. "Stowing away on a ship is a crime, remember?"

Carolina turned on her cell phone and pressed Lilly's name in the WhatsApp contact list. The ringing echoed throughout their suite until Lilly's face appeared on the screen. Carolina could see that Lilly was ready for bed.

"Good evening!" greeted Lilly. "It was getting so late, I was afraid I wouldn't hear from you tonight. What's up? Anything exciting?"

Eula Mae and Yasuko looked over Carolina's shoulder at their friend Lilly, who was curled up in her recliner with her cell phone. Behind her, they could see her husband Archie stretched out on the sofa, sound asleep. Must be another exciting evening in the Villas.

"We have lots to tell you, but first, do you know if you can go to jail for stowing away on a ship?" asked Carolina.

"Let me check," said Lilly, heading to her computer desk in the next room. Carolina always hated this, as the wildly moving images on her screen made her dizzy. Finally, Lilly sat down in front of her computer, anchoring her cell phone, while she Googled for information.

"Well, according to 18 U.S. Code Section 2199, you can be arrested and charged for stowing away on a vessel or aircraft." Lilly looked from her computer monitor to her friends.

"Lordy, Lordy," said Eula Mae.

"Is there any indication about fines or prison time?" asked Carolina.

"Yeah," joined in Yasuko. "Could they put you away for 25 years or more?"

Lilly turned back to her screen and scrolled down. "Says here that you can be fined under this title or imprisoned not more than 5 years, or both."

"Sounds like it's not a really bad thing, like say hijacking an entire ship," Carolina said thoughtfully.

"It's still a crime," pointed out Eula Mae," because you're stealing something not yours."

"True," put in Yasuko, "but if there are extenuating circumstances, then maybe a light fine or community service would be warranted."

"Hey! You folks cruising around the Caribbean! What's going on now?" Lilly's face filled the entire screen. "Don't leave me hanging here."

Carolina quickly filled Lilly in on the day's events.

"Wow!" Lilly exclaimed as Carolina ended with Colleen's rescue after being thrown overboard. "I hope you three keep your door deadbolted at night. I thought cruises were supposed to be fun and safe."

"That's probably the assumption of most passengers when they board a cruise ship," Carolina said. "No one wants to think about crimes committed onboard—like smuggling illegal drugs or homicides; or getting sick, falling overboard or dying. No one wants to admit that ships can crash into the dock or collide with another ship or catch on fire. And we've all seen on the news about terrible storms at sea that can capsize or sink a ship."

"Hold it right there," yelled Eula Mae. "Zip those lips. Not another word out of you. That's it for tonight."

Yasuko gasped, hopped in her bed and pulled the covers over her head. Carolina hastily bid Lilly good night. In less than a minute, all three women were lying silently in their separate beds.

"I apologize for losing my cool," said Eula Mae, breaking the silence. "I'm worried about Colleen, and I didn't need anything else to worry about."

"Apology accepted," mumbled Yasuko, from beneath her covers.

"It's all right, Eula Mae. We're all a little bit on edge tonight. But I think Colleen is going to be all right," Carolina said.

"But what about the Captain?" asked Yasuko.

"Exactly," said Eula Mae. "Have you considered that if he is the head of the smuggling ring, he might hurt Colleen?"

Carolina fluffed up her pillow and pulled out another Craycraft spy thriller. "Don't worry about it. How could anyone 'off' her in the medical center with all of those nurses watching."

Carolina glanced down at the sliced strawberries and bananas Dominic had placed in front of her. She couldn't help but notice that the banana slices looked darker than usual. She forked a slice into her mouth and chewed. She must have made a strange face, as a concerned Dominic approached her.

"Mrs. Cunningham, is everything all right?" he asked.

"I'm afraid this banana is too ripe for me, Dominic," Carolina said, after swallowing her one bite.

Dominic nodded. "This is what happens during a cruise, Mrs. Cunningham. At first, they are green. They begin to get riper. By the end of the cruise, they are very, very ripe."

"And only fit for making banana bread." Eula Mae pointed out.

"But once they turn totally black, they are too rotten for much of anything," Yasuko said.

After the women finished eating breakfast and were exiting the dining room, Dominic caught up with them. He handed Carolina a bag. "Here is your last picnic lunch this cruise. It is an extra special lunch I pack for you. Don't lose it." He smiled and twisted his mustache.

Carolina took the lunch and dropped it into her denim bag. "Thank you, Dominic. I promise to take special care of it. I'm sure whatever you prepared for us will be delicious."

Before taking a tender into shore to visit Charlotte Amalie, St. Thomas, the women paid a quick visit to Colleen in the medical center. Colleen, who was eating breakfast, seemed in good spirits. "I'll be fine," she told Carolina. "You go ashore and enjoy the day. Bring me back a surprise."

No one was happy about boarding a tender for the trip into shore. It was always easier to disembark the ship at the dock. Easy on and easy off. At least the ocean was fairly calm, which was good for Yasuko. For easy boarding, several strong crew members were present to help passengers step from the ship's platform onto the waiting tender.

As Carolina picked up her foot to step onto the tender, her elbows were grabbed, and she was lifted over the gap between vessels. Feeling like a drunken sailor, she steadied herself and walked carefully to a bench seat, followed by Eula Mae and Yasuko.

"Lordy, Lordy," exclaimed Eula Mae, edging closer to Carolina to make room for Yasuko. "I feel like a sardine in a can."

"If you really want to feel like that, wait until we have to abandon ship and they squeeze 150 passengers in here," said Yasuko, sitting snugly, thigh to thigh, next to Eula Mae. "I don't understand why the ship can't tie up at a pier and let us use the gangway. That would be much more civilized."

"Maybe their cruise ship dock was wiped out in the last hurricane and hasn't been rebuilt," explained Carolina. "Or maybe they ran out of space on the cruise ship dock." She hoped they weren't going to grumble their whole time ashore. Maybe she should have left them on board the ship. Too late now.

When the tender was full of passengers sitting elbow to elbow, crew members untied the ropes, and the small vessel pushed back from the *Emerald Dream*. A cooling breeze and ocean spray teased their faces through the open windows, as they headed toward shore. In the distance, Carolina watched sailboats circling two U.S. Coast Guard ships anchored in the harbor. Beyond the town loomed velvet green mountains, dotted with stark-white houses. It was a sunny, cloudless, blue-sky day.

"This place is beautiful," Yasuko said. "Do you think they have any retirement communities here?"

"I'm sure they do," said Eula Mae, "but they most likely have to rebuild them from time to time because of hurricanes and mud slides."

Carolina shook her head and watched two crew members tie the tender to the dock. "I doubt if they would allow troublemakers like us to live here."

Exiting the tender onto a solid dock was relatively easy, but crew members were still there to offer assistance and warn when the last tender left shore for the ship. Woe unto any passengers who missed the last boat back. How awful it would be, Carolina thought, to be stranded at any port of call without your passport or luggage. How would you get back home? She hoped she wouldn't ever have to find out.

Carolina glanced around casually to see if she could pick out the FBI agent who was protecting them. She didn't understand why the agent, who was looking after Colleen, didn't stop her from getting tossed overboard. But maybe they hadn't been able to locate her. Surely by now they knew she was in the medical center.

"It's about time you made it to shore."

The women turned in the direction of the voice and saw Ron leaning against a piling.

"I've been waiting 45 minutes. Thought I'd missed you." He fell into step beside them.

"We stopped by the medical center to check on Colleen," Carolina explained.

"She doing all right?"

"Oh, yeah, for nearly being drowned." she answered. "Dr. Sigman said she would probably be released this evening."

"I was in the Captain's office when he talked to her parents last night," Ron said. "They were frantic. Especially after they found out she wasn't at her friend's house. They didn't know what had happened to her. They'll meet the ship when it docks in Jacksonville."

The foursome strode along in silence for a few moments. Carolina could only imagine how upset Colleen's parents must be after losing their other daughter. "Maybe by then someone will be able to give the family answers about what happened to Garland."

"And Colleen," Eula Mae said.

"I hope they bring a good lawyer with them," Yasuko said.

Ron halted and turned Yasuko around. "Why do you say that?"

Eula Mae put a restraining arm between Ron and Yasuko. "We're all concerned about her being arrested for stowing away on the ship."

Ron shook his head. "I don't think that will happen."

"Really?" asked Carolina. "But it is against the law."

"It happens more often than you think," Ron explained. "Two years ago, two boys ages 16 and 17 were taken into custody for attempting to stowaway on a cruise ship in Reykjavik. But the majority of stowaway cases involve container ships. The International Maritime Organization, which maintains records of these incidents, reports it is a serious problem that is only getting worse."

"Lordy, Lordy. If I planned to stowaway, it wouldn't be on a container ship," Eula Mae said, thoughtfully.

"You're right about that," agreed Yasuko. "No frills, no midnight buffets, no nightly entertainment. Ugh! Why would they do it?"

"These stowaways—primarily people living in East, South, and West Africa—are seeking a better life," Ron explained. "There are organized stowaway networks operating in and around regional ports that help stowaways get on board a ship and hide."

Carolina watched passengers leave the *Emerald Dream* and board a bus. Since they were carrying towels and beach bags, she bet they were headed to a resort for a day of relaxing in the sun and snorkeling with the fish. "Those kind of stowaways are different from Colleen," Carolina pointed out.

"Exactly my point," Ron said and smiled. "Not only are they stowing away, their plan is to enter another country illegally. Colleen did not stowaway to commit multiple crimes, she only wanted to solve one. Considering all of the circumstances, I doubt the cruise line will press charges."

"Especially since they have other problems," Carolina reminded everyone.

"That is so true," Ron said. "So? What do you three plan to do today? Or do I really want to know?"

"Play tourists," Carolina said.

Eula Mae nodded. "Yeah, that's about it. Dominic said we should go to Magens Bay Beach. Want to come along?"

"I'd love to, but work comes before pleasure." He held up his digital camera. "Have to take a few photos of Bluebeard's Castle first. How about I join you in an hour or two?"

"Sure," Eula Mae said.

"If you aren't too late, we'll share Dominic's picnic lunch." Carolina opened her denim bag wide, so he could see the size of the lunch.

"Providing you don't lose it?" Yasuko asked.

"Or eat it?" suggested Ron. He laughed.

Carolina growled.

"See you soon." He grinned and left them standing on the dock.

At the end of the pier, a yellow taxi drove up next to them. A young black man in a tropical print shirt leaned out the driver's window. "Taxi, ladies? Leonardo will take you anywhere for cheapest price on the island."

He had the widest smile and the whitest teeth Carolina had ever seen, and the taxi appeared freshly washed and cleaned. "What do you think, Eula Mae? Yasuko?"

Eula Mae took a step closer to the taxi. "How much to take us to Magens Bay Beach?"

"For three lovely ladies like yourselves, I have very special price."

Carolina held her breath. The special price just had to be 20 U.S. dollars.

"Only 10 dollah."

"That sounds fair," Eula Mae said.

More like unbelievable, Carolina thought. But then the U.S. dollar was the official currency in the U.S. Virgin Islands.

The driver flashed his wide smile, again, hopped out of the taxi and opened the back door.

As soon as the three of them crawled into the back seat, he slammed the door, slid under the steering wheel, and took off in such haste his tires squealed, and the women fell forward.

"Hey," Eula Mae yelled. "We'd like to get there in one piece."

They stared at the driver in his rearview mirror. Unexpectedly, he slammed on the brakes, sending the three of them tumbling forward, causing Carolina to bump her forehead on the back of the front seat. "Are you crazy?" she screamed.

Carolina had just decided the three of them should jump out and look for another taxi, when the passenger door was snatched open. A middle-aged white male, wearing black trousers and a white polo shirt, jumped in and pointed a gun at them. The taxi took off, again.

Eula Mae and Yasuko gasped. Carolina gaped at Mr. Smith in horror and slid toward Eula Mae, who was reaching for the door handle.

"I wouldn't do that," the purser's friend said, pointing the lethal end of his revolver at Carolina's head. "Or this old biddy gets it."

In a good spy thriller, this is where a fellow agent would step out of the shadows and blow out the gunman's brains. But no FBI agent came forward. Carolina tried to remain calm and put together a plan.

Eula Mae slowly dropped her hand into her lap.

"That's a smart lady. Your friend wouldn't survive long with a bullet in her brain. Not only that, but it wouldn't look like an accident." He threw back his head and laughed.

Even though Carolina wanted to be brave like Agent Craycraft, she couldn't figure a way out of this situation. A sob escaped from her throat.

"Shut up! Nothing I hate worse than a sniveling old lady," he said, reaching over the back of the seat and slapping Carolina across the face.

Eula Mae put her arms around Carolina. "Leave her alone. What do you want with us, anyway?"

Carolina marveled at how Eula Mae was standing up for her. She knew Eula Mae was as scared as she was, because she could feel her entire body trembling.

"Surely you aren't that dumb. You three start snooping into our whole operation and you can't figure out what we want with you?" He pointed his gun at Eula Mae. "I'll tell you what we want—you and your stupid friends out of our business." He snarled and yelled at the driver. "Turn right here."

Carolina pulled herself upright. She needed to be brave. Secret agents did not snivel. Surely there was an FBI agent right behind them. "You won't get away with this. Lieutenant Lieberson knows everything, and the FBI is already on the case. They'll know that the Captain is the ringleader. If anything happens to us, they know who is responsible."

The driver and Mr. Smith burst out laughing.

That wasn't the reaction she had expected. What had she said that was so funny? They didn't look the least bit worried. She looked at Eula Mae and Yasuko, who were just as dumbfounded as she was.

Mr. Smith wiped his eyes. "You three aren't as smart as we thought. Imagine that, the Captain as the brains of our operation." He laughed, again. "By the time Lieberson gets through telling the Captain what ninnies you are, he and Dunten won't be surprised that you got yourselves drowned."

Drowned? What was going on here? Carolina shivered as icy fingers of fear cut through her backbone. As the car slowed down and stopped, her mind whirled with what she had heard. She tried to put the bits and pieces together into something that would make sense, but she didn't like what they were shaping up to be. The whole iceberg was beginning to surface in her brain. How could she have been so blind, she asked herself?

Carolina thought back to the day by the pool when she overheard the purser and Mr. Smith. Peter had been unusually upset to hear that she thought something was going on. He had to be one of <u>them</u>. He was probably on his way to meet them now.

And that night before the ship docked in Nassau, she remembered seeing Peter hours after he told Eula Mae he was going to bed. Then, too, if it hadn't been for Peter, Carolina wouldn't have taken the broken elevator or been choked nearly to death.

All those meals Peter missed—he must have been making plans for the smuggling operation. Mr. Smith is right, Carolina thought. She really was dumb not to realize why Peter was standing outside the luggage room. And to think she had spilled her guts and told him everything. Then she agreed to keep quiet, while he handled the rest. No wonder the Captain seemed so innocent last night. Carolina Cunningham, you are one real dumb butt.

Really angry now, Carolina glared at Mr. Smith. "You won't get away with this. Too many people will wonder what happened to us."

"You are quite mistaken, woman."

The driver stopped the car and both men got out. The driver opened the back door, and Mr. Smith waved his revolver at them. "Get out, ladies. This is the end of the line."

Chapter Nineteen
Disaster on St. Thomas

Mr. Smith gave Carolina a shove, knocking her into Eula Mae. "No funny stuff, ladies. Just follow that path. Nice and easy."

In a single line, Carolina, Eula Mae, and Yasuko began walking down a narrow dirt path, through a jungle of banana trees and undergrowth that smelled of rotten vegetation. Maybe rotten bananas, Carolina thought. The humidity was thick and clingy. The heat nearly unbearable.

Carolina heard a noise behind her and turned in time to see Eula Mae stumble and land on her bottom. She and Yasuko quickly pulled their friend to her feet.

"Lordy, Lordy," Eula Mae gasped. "It's hotter than forty hells in this jungle."

"Shut your mouth and keep moving," Mr. Smith yelled.

Carolina gently pushed Eula Mae ahead of her. Since Eula Mae was the oldest, Carolina was concerned about how the heat was affecting her. She wiped the sweat off her own face with the back of her hand and jumped, as something brown and black slithered across the path and into the bushes. Carolina stumbled, did a sharp intake of breath, and wondered if there were poisonous snakes in the Virgin Islands.

In a few minutes, they reached a small clearing, where an old weathered wooden shed leaned to one side. Its single window was shuddered and boarded up; the door, bolted and locked. A dense growth of banana trees, and other tropical trees and plants surrounded the shed, suffocating it in a blanket of eternal green.

The driver unlocked the shed's door and shoved the women inside with such force, they fell onto a rough, wooden floor littered with trash and gritty stuff that stuck to their sweaty arms and legs. Rat poop, guessed Carolina, as a squealing critter scurried across the floor. The three women sprawled on the floor and screamed in chorus.

Both men laughed.

"In case you nosy women are interested, your friend will be leaving the ship's medical center soon," Mr. Smith said. "Unfortunately, on her way to your suite, she will take a most unfortunate detour and end up here with you. Then tonight the four of you will go on a very short boat ride. Sad to say, it won't be round trip."

Angry now, Carolina pulled herself to her feet. Terrified, she straightened herself up as tall as she could get and used her tough agent voice. "We are supposed to meet a friend at the beach in a few minutes. When we do not show up, he will alert the authorities."

"Is that a fact?" Mr. Smith lowered his face into Carolina's personal space. "Don't concern yourself. If you're referring to Mr. Dunten, he won't be a problem. We're taking your towels, beach bags, and coverups, and leaving them in a prominent spot on the beach."

The taxi driver with the ultra-white teeth snatched Carolina's denim bag with Dominic's lunch, Eula Mae's straw beach bag, and Yasuko's brightly colored Totoro bag.

"Pull off them little coverups and hand 'em over," Mr. Smith said.

"No way!" Eula Mae yelled, stumbling to her feet.

Mr. Smith reached out and pushed her back down on the floor. "Don't tell me no, old woman. Either you take 'em off or I take 'em off, and I'd enjoy that."

That did it for Carolina. She wasn't going to let him be mean to her friend. She lunged forward, grabbed his right arm, which held the revolver, bit down as hard as she could, and hoped she didn't break her bridge in the process. Mr. Smith cursed, dropped the revolver and backhanded her with his left hand.

Shocked, but not surprised that Mr. Smith had so little respect for older women, Carolina kicked the gun across the floor and lunged at him, again. Grabbing him from behind, she wrapped her arms tightly around his neck. The other man dropped the bags and tried to pull her away from Mr. Smith, but Carolina hung on like a pit bull with a bone.

In all the chaos, Yasuko scrambled around the floor and grabbed the revolver. "Stop it!" she screamed, gripping the gun with both hands and pointing it at Mr. Smith.

Everyone froze in place for several long seconds. Then Carolina loosened her grip on Mr. Smith's neck and stepped away. What a shocker for Carolina to find that Yasuko was a closet secret agent. Most likely with awesome martial arts moves, too.

Mr. Smith rubbed his neck gingerly. "You little gutter snipe! You left teeth marks in my arm."

Carolina took two steps toward Yasuko, noticing that her hands and the gun were starting to shake big time. Eula Mae scrambled behind Yasuko.

The taxi driver, his hands in the air, tried to distance himself from Mr. Smith by moving closer to the door.

Mr. Smith took a step toward Yasuko.

"Stop right there, mister," Yasuko warned him, backing up a step. "Or I'll leave a bullet hole in your head."

Mr. Smith took another step forward.

"Shoot him!" Carolina yelled.

"She can't shoot me, you blithering idiot. The safety's on."

"He's lying!" Carolina screamed, but it was too late. Yasuko took her eyes off Mr. Smith to look at the gun. In one split second, he rushed forward, knocked the revolver from her hand, and threw her against the wall of the shed. She slid down the wall onto the floor.

Carolina and Eula Mae rushed over and knelt beside her. "Yasuko, are you all right?" But she just lay there with her eyes closed. Carolina glared at Mr. Smith with total hatred. "If you've hurt our friend, I'll kill you."

"Ha! You and what army, you old biddy?" He shoved Carolina to the floor and held her down with his foot on her chest. He leaned over and held the nozzle of the gun to her head. "I could shoot you dead right now, and it wouldn't bother me at all."

"No, please, don't hurt her," Eula Mae murmured.

"Leave her alone," Yasuko spoke from the floor.

Carolina's heart beat faster. Yasuko was alive!

Mr. Smith removed the gun from Carolina's head and his foot from her chest. "All right, now. Before I really lose my temper, take off those coverups."

Carolina and Eula Mae helped Yasuko to her feet. Silently, they removed the coverups, revealing their swimsuits underneath. Mr. Smith leered at them. "You look like three large, dried up prunes." He grabbed the coverups and backed towards the door.

The driver, who had been going through their beach bags, held out Dominic's lunch. "How about this, boss?"

"What is it?"

"Looks like their lunch. Can I eat it?"

Mr. Smith grinned wickedly. "No, let 'em enjoy their last meal." He grabbed the lunch, dropped it on the floor, slammed the door, and locked it. Except for a little bit of daylight shining through small cracks between boards, the shed was in total darkness.

In the unventilated room, Carolina found the heat and smell insufferable. Even in her swimsuit, sweat ran down her face and back, and between her sagging boobs. How long had they been trapped in the shed? Carolina didn't know if it had been minutes or hours. But it was long enough for her to do lots and lots of thinking. "Eula Mae?"

"Lordy, Lordy, leave me alone and let me continue dying in peace," her friend groaned. "I'm sweating like a whore in church. What?"

"I wanted to let you and Yasuko know how sorry I am."

"For what?" asked Yasuko.

"If I hadn't paid attention to the 'mysterious woman' on the gangplank, we could be lying on the beach today." Carolina sighed. She obviously didn't have what it took to be a secret agent. Mrs. Craycraft would be disappointed.

Eula Mae reached over and patted Carolina's knee. "Hush. Save your strength. We came along on this cruise with you voluntarily because you promised us excitement and adventure."

Carolina heard Yasuko chuckling in the darkness. "I believe you have exceeded our expectations."

The women sat in silence for a few more minutes. Then Eula Mae asked, "What's your plan, Carolina?"

"No, no more plans. I'm as dumb as a plank."

"That's not true," Yasuko chimed in.

"You always have a plan," insisted Eula Mae, ending her sentence with a shriek.

Carolina jumped. "What's wrong?"

"S-s-something just touched my foot," she squealed.

Suddenly, Carolina heard little squeaky noises and scratching. Uh-oh, the rat had returned. "Eula Mae, it's probably only a rat. Remain calm."

Eula Mae screamed and struggled to her feet. "I'm too old to deal with rats. Aren't they carnivorous? Don't they carry the Black Plague? Definitely rabies, I'm absolutely sure of that. Do something!"

Carolina felt around for the untouched lunch bag. "Listen, Eula Mae, he most likely smells our lunch. I'll throw him something." Reaching inside the bag, Carolina felt squishy bananas. "I cannot believe that Dominic included over-ripe, rotten bananas in what is supposed to be our extra-special lunch."

"Lordy, Lordy, how appropriate," Eula Mae said and chuckled. "Rotten bananas to end our special day."

"Right now," Carolina said, "I feel like one old rotten banana myself." She threw the bananas as far away from her as she could and listened to the rat scurrying and squealing in that direction. She wiped her nose with the back of her hand and wished the three of them were back in the Villas at Kensington Grove, enjoying their perfect lives.

Carolina was awakened by footsteps outside the shed. She didn't know how long she'd been asleep. Eula Mae stirred beside her. The lock clattered and the door opened. Brilliant daylight flooded the shed. Carolina had to shield her eyes from the brightness. Commotion and movement sounded outside the door. A woman screamed and fell whimpering onto the floor beside them. Then the door slammed shut, leaving them in darkness, again.

As footsteps receded, Carolina crawled towards the sounds of sobbing. "Colleen, is that you?" She carefully felt the floor in front of her until her fingers felt a face. With her fingers, Carolina gently brushed the hair from the teenager's face.

The sobbing slowed and stopped. "Carolina?" a quavering voice asked.

"I'm here." Carolina reached out and helped Colleen sit up. "Are you hurt?"

"Bruised is all." Colleen gripped Carolina's arm. "What about Eula Mae and Yasuko?"

"I'm here." Eula Mae crawled over beside them.

"Me, too," Yasuko called out of the darkness.

Carolina sighed. "I'm sorry to say it looks like we're all here to star in the grand finale."

"Oh no," Colleen said. "How did you get here?"

"We crawled into the wrong taxi," Carolina said.

"Yeah," Yasuko said, moving closer. "Mr. Smith's taxi."

"Lordy, Lordy, what a ride we had," Eula Mae said.

"I'm so sorry," Colleen sobbed. "I shouldn't have involved you in this. I should've gone to the police and told them about my last phone call with my sister. Now they'll kill us all."

"Don't beat yourself up," Carolina said. "It's not all your fault. My gut kept telling me Peter was the bad guy, but I didn't want to believe it. Good old gullible me."

"Peter? Peter really is in on this?" asked Colleen in disbelief.

"I'm afraid so," Carolina replied, repeating what Mr. Smith told them, plus the signs she had overlooked or ignored. "Looks like Peter is the ringleader. I never should have told him what we saw in the luggage room."

"And I should have told you that I suspected him from the beginning," confessed Colleen.

"What are you talking about?" Carolina asked Colleen.

She sighed a long sigh. "Remember when I told you about Garland seeing the purser with an officer in the hold?"

"Are you saying the officer was Peter?" Carolina asked.

"Garland thought so, but she wasn't sure. Guess she was right."

Carolina sat cross-legged on the floor. "Looking back now, I can see how it all fits together. How could I have been so wrong?"

Eula Mae gave Carolina a hug. "None of us knew who to trust. It's not all your fault."

Yasuko, who had been quietly listening, spoke up. "What we now know for fact is that ship stewards, who are part of the smuggling operation, hide the raw emeralds in items purchased onshore, and the passengers carry the unclaimed emeralds through U.S. Customs. The purser supplies passenger information, and Mr. Smith takes care of any problems that arise—like us."

"You are correct," Carolina said.

"What I don't understand," Colleen said, "is how the smugglers get the emeralds back after they get through U.S. Customs? They can't open passenger suitcases in public and steal them back."

Carolina thought about this for a moment. "Have you noticed that the items we've seen containing emeralds are too large to fit in a suitcase?"

"That's true," Eula Mae said. "My straw doll, Baby Dumplin's cloth dolls, the porcelain vase—"

"But how do they get the emeralds back?" Yasuko asked.

"Wait, I think I know that answer—at the cruise terminal," Colleen said. "Of course! It makes perfect sense. Everything is chaotic at final disembarkation. Hundreds and hundreds of passengers and officials. You have to claim your luggage—each piece is color-coded and marked with your name—and wheel it through Immigration and U.S. Customs."

"But with so many people running around, how could they possibly locate passengers carrying the emeralds?" Carolina asked, frustrated at not being able to figure it out.

Colleen sat silent for a few seconds. "Well, passengers usually go through U.S. Customs and Immigration with other passengers in their same color group."

"Once they get through U.S. Customs and Immigration," Carolina said thoughtfully, "they could be distracted by someone who knows when they will be exiting—a porter or a taxi driver or one of the hordes of folks waiting outside the terminal. Then by sleight of hand or bump and run, the emeralds could be removed or the entire item stolen."

"Or they might have people actually working at U.S. Customs," Eula Mae said. "They could open the box with the vase or doll to inspect it—"

"And remove the emeralds," Colleen said.

"I have another thought," Yasuko said. "Think of how many hundreds and hundreds of passengers ride the cruise line buses to the airport or to hotels for a post-cruise extension. Computers keep up with which passengers are on which bus. Crew members check each passenger off as they board the bus. Luggage and carry-ons are stored under the bus. Easy enough to remove the emeralds then."

The four women sat in silence for a few moments, considering the possibilities. "A lot of good it does us now to figure this out," Eula Mae said. "Lordy, Lordy, we'll never be telling anyone anything."

"Don't say that," Carolina said, pausing in mid-sentence. "But it's true," she said, her voice cracking. "It's all my fault. I had to have an adventure. I had to go on this Caribbean cruise. The brochure made it sound exciting and romantic." A sob escaped from her throat. "I'm sorry. I know none of you really wanted to come along."

The women reached out for a group hug.

"We all have to share the blame," Eula Mae said. "Stop feeling sorry for yourself. We can't go down without a fight."

Carolina wiggled out of the "pity-party" huddle. "I have a plan." She grabbed Eula Mae's hand and pressed it down on the floor. "Feel this loose board? Everyone. Help pry it up. Maybe we can get out through the floor."

With sandy soil clinging to sweaty palms, the women took turns working the loose board. Like playing with a loose tooth, they worried it looser. In spite of broken fingernails and numerous splinters in their fingers, they eventually pried the board loose, its nails intact. Unfortunately, the crawl space underneath the flooring was barely 4 or 5 inches deep. Only a rat could crawl through that—or a snake. Carolina shuddered at the thought.

Panting from the wasted physical effort, the women fell over exhausted and rested. "That was a bummer," Carolina said. But wait a minute, she had another plan—a deliciously awesome plan that any super agent would appreciate. "Listen up! I thought of something else, but we'll need to pry up more boards. Feel around for more loose ones."

"I don't like feeling around the floor in the dark," Eula Mae said. "What if I touch a rat or worse?"

"You'd probably scare him to death," Carolina replied. "Whoa, what's this? Another loose board?"

"Here's another," Colleen called out from the other side of the shed.

Soon the women were the owners of four boards. "This is great," Carolina said. "The nails can turn these boards into weapons. Makes our game plan even better."

At dusk, the women heard voices and footsteps outside the shed and took up positions on one side of the door. They heard the lock being unfastened, then the door swung inward, hiding them from view. Someone shined a flashlight around the shed.

"Huh? Boss, they're not here."

"Impossible!" Mr. Smith's voice boomed.

Two men entered the shed, lighting the floor with the flashlight. As soon as they reached the center of the shed, the women sprang from behind the door, and began beating the two men on their heads and backs with their nail-infested boards. Caught off-guard, the men fell, yelling and cursing to the floor, temporarily stunned by the attack. The women ran out of the shed and locked the door.

"That door won't hold them for long," Carolina shouted. "Run for the car."

When the women reached the end of the path and the taxi, they heard gunshots and the sound of splintering wood. "Hurry," Carolina called out urgently, opening the driver's door. "Get in and let's get out of here."

"Hurry, Carolina," Eula Mae said from the passenger's seat. "They're coming."

"What's wrong?" Colleen asked from the back seat.

"I don't have my driver's license," cried out Carolina.

"Doesn't matter," screamed Yasuko. "Get us the hell out of here."

"I can't," Carolina said.

"I'm fixing to have a duck fit," yelled Eula Mae. "What's your problem now?"

"The key isn't here."

"Hell's bells," cried out Eula Mae.

Stampeding footsteps sent the women scurrying from the car into the heavy jungle undergrowth. Even with some moonlight filtering through the leaves, they could barely see in the darkness. Branches swatted their arms and faces, thorns tore at their naked flesh, bugs flew up their noses and into their mouths and ears, clingy vines slowed them down, but they kept moving.

When Eula Mae slowed and stumbled, Colleen and Yasuko grabbed her shoulders and kept her moving. Carolina could feel her heart racing. Her lungs ached. But her adrenaline was pumping; the super agent rush had kicked in. That and fear of a bullet in her back kept her going. Finally, when they couldn't take another step, the four women crawled underneath dense foliage and collapsed gasping on the ground.

Carolina squirmed uncomfortably in her near nakedness. It wasn't fair, she thought, that they had to deal with all of this. Although she wasn't squeamish when it came to most critters like rats or frogs or spiders or bugs, like Indiana Jones, she had this deep fear of snakes. Carolina just knew that this banana tree jungle was crawling with them. And now that they were no longer moving, the blood-sucking insects were attacking with a vengeance.

Gasping and gulping down mouthfuls of air, Carolina tried to calm down and regain some strength for what was to come. She smelled the sweat and felt the body heat of the other women as they huddled together in terror. In the distance, she heard the sound of voices, the breaking of branches, and the trampling of underbrush. The four women lay quietly on their stomachs in the rotten vegetation. Carolina gritted her teeth when something began crawling up her leg. She could hear the men coming closer and closer to their hiding place. Then suddenly they stopped only a few feet from Carolina's head. She willed herself not to breathe or scream out loud as whatever continued crawling higher up her leg.

"I can't hear 'em any more, boss. We must've lost 'em," came the voice of the taxi driver.

"Shut up, be quiet. I heard something. They couldn't have gotten far in this dark jungle. I know they're close. Listen. Maybe we can hear them breathing."

Seconds of silence ticked by like an eternity. Something stung Carolina on her thigh. She wanted to scream, but bit her lower lip instead. If a rat ran over Eula Mae's leg or a snake slithered out of this bush next to Yasuko, she knew the four of them would be doomed.

"Say, boss, listen up."

Carolina strained to hear what she thought were faint sounds in the direction of the shed.

"Maybe they're headed back to the car," Mr. Smith said. "Move it."

"Uh—Wait up, boss. Them noises are coming this way."

"Maybe they got turned around?" Mr. Smith said.

"No, no way, boss. They couldn't have got around us without us knowing it. It has to be somebody else, and I'm not waiting here to see who."

Mr. Smith and the taxi driver turned in the direction of the women's hiding place and stumbled over them. Sheer chaos followed. The women began attacking their assailants—screaming, kicking, biting, and clawing. Yasuko jumped on the back of the driver and tried to choke him, while Colleen pummeled her fists into his abdomen.

Reaching for the revolver he'd dropped in the dirt, Mr. Smith stumbled to his feet, pointed his gun at Eula Mae and yelled. "All right, everybody, stop where you are before I shoot this dried up old hag."

Colleen ran behind the driver, who still had Yasuko on his back. Carolina lunged her full body into Mr. Smith, knocking him off balance. The gun fired wildly, hitting the driver in the shoulder. Then Carolina kicked Mr. Smith's tender spot and broke away. She was only able to run a few yards before colliding with another man, who grabbed her around the waist with one arm and lifted her off the ground. Confused, Carolina struck at the man wildly, trying to free herself from his grip.

The man shook her and shined a light in her face. "Carolina, stop it!"

Somewhere in her subconscious Carolina recognized the familiar-sounding voice. She froze. "Ron?" How could that be? Unless— "Oh no," she said, sobbing and beating his chest with her fists. "You're one of them, too!"

Chapter Twenty
Clarity

Ron grabbed Carolina's fists and pulled her toward him, holding her so tightly against his chest, she could hear his heart beating. Unable to move, she screamed and howled, and tried unsuccessfully to kick him.

He eased Carolina down and shook her. "Will you shut up!" he yelled. "I'm here to save you."

Carolina shut her mouth. Even though she couldn't see his face in the dark, she wanted to believe him. She needed to know they were safe. "If you aren't one of <u>them</u>, where are Eula Mae, Yasuko, and Colleen?"

A man with a flashlight stopped behind Carolina. She stiffened, not knowing if he was going to stab, shoot, or garrote her. Was she a lousy spy or what? Was her brief spying career coming to a deadly end?

When the man walked around her and approached Ron, Carolina saw he was dressed in a uniform. "The other women are all right, sir—considering the ordeal they've gone through. The doctor is checking them out now. Lots of cuts, scratches, insect bites, and some bruising, but no apparent broken bones."

"And the men?"

"Handcuffed and waiting to be transported to jail, sir. The doctor sent this for Mrs. Cunningham."

"Thank you, Ed." As the policeman disappeared into the darkness, Ron wrapped a sheet around Carolina's shoulders and pointed his flashlight straight ahead. "Shall we join your friends?"

"Yes, I need to see for myself that they're all right." Carolina started to tremble at the thought of how close they'd come to dying. She bit her lower lip. "Was that you and the police we heard coming through the jungle?"

Ron wrapped his arm around her shoulders and pulled her closer to him. "Yes, when we found the taxi and the empty shed, we had only to follow the noise. Never heard so much screaming and yelling. Then you ran out of the bushes and crashed right into me."

"I'm glad you found us before Mr. Smith dumped us in the ocean."

"I am, too," Ron said, squeezing Carolina's shoulders. "You just don't know how glad."

Finally, at last, she felt safe. "I'm happy you turned out to be a good guy, after all." Because, she told herself, she was starting to have feelings for Mr. Hunky Spy. After Arthur died, she never thought that would be possible.

After the doctor checked out Carolina, she joined Eula Mae, Yasuko, and Colleen in a St. Thomas police mini-van for a ride to the pier. Ron sat up front with the driver.

Carolina felt blessed to be alive. But now she needed to hear the whole story.

"Ron, how did you find us?" Carolina asked.

"Through my superior qualities as an investigative reporter."

Even though it was too dark to clearly see his face, Carolina knew he winked at her and grinned. It annoyed her that he seemed to find her amusing. "I don't think so," she said.

Eula Mae leaned forward. "Mr. Dunten, be serious."

"I thought we were trying to keep the conversation light. No?"

"No!" the four women chorused.

Ron sighed loudly. "Seriously, huh? Well, let me see. When I arrived at the beach, you were nowhere to be found."

"But that creep carried our things to the beach," Yasuko pointed out.

"Yes, I did find your towels and other personal items. However, Dominic's lunch bag was missing. After all the times Carolina lost that lunch, I knew she wasn't going to let it happen, again. Especially after promising to share it with me. Then a couple sitting nearby on their beach chairs—the Ferdinands?"

The women looked at each other. "Baby Dumplin'!" they chorused.

"Plumpish woman with fire-engine red hair?" he asked.

"Wearing a red string bikini?" Eula Mae asked.

"No."

"No?" they asked in disbelief.

"International orange."

"Okay," Colleen said. "Same woman. Continue the story, please."

"The Ferdinands remembered seeing a man drop the clothes and personal belongings on the beach. I contacted the St. Thomas police and called the Captain, who reported that Peter told him all of you were crazy. I pleaded in your behalf, of course."

"Thank goodness," Carolina said.

"The Captain immediately confronted Peter with all of the evidence we'd collected and our suspicions."

"Like he was head of the smuggling ring?" Carolina guessed.

Ron stopped startled. "You finally figured that out?"

"Mr. Smith let it slip. He didn't think we would live to tell anyone," Colleen said.

"I can't believe how stupid I was to believe everything he told me," Carolina said.

"What a waste!" exclaimed Yasuko. "He was charming, easy on the eyes, well mannered, a great dancer …"

"Yasuko, shut up," interrupted Eula Mae. "You still have Charlie Chan, and I really think he's smitten with you." Eula Mae elbowed Carolina. "As for you, Carolina, will you stop beating yourself up?"

"I'm working on it. Ron, what happened next?"

"Peter knew you three were scheduled to be disposed of tonight, but he didn't have the details. Once the purser heard Peter had talked, he sang like the proverbial canary. But then, again, he only knew that Mr. Smith was working with a local taxi cab driver. Then enters Mrs. Coolhardy."

"The little old lady with the stuffed bulldog named Napoleon?" Carolina asked.

"That's the one. She insisted she had seen a man, fitting Mr. Smith's description, stuff a body in the trunk of a taxi."

Carolina's eyes widened. "Colleen?"

Ron nodded. "Apparently so. She actually wrote down the number of the taxi, as well as the tag number. Under any other circumstances, she'd probably have been written off and ignored."

"Ahh, but you had prior experience with that nice old lady and Napoleon. So you had the local police locate the taxi?" Carolina asked, because that's what any sane secret agent would have done.

"Yes, they staked it out, and we followed Mr. Smith and the taxi to the shed."

"Where were you while we were being chased through the jungle?" Yasuko asked indignantly.

"Being very cautious," Ron said sheepishly. "In my defense, we got lost when the taxi turned off the main road. By the time we turned around and found the dirt road, the car and shed were empty. If you hadn't escaped into the jungle, they might have hustled you out of there before we showed up."

"Let's not even go there," Colleen said.

"Now, have I answered all of your questions?"

"No," Carolina yelled, making everyone jump. "One more: Who are you?" Carolina felt Eula Mae tense up beside her.

Ron let out a long sigh. "You never give up, do you?"

"No, never. You have to tell us."

Ron reached into his pocket and handed Carolina a leather billfold. He shined his flashlight on it.

With Eula Mae, Yasuko, and Colleen looking over Carolina's shoulder, she opened the billfold. Inside was a badge and an identification card: Ronald Williams, Special Agent for U.S. Customs and Border Protection.

"Satisfied?" He took back his badge and flashlight.

"No, not yet."

"Carolina!" Eula Mae squealed.

"Who is Ronald Dunten?"

Ron chuckled. "My brother-in-law. My sister says if anything ever happens to him—I use his name as an alias on occasion—she's going to come gunning for me."

"We're almost to the pier, sir," the driver said. "A tender is waiting to take you to the ship."

"Thank you," Ron told him.

"I wish we'd known your true identity a few days ago," Colleen said.

Ron sat silent for a few seconds before answering. "When I work under cover, no one knows my real identity. It's my job to follow a trail of smugglers and find out who's involved before seizing what's being smuggled and arresting the smugglers. Because you three were so determined to find out what was going on, my partner and I were able to put the pieces together faster than we expected."

"Partner?" Carolina asked.

"Mr. Gallenkemp."

"Mr. Gallenkemp?" Carolina's voice rose in pitch. "Then I was right. He was always snooping at our door."

"Not really snooping. Just keeping an eye on you and your activities. We knew you were up to your ears in something. We just couldn't quite figure out what."

"Excuse me, sir," the driver said, halting at the pier's security check point, "but we're here."

As Ron helped the women out of the police car, Colleen paused. "How did you find out that raw emeralds were being smuggled into Jacksonville?"

Ron glanced over Colleen's shoulder to the security office door. He smiled at her. "From your sister Garland." He pointed behind her.

Swirling around, Colleen saw a slender young woman step through the door. "Garland!"

Carolina, Eula Mae, and Yasuko watched as the sisters embraced. "But I thought she died," Carolina said, staring at Ron.

"Mr. Smith did throw her overboard, but she was rescued by two teenagers in a sailboat. The teens chose not to call the Coast Guard because they were smuggling untaxed liquor into Miami. When she approached us, we decided to let everyone believe she was dead. That way the emerald smugglers would feel safe enough to continue their operation. She's been living in a safe house on St. Thomas for her own protection."

The last launch to the *Emerald Dream* cast off its lines. As crew and passengers headed toward the ship, the lights of St. Thomas faded in the night. Colleen and Garland hugged and talked a mile a minute. Yasuko and Eula Mae huddled together, deep in conversation. Ron sat beside Carolina in peaceful silence.

Carolina sighed happily. She felt warm and fuzzy all over. Was this the way all secret agents felt after a successful mission? She also felt something else—a gnawing hunger for chocolate éclairs.

Early the next morning—one of two scheduled days at sea—the Captain announced the *Emerald Dream* would make a brief unscheduled stop in Miami. He explained that the ship would still arrive on time as scheduled for disembarkation in Jacksonville. He did not have to explain why the ship would be stopping in Miami. Every passenger, ship's officer, and crew member had heard the news, which had gone viral throughout the ship the night before.

Carolina was disappointed that Ron did not show up for breakfast, but she figured he was busy interrogating everyone involved with the smuggling ring and tying up loose ends before Miami. A surprise for her and Eula Mae was the appearance of Charlie Chan, who asked to join them. He sat next to Yasuko. Carolina couldn't help but smile as she watched them whispering together and giggling like young lovers.

"Dominic happy to see his ladies smiling this morning." He set down a small bowl of blueberries and strawberries in front of Carolina. "No rotten bananas for Mrs. Cunningham this morning."

Carolina laughed. "Thank you, Dominic!"

"Looks like the only rotten bananas at this table are us," Eula Mae said.

Yasuko placed her hand over Charlie's hand. "I certainly don't feel like a rotten banana today."

"Is this an inside joke or something?" asked Charlie.

"Yes, exactly," Carolina responded. "Eula Mae was just teasing. Yasuko can explain it to you."

After breakfast, Charlie and Yasuko excused themselves to play in the mahjong tournament. Eula Mae and Carolina headed back to their suite to call and update Lilly on their adventures.

Lilly was still in her pajamas when her face popped up on WhatsApp. She squealed delightedly. "I have been quite worried about you. I had this awful feeling all day yesterday that you were in terrible trouble. I tried to reach you, but you didn't answer."

"That's because we were separated from our phones," explained Carolina.

Eula Mae edged her face into the cell phone screen. "We were kidnapped and almost killed. Lordy, Lordy, I nearly keeled over and died of a major coronary several times over. Praise Jesus, I survived."

"What!? That is unbelievable!"

"We're not making this up," insisted Carolina, and in great detail, she told Lilly how their day on St. Thomas had gone.

A shocked Lilly hung on every word. "Oh, my goodness! How scary and awful!" was all she could say when Carolina finished. "I'm so glad this cruise is coming to an end. Everyone here at the Villas can't wait to see you."

"We stop in Miami tomorrow and disembark in Jacksonville the next morning," Carolina said.

"Anything interesting happening in the Villas?" Eula Mae asked.

Lilly grinned. "We have a new resident."

"Male or female?" asked Carolina.

"Male. By the name of Geoffrey Winston Churchill. He's originally from Rustington, England, and he looks like Harrison Ford with white hair. All the women are going gah-gah over him. They fight to sit at his table for meals, and they shamelessly throw themselves at him."

"Details?" persisted Eula Mae.

"Geof just turned 80, works out every day, and is in perfect health. He drives a new Mercedes, still has his teeth, no toupee, has a great personality, and a bass voice with a sexy British accent that I could listen to all day. I think we should set him up with Eula Mae."

"Lordy, Lordy, a man is the last thing I need," Eula Mae said.

"We can discuss this more once we're back at the Villas," said Carolina.

"Wait, before you go, Carolina," Lilly put in, "you should know that your daughter came by for a visit on Sunday. She was most distressed that you weren't here. And really upset to hear that you were on a Caribbean cruise."

"Lordy, Lordy, there will be hell to pay when you see her, again," predicted Eula Mae. "Can't say I didn't warn you."

Ron didn't make it to lunch, either. Carolina told herself that she really didn't care, but she knew that was a lie. She heard that he would be disembarking in Miami with the rest of the agents and members of the smuggling ring. That was fine with her, she thought. He would soon be out of her mind and forgotten. A bleep in her memory banks, which seemed to be getting worse the older she got. Another lie. She would never forget him. She rolled her eyes upward and mumbled, "Sorry about that, Arthur, but you know I dearly loved you for as long as you were alive. And I'll always love you until the day I drop dead."

At 4 o'clock, while Eula Mae took her pre-dinner nap and Yasuko was doing who knew what with Charlie Chan, Carolina grabbed her latest Craycraft novel and headed up for tea. Strawberry pie with clotted cream and a couple of chocolate éclairs would improve her mood.

Carolina staked out a small round table directly in front of floor-to-ceiling windows overlooking the ocean. A floor-length, white linen cloth covered the table, which was set for two with linen napkins, fine china, and real silverware. Seconds after she sat down, a waiter placed a teapot full of hot water and opened a large wooden box full of assorted tea in front of her. Carolina chose the Jasmine green tea.

Before she had finished two pages in her book, a waiter appeared with a silver tray covered with tea sandwiches, including cream cheese and cucumber, chicken salad, egg salad, and pimento cheese. Carolina picked one cream cheese and cucumber. She wanted to have plenty of room for the yummy, high-carb choices that would be coming soon.

Carolina didn't have to wait long before another waiter, pushing a three-tier cart, stopped next to her and pointed out what he had to offer. Too many choices, she thought, but finally decided on an apple tart with clotted cream, a slice of strawberry pie with clotted cream, chocolate mousse with whipped cream, and a chocolate éclair.

Attempting to read, eat, and sip tea at the same time, Carolina had reached the part in her book where Agent Craycraft was crossing the Sahara Desert by camel in search of a family of nomads who could help her escape a terrorist. The terrorist, astride a sleek black steed, appeared at the top of a dune, yelling and waving his rifle. Totally absorbed in the story, her heart began to race.

"May I join you?"

Carolina jumped in her seat, as Ron sat down beside her. She felt her face warming and a fluttering in her stomach.

"Sorry, I didn't mean to scare you," he said, flashing her a smile. "You were so absorbed in your book, I guess you didn't see me." He looked at the cover of her book and laughed. "Another Craycraft book? I would think your own real adventures are more exciting than any of hers."

"My adventures have come to an end. I will have to continue to live vicariously through these books." She watched Ron plop an English Breakfast tea bag in a teapot of hot water and select a scone with jam and clotted cream from a cart. "You know, Ron, I wasn't sure I would see you before you disembarked in Miami."

Ron dunked his tea bag up and down in the teapot a couple of times and poured tea into his cup. "Yet here I am, talking to you." He took a sip. "You know I couldn't leave without seeing you, again." He looked into her eyes and smiled.

Carolina liked his smile. It wasn't the fake smile of a smuggler or an assassin. It was a sincere smile of a good man, who had a difficult, risky job. She wiped the clotted cream off her mouth. "I'm glad we have this chance to talk, also."

"Good. Then let's not waste the moment. Since you know who I am not, I want you to know who I am."

"I know who you work for. Is your office in Miami?"

Ron spread jam and clotted cream on his scone. "No, I work out of an office in Jacksonville."

Carolina watched Ron take a bite of his scone. Why did she feel happy hearing that he worked that close to the Villas? Why should she care about that?

"What else would you like to know?"

"You know that I live in the Villas at Kensington Grove in the Marshes of Glynn," she took a sip of tea. "Do you live anywhere near the beach?" He looked so tan and fit, she could picture him jogging shirtless, up and down the beach.

"No beach house for me. I live in a condo on the St. John's River, where I like to go kayaking. Do you kayak or go sailing?"

"No. Before Arthur died two years ago, we liked to take long walks on weekends. He especially liked to walk along River Street in Savannah and watch the big ships sailing up and down the river." A steward stopped with a platter of chocolate éclairs and presented one to Carolina. "Does your wife like to kayak?"

Ron swallowed the last of his scone and chuckled. "No, my wife divorced me after 18 months of marriage. She didn't like my career choice. And before you ask, I have no children. Just a dog, Sherlock, who loves to go for long walks."

"Okay, so you like kayaking and long walks with your dog." Carolina licked some chocolate off her finger. "What about indoor activities?"

Ron raised his right brow. "In my free time, I like to play computer games, read books by Tom Clancy or Stuart Woods, and cook gourmet meals for friends." He took another sip of his tea. "What about you? Besides loving to read Agent Craycraft books?"

Carolina took a deep breath. "I'm in a bridge group at the Villas with Yasuko, Eula Mae, and Lilly. I like to go out for lunch with my friends, who are still working at Rose Dhu College, where I taught ceramics for many years. They say they're jealous that I'm retired."

"I'm jealous, too, Carolina." Ron reached out and clasped her hands. "I have two more years before I can retire at 62 with a government pension."

Carolina blinked. She was surprised that he was only two years younger than she was. "Then what are your plans? Will you stay in the Jacksonville area? Or move somewhere to be near family?"

"You know about my sister, Sandra and her husband Ron. They live in New York City. We see each other once or twice a year. Both parents deceased. I have a couple of cousins in the Miami area, but I rarely hear from them. Did I hear that you have children living near you?"

"I have a married son Charter and two granddaughters, who live in Savannah, and an unmarried daughter Caitlyn, who is in the Coast Guard," answered Carolina, thinking how lonely it must be for Ron having no close family. She couldn't imagine what her life would be like without hers.

"I am curious, Carolina," Ron said, reaching out and squeezing both her hands with his. "I'm assuming—since you taught at Rose Dhu College—that you and Arthur had a house in the Savannah area?"

Carolina nodded. "Yes, we did, but after retiring, I decided to sell it and move to the Villas at Kensington Grove in the Brunswick area. I thought it would be the perfect place to spend my retirement years."

Ron finished off the last of his tea. "And has it been?"

"Been what?"

"The perfect place?" Ron leaned forward, closer to Carolina.

"At first, I thought it was perfect. Then it started feeling too perfect and almost boring. Finally, I decided something was definitely missing."

Ron raised his right eyebrow. "Let me guess." He placed his hand over hers. "You weren't experiencing any excitement or adventure like Agent Craycraft?"

Carolina shivered. She couldn't believe that he understood. Here was someone who "got" her. Not since Arthur, and suddenly, she felt guilty. Even unfaithful. "Yes, that was exactly it."

Ron leaned back in his chair and grinned. "So, you talked your friends into a cruise." He laughed softly. "I bet you experienced a little more excitement and adventure than you wanted."

Carolina felt more warmth in her cheeks. Wasn't she too old to blush, she asked herself? "Possibly," she admitted.

Ron looked around the tea room and stood up. "Tea time is over. They will be running us out of here any second. Shall we take a stroll outside?"

Ron pulled back Carolina's chair, took her hand, and led her outside. They walked the length of the deck to a quiet spot and stood at the rail. Ron reached out and gently pulled Carolina closer to him. "Carolina, I like you. You're smart and feisty, and fun to be around. A little bit opinionated, obstinate, and stubborn, but that's okay. I'm not perfect, myself. I'm overly passionate about my work because I want to make a difference. That's probably why I never remarried."

"But?" Carolina felt confused, and wondered where he was going with this.

"Jacksonville is not that far from Brunswick. Unless you totally despise me for lying about my identity and other questionable behavior issues, I would like to see you, again. I would like to get to know you better. Do you think that might be possible? Would you be willing to do that? To take a chance on me?"

Carolina took a deep breath. She had not expected this. Did she want to see this man, again? Her Mr. Hunky Spy? She remembered all the times he frightened and angered her. But he was only doing his job. Did she want to take a chance on him? What did she have to lose? "All right, Ron. As long as you don't lie to me, I would love to see you, again, too."

When the *Emerald Dream* tied up in Miami the next morning, passengers lined the top deck rail or watched from their balconies, like Carolina, Eula Mae, and Yasuko. They leaned over the rails, jockeying for good views, and taking photos with their cell phones. They cheered when the Captain and Dr. Sigman, walked Colleen and her sister Garland down the gangway, where they were greeted by a middle-age couple, who tightly hugged their daughters. Members of the Burgess family were not the only ones who cried with joy that morning.

After the Burgess family disappeared into the terminal with cruise line officials, passengers remained at the railings for the rest of the show. Everyone watched as uniformed authorities boarded the ship and escorted all crew members and ship's officers involved in the smuggling operation—plus Mr. Smith—off the ship and into waiting black SUVs. Carolina's heart fluttered as she watched Ron disembark with Mr. Gallenkamp. She felt sad to see him get into one of the SUVs, yet hopeful that she would see him, again. In less than an hour of arrival in Miami, the *Emerald Dream* blew its horn and cruised toward Jacksonville.

Docked the following morning in the Port of Jacksonville, Carolina, Eula Mae, Yasuko, and her new BFF Charlie Chan ate a final breakfast in the main dining room. After bidding Dominic farewell, they found comfortable places to sit in one of the lounges and waited for the color brown to be called. Passengers with early morning flights or morning shore excursions were called to disembark first. Passengers disembarking last included those going to local hotels or those with late flights or those who would be driving back home, like Carolina, Eula Mae, Yasuko, and Charlie.

"You know what?" asked Yasuko, who was sitting shoulder to shoulder on a small sofa with Charlie.

"What's that?" asked Eula Mae.

"I've been thinking about how dull and boring our lives will be after we get back to the Villas."

"I don't know, dull and boring might be nice," Eula Mae said.

"Maybe at first," agreed Carolina. "But after a few days or weeks, I think our perfect lives at the Villas will be missing something, again."

"Exactly my point," said Yasuko.

Eula Mae squirmed in her seat. "You mean like we'd go through excitement and adventure withdrawal?"

"Yes, we will miss the thrill of adventure," said Carolina. "That adrenaline rush."

"Mmm. Maybe we could start an Adventure Club?" Eula Mae suggested.

"An Adventure Club?" asked Charlie, stroking his beard. "And club members would do adventurous activities like bungy jumping or cliff climbing or skydiving?"

Carolina's jaw dropped. "Oh, no, I'm sure that's <u>not</u> what Eula Mae meant." Everyone turned to Eula Mae for clarification. "Right?"

Eula Mae blinked and twisted her mouth to the side. "Lordy, Lordy, I was thinking about road trips to Atlanta to visit the Georgia Aquarium or Zoo Atlanta. Maybe a weekend trip to Charleston or a long weekend in New York to see a Broadway play. But—" She chewed thoughtfully on her lower lip. "—if some folks were interested in doing more risky and exciting activities, we could consider other possibilities."

"Not for me," Yasuko said.

"Or me, either," agreed Charlie. "I merely needed a clear definition of adventure." He held up his cell phone. "Because my online dictionary says it is—and I quote—'an unusual and exciting, typically hazardous, experience or activity.'"

An image of a very annoyed Caitlyn and Charter instantly popped into Carolina's mind, as she thought about their reaction to her jumping out of an airplane or riding a motorcycle down the Tail of the Dragon highway in North Carolina. "I think an Adventure Club is an excellent idea. We can discuss it in detail once we are back in the Villas."

It was at this point in the conversation that passengers with brown luggage tags were called to disembark in Jacksonville. Carolina, Eula Mae, Yasuko, and Charlie followed a steady stream of passengers outside, where their key cards were scanned one last time. A line of crew and officers bid them farewell and wished them a safe journey home.

As Carolina reached the Captain at the end of the line, he handed her a large white envelope. "This is for you, Mrs. Cunningham. To show our sincere thanks from the *Emerald Dream* crew and officers for your help in solving crimes committed onboard the ship. We hope you will come back and cruise with us, again." He shook her hand, and Eula Mae's and Yasuko's.

The three women and Charlie trudged down the gangway and into the large cruise terminal, where they quickly found the section with rows and rows of luggage with brown tags.

After locating and claiming their luggage, they made their way through Immigration and U.S. Customs. Outside the terminal, passengers scurried to find a taxi, the right shuttle bus, or friends and family.

On the sidewalk, standing side by side—like in a police lineup—were Carolina's son and daughter, Charter and Caitlyn Cunningham, and Eula Mae's daughter and son-in-law, Georgia Davis and Carl Overstreet.

Caitlyn, looking worried and concerned, rushed over to Carolina and hugged her tightly. "Mom, you scared us to death. We didn't even know you had gone on a cruise, until I dropped by the Villas for a visit. Then the next day the cruise line called and said you were missing."

Charter gave Carolina a hug, after Caitlyn backed away. Gripping her shoulders, he looked her solemnly in the eyes. "Mom, didn't I tell you that taking a cruise could be dangerous?" he asked sternly. "If I'd known you were thinking about doing it, I would have advised against it."

Carolina sighed. How she hated it when her own children acted like her parents. "That's exactly the reason I didn't tell you."

"Mom, you're hopeless." He gave her another hug. "Welcome back! I'm glad you're safe. No more running around like you're Agent Craycraft. If you want some excitement, why don't we plan a family trip to Disney World. The kids would love it."

Oh, definitely, yes, thought Carolina. Absolutely, that's what we should do. Disney World with the grandchildren. A week of following them around the Magic Kingdom, standing in long lines to ride Peter

Pan and It's a Small World. No one would want to ride Space Mountain or the Rocking Roller Coaster or Dwarfs Mining Cars with her. She sighed. Nothing but a big bunch of wussies in her family.

Charter turned to his sister, Caitlyn. "You're still driving Mom back to the Villas, right?"

Carolina snapped to attention. "What? Wait! That's not necessary."

"Not necessary, but a good opportunity for me to hear the details about your infamous cruise," Caitlyn said. "Is this your luggage?"

Carolina turned around and looked for Eula Mae, who was talking to her daughter Georgia and pointing to Carolina. Eula Mae stepped over next to Carolina. "Georgia and Carl insist on driving me back to the Villas. Is that okay?"

Carolina nodded. "Caitlyn is going with me back to the Villas."

Yasuko quietly approached Carolina. "I have my luggage, but I have my own transportation back to the Villas." Yasuko reached behind her and grabbed the hand of Charlie Chan. "Charlie lives in Savannah, but he's been looking at retirement communities. He offered to give me a lift back to the Villas, so he can check it out."

Carolina stood in shocked silence. She could not believe that her traitorous friends were bailing on her. It would be a really long drive back to the Villas with Caitlyn in the passenger seat.

Yasuko stepped over to Caitlyn and Charter. "Hello, I'm Yasuko Crane. We met at the Villas open house. This is my friend Charlie Chan." She smiled at him. "Charlie, meet Carolina's children, Caitlyn and Charter Cunningham."

Caitlyn reached out and shook Yasuko's hand. "Yes, I remember meeting you. You're in Mom's bridge group, right?"

"That's right." She shook hands with Charter.

"My mom talked you into going on this cruise, too?" Charter asked.

"It didn't take much persuasion after I heard the grand bridge champion would be teaching classes on the ship. It was an opportunity I couldn't pass up," she explained.

"I hope the bridge classes were worth the danger you put yourself in," Charter replied.

Yasuko shook her head. "Unfortunately, after we boarded the ship, we found out he had to cancel and would not make the cruise."

"That must have been terribly disappointing for all of you," Charter said. "If you had been in bridge classes every day, you wouldn't have had time to get into trouble."

Yasuko laughed. "It was definitely not your typical Caribbean cruise, but it was memorable." She squeezed Charlie's hand. "I wouldn't have met this fellow here, either."

Carolina finally found her tongue and gave Yasuko a hug. "I'm glad the cruise wasn't a total loss for you."

"Hardly," said Yasuko, smiling at Charlie. "I think in spite of the stress of too much adventure, things are ending on a positive note for me. Charlie and I are off. See you back at the Villas."

Charter watched Yasuko and Charlie leave, and turned to Carolina. "Here, Mom, let me help you with your luggage. You do remember where you parked the car, right?"

Carolina shook her head. "Of course. I haven't lost my brains yet."

Charter glanced at the large, white envelope she was carrying. "What is that?" he asked.

"Something the Captain gave me when we disembarked the ship," Carolina said, examining it. "Should I open it?"

Eula Mae walked up with her daughter and son-in-law in tow. "We're headed back to the Villas." She stopped to watch Carolina open the envelope and pull out a gold-seal certificate—good for any 21-day cruise on the *Emerald Dream* with accommodations in the three-bedroom Captain's Suite.

Eula Mae rolled her eyes and glanced at Carolina, whose mouth was opening and shutting with nothing coming out.

"Wow!" exclaimed Carolina, her eyes widening. "Look, it includes free business class air to the port of embarkation, plus a personal butler."

"What's that?" questioned Charter. "Another cruise? Absolutely not, Mom! I forbid it. Passengers fall overboard on cruise ships—plus smuggling, stowaways, pirates hijacking ships, and passengers getting kidnapped and held for ransom. Uh-uh. No way."

"Calm down, Charter. Did you hear me say I was going on another cruise?" She turned to Eula Mae. "I will see you back at the Villas, dear friend. Good to see you, again, Georgia and Carl." She put the certificate back in the envelope. "Caitlyn? Are you ready to escort me back to my perfect life in the Villas?"

"Yes, Mom, I will be relieved to get you safely back." Caitlyn took Carolina's luggage from Charter. "I'll take that, brother. I think we can find Mom's car. I'll talk to you later."

Carolina took one last look at the *Emerald Dream*, towering above the cruise terminal. As she led Caitlyn in the direction of the parking garage, Carolina realized that there were many places on her "bucket list" that she wanted to see. Exciting places, full of adventure—like Egypt, the Suez Canal, and the Holy Lands; Brazil and the Amazon River; Greenland, Iceland, and the Faeroe Islands; Morocco and Tunisia; India, Thailand, Malaysia, and Indonesia; and South Korea, Hong Kong, Shanghai, and Japan. So many places to explore; so many cultures to experience. Surely seeing those parts of the world from the safety of a cruise ship wouldn't be all bad, would it? What could possibly go wrong?

THE END

NOTE FROM THE AUTHOR

Word-of-mouth is crucial for any author to succeed. If you enjoyed the book, please leave a review online—anywhere you are able. Even if it's just a sentence or two. It would make all the difference and would be very much appreciated.

Thanks!
Muriel

Muriel Ellis Pritchett writes fun fiction about older women, who are feisty and smart, who are often wronged or exploited, but who always climb out of the muck smelling like a rose. An award-winning author, Muriel lives in Georgia. When not cruising around the world with her computer guru husband, Muriel enjoys sculpting humorous creations in clay. She and her husband are both Disney-holics. *Rotten Bananas and the Emerald Dream* is Muriel's third novel.

Thank you so much for reading one of
Muriel Ellis Pritchett's novels.

If you enjoyed the experience, please check out our recommended
title for your next great read!

Making Lemonade by Muriel Ellis Pritchett

"A woman gets a chance to start over in this romantic novel...
centering on wish fulfillment." *-KIRKUS REVIEWS*

View other Black Rose Writing titles at
www.blackrosewriting.com/books and use promo code
PRINT to receive a **20% discount** when purchasing.